Praise for R. J. Lee and his A Bridge to Death mysteries!

PLAYING THE DEVIL

"Entertaining . . . Lee does a good job rendering Southern speech patterns in the conversations between Wendy and her friend Merleece." —*Publishers Weekly*

"Solid small-town cozy fare." —*Booklist*

GRAND SLAM MURDERS

"Lee deals a winning hand . . . An attractive protagonist, plenty of Southern charm, a long suit of colorful characters, and a plot that comes up trumps at the surprising end all bode well for future installments." —*Publishers Weekly*

"A compulsively readable series debut, dripping in Southern charm, with a clever sleuth whose bridge skills break the case." —*Kirkus Reviews*

"Lee vividly captures life in a quirky Southern town ruled by a rich elite, and heightens interest with a plot that exposes past secrets and a budding romance." —*Booklist*

"Set in a small Mississippi town rife with stereotypical prejudices, gossip finger-pointing suspects, and an interesting mystery with an unlikely detecting team that puts their entire focus on finding out whodunit. . . . The author cleverly uses knowledge of the game of bridge to uncover what really happens—and it all leads to one heck of a jaw-dropping ending. Book two will be highly anticipated." —*Mystery Scene*

"A promising introduction to R. J. Lee's Bridge to Death mystery series. I look forward to the next one." —*Suspense* magazine

"An impressively original and deftly crafted mystery from first page to last, *Grand Slam Murders* by R. J. Lee will prove to be an inherently riveting read." —*Midwest Book Review*

"Pick up a copy of *Grand Slam Murders: A Bridge to Death Mystery*, and find out just how delightfully devilish the game can be." —*The Baldwin Times*

"The book is set right here in Mississippi, which is quite appropriate since the author is one of Mississippi's literary gems." —*Tupelo Daily Journal*

Books by R. J. Lee

GRAND SLAM MURDERS

PLAYING THE DEVIL

COLD READING MURDER

THE KING FALLS

Published by Kensington Publishing Corp.

The
King
Falls

R.J. LEE

Kensington Publishing Corp.
www.kensingtonbooks.com

ISBN: 978-1-4967-3150-0 (ebook)

ISBN: 978-1-4967-3149-4

First Kensington Trade Paperback Printing: April 2022

10 9 8 7 6 5 4 3 2 1

Printed in the United States of America

For my beloved Will

CHAPTER 1

On a cool May morning in Rosalie, Mississippi, Wendy Winchester Rierson sat across from her husband, Ross, at the kitchen table, listening to the usual "turkey-gobbling noises" the back of the refrigerator was making while she shuffled through the Saturday mail. They had just enjoyed a light breakfast of coffee, fresh-squeezed orange juice, and whole wheat toast with Rosalie muscadine jelly. While Ross was entirely preoccupied with their bills—which he stubbornly refused to pay online because of a one-time computer glitch that had annoyed him to no end—she retrieved a greeting card-sized envelope from her stack and tore it open with great relish, giving out a light gasp.

"Well, he's at it again," she said, flashing the card at Ross, as if he could actually make it out in such a short interval of time.

"Who's at what again?" he asked her, after she had returned it to the palm of her hand. She was always doing that to him—making him guess at the gist of things that flew out of her mouth.

"King Kohl is having another of his bridge parties," came

the reply. "This will be the third one since he joined the Bridge Bunch a couple of years ago. Plenty of booze, and a big spread for those who don't want to play half-buzzed, and a selection of Rosalie socialites to beat the band. Of course, he's always the center of attention."

Ross frowned, bringing a blush to his Nordic coloring. "Of course he is. What else would you expect from the scion of the Kohl and Son real estate firm? Their FOR SALE and SOLD signs are planted all over town, and new ones seem to sprout every day on lawns just like crabgrass. To use an internet term, their business went viral a long time ago."

"An understatement. Sometimes I think they founded Rosalie and divvied up all the original tracts the Spanish laid out way back when. Of course he's not a bad bridge player. Except he's always got an eagle eye for the ladies he invites. The guest list always tilts that way, it seems."

"Just as long as he doesn't try to hit on you," Ross said. But his tone suggested she was not to take him seriously.

"I can handle myself," she told him, raising her right eyebrow.

"I know you can. All of Rosalie knows you can. You're the best investigative reporter and crime solver this town has ever had, all rolled into one."

Wendy feigned being taken aback with a sideways glance. "You know Daddy would disagree with you, sweetheart. There are plenty of officers being paid to catch criminals that I couldn't hold a candle to. I'm strictly an amateur who can't help but meddle."

Ross made a face after tearing open a bill and staring at the amount that greeted him. It seemed he had forgotten how to blink. "Hmmm. The utilities keep going up and up. It's not like we're abusing the thermostat. But whaddaya gonna do? Summer in the Deep South is an outdoor sauna. Anyhow, I agree that you are your daddy's daughter. Bax Winchester is the best chief of police this town's ever had, and I think we both know you got your crime-solving genes from him."

Wendy brightened considerably, tossing back her shoulder-length auburn curls. "Probably."

"No, definitely. First, you solve the murders of the Gin Girls, who were poisoned at their own bridge luncheon; then you help figure out the murder of that horrible Brent Ogle, who was clobbered in the hot tub out at the country club; then you come up with just the right angle for the murder of Aurelia Spangler, that psychic who rented Overview on the High Bluff. You're about ready for another murder to solve, aren't you? You don't want your talents to run dry, do you?"

Wendy shuddered. "Don't even say something like that, Ross. I'd like to go a decent period of time without having my love for the game of bridge connected to someone's untimely death. Of course, I have had my share that were unrelated."

"I was just kidding anyway."

"But these things have a way of happening to me," she continued. "You and Daddy do your part in these investigations, but why do all these breakthroughs seem to fall into my lap?"

Ross began writing a check for the utility bill and did not look up. "Because you are gifted, my girl. You have that puzzle-solving ability that few people have. You line things up in that beautiful brain of yours, and then something clicks. *Voilà!* The solution that nobody thought of. Or at least not the entire solution." Ross finished with the check, put down his pen, and finally looked up. "So when is this bridge to-do that King Kohl has invited you to gonna take place?"

"Next Saturday." She paused, reviewing her newspaper schedule, remembering that her editor and now her father's second wife, Lyndell Slover, had given her the day off again. The bond between the two women had only grown stronger over the past couple of years as stepmother and daughter, and Wendy was often granted special requests regarding time off. "Remind me. Do we have anything on the calendar from your end that I've forgotten about?"

He glanced briefly at the ceiling as if it had the answer for him, narrowed his eyes, and told her that he didn't think so.

"The invitation doesn't say *and guest*, of course. So I'd have to go it alone if I decided to go."

He snickered. "You can always decline."

"I . . . know that."

Ross cocked his head at the hesitation. "What's wrong? What are you thinking?"

"I don't know."

"A premonition, perhaps?"

She pursed her lips and shifted her weight slightly, leaning against the back of her wicker chair. "I just don't know. Something just went up my spine. I can't explain it, and you know I hate it when I get that feeling."

Ross returned to his bills and left the matter hanging. "You could try to explain it if you really wanted to."

"I wonder what they could have been thinking?" Wendy said at last, posing the question more to their bright, yellow, redecorated kitchen with its bell-pepper–dotted curtains than to her husband.

"I love your lack of segues, as usual. What *who* could have been thinking?"

"King's parents. Who saddles a child with a name like King Kohl? I'm sure he's been teased all his life by that nursery rhyme. Can't you just hear his classmates now? Endlessly chanting it at recess and in the cafeteria when he sits down with his tray."

Ross looked amused. "Ah, yes. *And a merry old soul was he,* right? It's been a lifetime since I've thought of that nursery rhyme."

"Actually, he does always appear to be merry enough. He's a very handsome man—tall, with that deliberate, dark scruff that's so popular these days, and one of those jutting chins that looks like it's made out of rock. He does have the first signs of a receding hairline, but he obviously doesn't let it bother him. He's always telling jokes, mostly aimed to charm the women around him. But I found him to be a bit much. He knows he's good-looking, and there doesn't seem to be a modest bone in his body. He's always *on*, and that's just not for me. You are, of course."

"By that, I'm assuming you don't think I'm *off*?"

"You're neither on nor off. You're very secure in your masculinity. You know exactly who you are, and you have nothing to prove."

"Thanks." Ross frowned at another bill, shaking his head. "So, are you gonna accept the invitation to this little bridge to-do or not?"

"I've been thinking that it might be fun just to see what he's up to."

"Does he have to be up to something? Can't he just be being himself?"

Wendy sat up straight and tried to sound matter-of-fact. "Yes, he could be, I suppose."

"Well, I didn't mean anything by my question. Just making conversation." After a pause, he continued. "So, are you going?"

She picked up the invitation again and studied it closely. The font was flowery and fussy, the heavy stock a shade of lavender, and it was even scented—none of that particularly masculine, in effect—something a woman might have conjured up and sent. The thought continued to occur to Wendy that she should go because King might be up to something. His bridge parties at his brick townhouse on prestigious, crepe myrtle–lined Minor Street were quite festive to date. Something kept telling her that she should attend. She would accept the invitation from King Kohl—the merry *young* soul.

"I'm going," she told Ross at last.

His smile was wry and brief. "Was there ever any doubt?"

Campbell King Kohl sat at his highly polished plantation desk in his den, lost in thought. The room was too full of period furniture—antique lamps and conservative window treatments that his mother had coordinated for him—to be called a man cave, but that was its purpose, nonetheless. In fact, the entire Federal-style townhouse, flush with the sidewalk, had been decorated by her since Jackson and Ethel Kohl had bought and restored it after the business had taken off some thirty years ago; and then they had conveniently turned it over to their son a few years back and retired to the slave quarters in the backyard. They weren't giving up much in the way of comfort and style, since the two-story, brick outbuilding had been as lavishly furnished as the main house; they were perfectly happy with the downsizing, so to speak, now that they were entering their sixties.

Kohl had been reviewing the guest list for his upcoming bridge gathering for some time now, although he knew it would turn out to be much more than that. For one thing, the list was far shorter than the ones for the other parties he had thrown. There had been three tables of players invited to those. But then, those had been genuinely devoted to bridge and lots of drinking and socializing, and everyone had left buzzed and anticipating another gathering down the road. That would not be the case this coming Saturday.

Of course, he had to have his parents there as the star guests—Jackson and Ethel Kohl. They had brought him into the world and had always had such high expectations of him. His father, Jackson, had shown him every angle of the real estate business since his college graduation from Ole Miss five years ago—including some hacks about cutting corners that weren't exactly by the book. Nonetheless, they worked and brought in more business, and that was the point. Kohl and Son was more than just a corporation. It was a generational gift.

"I want you to start taking over more and more of the business, son," Jackson had told him more than once. "I think maybe by the time you're thirty, I'll be ready to take a back seat and let you run most of the show. We've already given you the house. Why not give you the business, too? Besides, I've done most of the heavy lifting. Now it's time for you to reap the rewards for the next generation."

King remembered the gleam in his father's eye every time he dredged up that sentiment. He knew how much Jackson Kohl looked up to him. Literally. What a thrill it had been for his parents when King had sprouted up past six feet as a teenager. It was the summer between his sophomore and junior years in high school, and his appetite had exploded. He ate and drank everything in sight and had been especially fond of apple juice, beef jerky, and tuna fish sandwiches made with sweet pickle. He couldn't get enough of them all. If he knew nothing else about his father, it was that the man hated his short stature—straining at 5'4" in his best shoes with lifts. And there was that time recently when Jackson had taken King aside and given him the unwelcome revelation of a lifetime, every bit as ponderous as any he had divulged over the years at St. Mary Basilica to Father LeBlanc or another priest on the other side of the confessional.

"I never thought I'd tell anyone this, son," he'd said. "But for some reason, I think now is the time to tell you . . . I've never really loved your mother the way everyone thinks I have. Everyone has always thought of us as the perfect couple. In many ways, we are. But that's not the whole story."

King had been unable to keep the shock out of his voice

and his face. "You don't mean that, do you, Pop? And if you do, why are you telling me now? I think I could've gone the rest of my life without knowing this."

"I do mean it, and I had this frightening dream the other night that time was running out."

King looked horrified. "You're basing this on a dream? About what?"

"I don't know. I had the sense that it was just a matter of time before things changed drastically," he had begun, but the pause he had taken next was significant, uncomfortably so for King. "But I can tell you about the rest of it, apart from the dream, that is. I did like your mother well enough. I just never loved her. I had an ulterior motive in marrying her, and you must never tell her I told you this. In fact, you must never tell anyone. You must take this to your grave."

That last word found its way into King's bloodstream, chilling it at once. "Why did you put it that way?"

"What way?"

"The mention of death. Are you trying to tell me that you're dying? Or Mom's dying?"

"No, nothing like that. It's just . . . a trite expression, that's all."

Even so, King knew the upcoming explanation would not be good news. "That's all quite a buildup. Will you please get whatever it is over with?"

Jackson had looked down at the floor as he spoke, clearly revealing that he was less than proud. "It was because I was so short, and your mother was taller than I was by several inches. And your uncle Murl was over six feet before he started shrinking there at the end. I admired him so. He looked down on nobody. That's why."

"Would you care to elaborate, or are you gonna just leave it at that? Uncle Murl was one toxic male specimen, I have to say. A couple of rape charges that got dismissed, as I recall, and

I'm willing to bet that he never set foot in church after his first communion."

"Okay, so he wasn't a saint. Who is? The thing is, I wanted tall children, taller than I was, at least. Specifically, I wanted a tall son, tall as your uncle Murl. And . . . and here you are. I got my genetic wish."

King could find no words.

"I'm so proud you're tall," Jackson had continued. "You've never had to put up with what I've had to in my life. They smirk and call it the 'small man syndrome.' I'd have to say it's real, based on my experience, but it's a battle you've never had to fight. To have more women taller than you are is something you don't want on your plate, believe me."

King found the comment even more unsettling than the one about his mother. "I hope you're proud of more than my height, Pop. That's kind of a backhanded compliment, if you think about it. I may have started out like Uncle Murl, but . . ."

"Wait . . . whaddaya mean, you started out like Uncle Murl? Is there something you haven't told me, son?"

King shrugged but also looked uncomfortable. "I just meant my attitude toward women, that's all. I think it's not what it should be."

Jackson had blanched. "Please tell me you aren't gay. Not after all the girlfriends you've had. You can't be."

"Hell, no, Pop. That's not what I meant at all."

Jackson had gone on to tell him that of course he was proud of him, but it had stuck with King all this time that perhaps his father didn't really see who he was; that his presumption was that all his son wanted was to continue being a part of the business. A tall part of the business. It had seemed so superficial—without any true depth of feeling. It was all a matter of inches. Was that the extent of the relationship between father and son? If so, what loyalty did he really owe to the man?

And then there was that dream his father had detailed.

King had read up on dreams afterward, even though he knew from his catechism that the church did not exactly endorse such a diversion as gospel. The book he'd skimmed insisted that information could sometimes be imparted in dreams that could be obtained nowhere else—including waking life. If that were true, then that description of "time running out" truly disturbed him. How could his father know anything? Was this just a random thing? How could anyone know, other than Father LeBlanc?

King snapped out of that particular reverie and thought about his mother for a moment. How would Ethel Mayes Kohl handle such a revelation about why his father had married her, assuming she ever found out? He knew he would never tell her such a cruel and calculating thing. Nonetheless, she was a formidable woman, and she had never been concerned about the business. Instead, her mantra was *family, family, family.* More than ever lately, she had been pressing him about getting married and giving her grandchildren before she got too old to pick them up and play peekaboo without too much of an effort. She had even told King that she had some names picked out for them when they came. That had been an annoying revelation for him, to say the least. He hadn't even begun to think about such a thing as baby names. That not only wasn't on his plate, but the plates weren't even in the cupboard.

"King, honey," she had begun in that smoker's voice of hers that had long ago become her trademark in the days before she had quit, "I want you to keep these family hand-me-downs in mind when you and your wife get pregnant. I fully expect grandchildren to spoil." They were both sitting on the wicker sofa on the back screen porch underneath the whirring of the creaky old ceiling fan that they'd been meaning to replace for years. They certainly had the wealth and wherewithal to do it, but for some reason just hadn't. With great wealth sometimes came great inertia, and wealthy people could get away with this and that being run-down or out of order for a while. They were just termed *quirky* and given a jet runway's worth of the benefit of the doubt by their peers.

Caught off-guard, King had said, "But I'm not even married yet. And what do you mean—hand-me-downs? Are you talking about clothes? I can buy my own clothes, Mom. I stopped letting you dress me back in high school, if you recall."

The remark seemed to wound Ethel, and before continuing, she had taken another sip of her mimosa that she was never without past noon in hot weather. "Heavens, no. Forget about clothes. I mean handing down our family names. Now, if you should happen to have a girl first, I think Lorien would be nice. That was your great-grandmother's name, and no one has ever bothered to honor her. We can't let her slip between the cracks, can we?"

"I don't mean to be disrespectful, but Lorien sounds like a sports car, Mom. We might as well be calling her Jaguar."

"Don't be silly. It's perfectly respectable." There had been a pause in between further savoring of the mimosa. "And then, if you should have a boy, I favor Belfast."

King was unable to restrain himself. "You're kidding? A kid having to live with that all his life? Wasn't that the name of one of Rosalie's mansions that got burned down during the Civil War? Didn't a Union officer blow it up on the High Bluff because he wasn't invited to one of those elaborate soirées the planters were always giving to keep the Union brass happy and at bay?"

"No, you're thinking of Belforest. That was the Forest family. They say Franklin Forest committed suicide after that because he just couldn't take the loss of his magnificent mansion. Just up and cut his wrists and bled out all over the Belter parlor love seat. They had to throw it out because of all the bloodstains that just wouldn't come out, no matter what they did. Of course, I suppose an upholsterer could only do so much back in those days. Now try to keep up."

That was another thing. How ironic that Ethel had told him to "try to keep up." It was she who seemed to be slow on the uptake these days, asking people to repeat things all the time. King had even suggested she have her hearing tested, but she would have none of it. Just the mention that she might be hard of hearing sent her into what Southerners referred to as a hissy fit. Still, something about her seemed to have changed and wasn't quite right.

Matters had gone even further downhill during their baby names discussion, and King had not bothered to try and retain the succession of inappropriate monikers his mother had trotted out in dizzying and ditzy fashion. He only knew that she continued to press him these days about the women he had been dating—particularly, the two he had seen the most of since college had ended five years ago—Bella Compton and Patrice Leyton.

King returned to his bridge party guest list, smiling at the next name he was viewing.

Ah, Bella! Short for Isabella, which he always thought had a medieval flair to it. Or was he thinking of Queen Isabella of Spain, ordering the *Niña*, *Pinta*, and *Santa María* to set sail for the New World? He had invited her up to his college graduation, and that's where they had first done it—at the Holiday Inn, instead of on campus. Few could afford the price of their rooms, but King had paid for their best suite and ordered up room service to gild the lily. It had all seemed so adult to the both of them, giving them a feeling of smugness and superiority. Champagne, smoked salmon, and sex. Could anything be more illusion-building?

After that, they continued seeing each other in Rosalie and became identified as a couple socially. Ethel and Jackson were beside themselves in anticipation of a wedding, which would genetically bring together the wealthy Kohl and Compton families in perfect union. And what a looker Bella was: nearly as tall as he was, but blond where he was dark; freckled across the bridge of her nose and prone to sunburn, she had the sort of smile that suggested she should be modeling toothpaste or moisturizer out in California. Plus, Jackson never tired of pulling his son aside about the important matter of proposing.

"I'm tired a' asking this. When are you two gonna tie the knot?" he had said during their most recent discussion. "Your children are sure to be tall, you know."

But King had thrown cold water on his father's enthusiasm with no qualms, having not fully recovered from the revelation about his mother's family's tall genes in that previous confrontation. "On the other hand, Pop, we could have a throwback. After all, you're short, so the odds favored me not being as tall as I am. Genetics are a crapshoot, and then there's always that 'skipping a generation' thing. That's not out of the realm of possibilities."

Jackson scowled, stopping short of wagging a finger. "Why in hell would you wanna go there, son? Are you just trying to annoy me?"

King just let it lie there. He disdained a serious discussion on the subject of settling down. Besides, Bella Compton was willing to wait, anyway. Forever, if she needed to, as she had told him before their falling out, and that had been fine with him. "I want to be with you 'til death do us part," were her exact words.

King pulled out of his contemplation. *Death. Time running out.* Was it all as simple as that? Was there some hope for him yet?

As for Patrice Leyton, she was a different proposition altogether. There had been that summer when King and Bella had had that big falling out, and he had told her in a regrettable fit of rage that their courtship, so to speak, was going nowhere fast. It was somewhat of a lie, since he still cared for her, but he chose not to clear up the matter. Sometimes, he thought commitment was not to be found in his DNA. There seemed to be something perverse in his makeup that he couldn't control.

So he had started seeing Patrice on the rebound, and he was not naïve enough to believe she was going out with him for any other reason than she had an eye to the main chance. He knew the Leyton family was not to the manner born—as blue-collar as they came. He would never have been caught dead dating her in high school, but she had come onto him more than once in a private moment or two at their lockers in between classes. He had filed it away and made good on her "offer without an expiration date" that she had granted him. She had even written him a little note on one of those blank greeting cards from the pharmacy and slipped it into his hand. It had read: *ANYTIME, BIG MAN, ANYTIME.* And then had been signed: *YOU KNOW WHO.*

Patrice's beauty was a striking contrast to Bella's. Whereas Bella seemed to have found a way to bottle sunshine at high noon, exuding it at a moment's notice, Patrice had mastered the art of looking downcast and vulnerable with her long lashes, darker coloring, and exquisite, pouting mouth. The combination was capped off by her generous bust, which had been her calling card since she was fourteen. She'd long had the boys swarming around her like fruit flies, and she hadn't exactly swatted them away, but she'd made it all too abundantly clear to King that it was he she really coveted.

King stopped himself from reviewing his relationship with Patrice any further. That smile he had generated at his thoughts of Bella had now morphed into an ugly frown, one that was more than painful. Maybe that chapter of his life with Patrice was the real beginning of what he was planning to tell them all at the party. His confession to Father LeBlanc had not really cleared up the matter for him. At least, not in any way deep down in his core, where he had to live with himself. The Hail Marys had rung hollow, just an exercising of fingers over rosary beads. Texture, but nothing in the way of real absolution. Perhaps there was only that one thing that really would turn his world right side up. That was the payoff he was hoping for, and then everyone would let him off the hook—Bella, Patrice, his parents and their expectations of him—every one of them—at the party. True, he imagined that none of them would likely view it the way he would, but it was his life, not theirs. Even if his father mentioning that phrase from the dream—*time running out*—continued to shake him to his roots. Was that an indication from unseen sources that it was too late?

Last on his list was Wendy Rierson, president of the Rosalie Country Club Bridge Bunch and reporter for the *Citizen*. Among the invitees, she was the true outlier. She did not really fit in as an integral part of his life, but he wanted her there anyway for some reason that he couldn't quite identify. Perhaps it was because he had found a way to lighten his load by getting back into the swing of playing bridge after he had first joined the club. She had been so welcoming, and it was there, while bidding and making a grand slam, that more of the idea had occurred to him. Plus, even though he knew she was married—and to a police detective, at that—he could not entirely banish the slight crush he had on her. It was the auburn hair and the blue eyes and the way she put all her players at ease every time they met and spent a few hours trumping tricks and counting points and winning rubbers. It had all further developed a new way of thinking and viewing his life for the young scion: a secret world that no one else knew anything about, yet which he fervently desired to enter. But that small group would soon know about it at the party, and he would take it from there, no matter how negatively any of them might react. And who knew? Maybe one or two of them would even understand his decision. Stranger things had happened in this world.

That last thought gave him pause. There was another way he could do this. Maybe he was making it too public all at once. Should he be more private about it? Was that the right way to go? One-on-one? What about Marcus Silvertree? He probably wouldn't even consider responding to an invitation, and wouldn't that seem like rubbing it in, at least on the surface? There was too much bad feeling between the two of them. Their last confrontation had been as rough-edged as they come.

"I may be out," Marcus had told him, standing rigidly across from him as King sat behind his office desk looking supremely smug. "But I'll find some way to get even with you, I swear. You and that daddy a' yours didn't play by the rules, and you know it. You stole customers from me right and left. You have no ethical standards, and you know it." Marcus had sounded and looked as fierce as his great, dark handlebar mustache, which had always made him look like part of an old-fashioned barbershop quartet, even though the man couldn't carry a tune.

"I doubt that very much," came the bored reply from his real estate competitor. "You make me want to yawn."

Then Marcus had stormed off, and there had been no contact between the two of them since, although King had shared the confrontation with his father, who had taken grand delight in the details.

"We got him, son, we got him." And there had been not a drop of empathy in Jackson Kohl's reply.

King went down the existing list and considered once again. But each time, something froze him in place, making him unable to pick and choose. Maybe he should just leave it all the way it was. He'd gone to all this trouble and planned nearly every detail, even though he'd had his mother help him design the invitations and pick out the stock; he was supremely annoyed that she had dipped her index finger in her perfume and touched it to the back of each envelope. Ugh! No man should send out scented invitations. But why turn back now and dump this format?

King got up from his desk and stretched his long legs. He glanced at his watch and was startled to discover how much time had passed since he had sat down with the list and reviewed everything. No matter. He exhaled and then headed for the kitchen, full of beef stew–preparation smells, where his part-time cook and housekeeper, Wyvonne Sidley, awaited him at the stove with an eager smile.

Young and single with a distracting head of trendy, long-flowing, rainbow-colored hair, she was putting herself through the College of Rosalie by working several afternoons a week for various wealthy families. She'd even worked her class schedule around her duties. It had taken King aback when she had made quite the production of telling him how to spell and pronounce her peculiar name properly.

"You see, the W and the Y combine into just the one letter Y all by itself and that's the letter you pronounce, followed by the ordinary VONNE part, if you get my drift," she had explained. Then she had said that her parents wanted something unique for her that people would remember, but also that to her way of thinking, they never really thought things through.

"My parents were like that with my name, too," King answered back, giving her a wink.

"Sometimes I think my parents should just have gotten some sense into their heads and just spelt it WHY-VONNE to avoid all the confusion," she had continued, and then left it at that.

"Is there something you need right now, Mr. Kohl?" Wyvonne was saying at the stove back in present time. "Your favorite stew should be ready in about another hour or so. I know how much you love it. I mean, I could actually serve it now in a pinch, but it gets better the longer it simmers."

He told her no, he needed nothing right now, and the stew smelled delicious as usual. Then, "I'm going out for a little spin. I need to get outta the house. I've been cooped up with my guest list all afternoon. I worry too much about everything, as you know. I shouldn't overthink things, but I guess it's in my nature."

"I know you want all your parties to go just right, and I think the ones I've helped out with have turned out that way. This one will, too."

King hesitated for a few awkward seconds, but then recovered his resolve. "There's no question about that, Wyvonne. I don't know what I'd do without you."

"Thanks. Well, when do you think you'll be back, sir?"

"Not sure," he told her. "It may take a little while. I'm gonna try to see if I can count every single KOHL AND SON sign all over Rosalie. I especially like the SOLD ones. More money in our pockets these days when things are tough, as Pop would say. That won't be an easy task to cover all that territory, since I don't intend to miss a one."

Wyvonne drew back, the wooden spoon she had been using nearly falling out of her hand before she awkwardly rescued it with an "Oops!" Then, "Wow! I guess that would take a while. You and your father must sell every piece of property in Rosalie, from what I've seen on every corner."

He smiled big for her. "Just about. We really are the only game in town now. The Silvertree Firm finally had to fold just recently after making a serious run at us these last few years. But I have to say that Marcus Silvertree just couldn't compete with me and Pop in the end. We put him out of his misery, and I know he didn't appreciate it one bit. In fact, I had quite a row with Marcus the evening he came to my office and told me he was hanging it all up now—that it was all over but the shoutin'. The man didn't take defeat graciously, lemme tell you."

"Well, I don't know anything about that, I'm sure, but I'd be interested in knowing how many signs you come up with," she said, tossing her carnival-sideshow hair back for dramatic effect.

"I promise to tell you, Wyvonne. I ought to know how many we have just by looking at the books. But I'm in the mood to verify my empire all for myself. Sometimes, you just have to experience things firsthand to believe they really exist, and you've accomplished what you've accomplished. I know that probably sounds strange to you, but that's where I am in my head right now."

"No, sir, I don't think it sounds strange at all. Everyone knows how successful you are. I've known it for some time now."

"Anyhow, I promise I'll text you if I get too far behind and run late. I wouldn't want you to burn that stew. I've been waiting to taste it all afternoon."

"Yessir, I know you have. And I'll be on the lookout for your text."

King took his keys off the wall hook and walked through the kitchen door into the spacious garage, with its hoses and leaf blowers and other handyman tools, and where his spotless, shiny BMW awaited him. He did so without turning around and waving, and thus missed the dreamy, laser beam of a look that Wyvonne was shooting his way.

Then she turned around and resumed stirring the stew, gazing down at it lovingly, as if it were actually liquid gold fit for a king.

*   *   *

King sat in his car, which was parked in front of the Kohl and Son office on Lambert Street, staring at the building with what he felt was conflicted affection. They were officially closed all week, since their secretary, Vera Maloney, was on vacation, and father and son had chosen to take the time off, as well. Lambert Street was a mixed neighborhood; that is, it was mostly residential, but a handful of lawyers, doctors, and Realtors had decided to spruce up a few of the raised cottages, gentrifying them and turning them into offices. Under Ethel's guidance, their cottage had been painted a robin's-egg blue with white gingerbread trim, and as a result, had come off looking more like an art gallery. Yet it was still pleasing to the eye, and the flower beds and pink crepe myrtles in the front yard made it even more inviting.

Farther down the street and just out of sight was the family home of the late spinster, Evadee Appleby, a listing King had stolen from Marcus Silvertree right under his nose. His approach had been underhanded yet effective.

"I need you to keep this strictly confidential," King had said to Evadee at one of Rosalie's Mardi Gras parties. "But I want you to have the best representation possible for your beautiful cottage. I know you'll be selling soon so you can move in with your daughter up in Port Gibson. Word is that Marcus Silvertree has been wooing you for your business. I feel you need to be kept in the loop in this particular situation."

Evadee had taken a swig of her teetotaler's soft drink and eyed him warily. "Do you know something I don't know?"

King had lowered his voice even further and leaned in with a wink. "I'm sure you know that Mr. Silvertree is a confirmed bachelor. Need I say more?"

Evadee had frowned. "I think you'd better. I'm not at all a worldly person."

"It's just that you don't want the wrong type of person to

be moving into your childhood home. You want it respected and cared for," King had continued, exploiting quite well Evadee's evangelical, dogmatic fervor. "Suppose he sells it to one of his . . . ahem, *friends*, and they decide to have all kinds of wild parties. Mr. Silvertree is well-connected that way, shall we say? I'm sure you don't want me to go into detail, being the grand lady that you are."

And that had done the trick. Promising to keep King's revelations in strictest confidence, Evadee had given him the listing, and Marcus Silvertree was none the wiser but all the poorer.

King came out of his remembrance of things past. He was halfway through his tour of the real estate signs, which was taking him all over the city, and he wanted to come to a stop and contemplate everything again. Suddenly, something began churning in the pit of his stomach. It wasn't painful or anything close to that, but it definitely felt intuitive to him, demanding his full attention. Yes, the tour had its purpose—surveying the kingdom was certainly appropriate at this point. There truly were signs galore on nearly every block, particularly since both Rosalie and the country were going through a recession. As a result, not everyone was a winner. But the mental debate about the method of delivering the message to the important people in his life had made an appearance earlier in the day when he had been reviewing the guest list. Was the party indeed the right format to announce such a thing?

He decided to discontinue the tour that he had disclosed to Wyvonne and made his way instead to the parking lot in front of the St. Mary Basilica Rectory, where he knew Father LeBlanc would advise him as he had been doing lately. He idled the engine for a while under the shade of one of the great live oaks that had been preserved when the lot had been paved about ten years ago. A group of very vocal, wealthy, older historians of the female, poofed-hair persuasion had picketed the construction site, demanding that several of the trees be saved from the buzz saw and the bulldozer, and they had succeeded. As a result, those mature, muscular branches still provided their shade to the concrete below, branches that had taken at least a hundred years or more to reach their size. Such treasures, the ladies insisted, were not to be cast aside so callously, and their voices had been heeded.

Finally, King shut off the engine and sighed. Whatever Father recommended at this point would determine his final decision. He would either go through with the bridge party that really wasn't a bridge party, or he would tell each person on a one-to-one basis, face-to-face, pulling no punches. That would ensure some measure of privacy should the revelation run someone off the rails, which might be a real possibility. Hell, there might even be an actual train wreck, with boxcars spilling all over creation and first responders speeding to the rescue. After all, this wasn't business as usual he was going to discuss.

As he entered the two-story brick rectory that stood next to the mighty Gothic basilica itself—the center of Catholicism in the early years of Mississippi history—he tried to envision his parents, as well as Bella and Patrice, reacting to it all. But images refused to pop up in his brain. Instead, there was only a curious but impenetrable fog, one composed equally of self-doubt and stubborn determination to go through with it. How could those two things exist at the same time? Yet, they did. King could only hope that Father LeBlanc would clear things up as quickly as reciting the rosary usually did for him. Except in the matter of Patrice. There was always that.

But the lanky, balding priest with the pockmarked face didn't seem to be in such a seamless, straightening-things-out mood once they had settled into his crowded little office with one square, stained glass window as the only source of multi-colored incoming light. In fact, there was a decided lack of empathy in his tone for the face-to-face session.

"Before we go much further," Father LeBlanc said, "are you having second thoughts about this?"

"You mean . . . ?"

"Of course I mean."

King gave him a most emphatic, "No! Absolutely no second thoughts."

"I believe you, son. I don't think there's any way you could fake such emotion. Then, full speed ahead, but I think one-on-one is your best option. You were right to balk at that party idea. I wouldn't have advised it had you come to me first. This makes everything so much more private, and I think that's what you need in this situation. Incidentally, were you actually going to play bridge on such an occasion? Truthfully, I can't see the two mixing very well."

King managed to crack a smile. "Well . . . yes. I thought we could start with that, and then when everyone had had enough to eat and drink, I was going to make the announcement. Aren't things easier to take when people have full stomachs?"

"Depends. Sometimes it's best to reveal things to empty stomachs. That way, people won't get sick if the news upsets them." Father LeBlanc briefly turned his head to one side, seemingly mesmerized by the stained glass. "I know what grand parties your family throws—I've been invited to more than a few and enjoyed myself thoroughly. But you need to sit down and decide your pecking order, who gets the news first and who needs a little more careful handling. But I believe you're up to it. Because if you can't handle this, you won't be able to handle all the rest that will surely follow."

"Point well-taken," King told him with a gentle nod.

Now, there was nothing left to do but go home, eat Wyvonne's dependably delicious stew, and then work out the all-important logistics of the multiple sessions that lay ahead of him.

* * *

About an hour later in his den, King's pecking order wasn't even beginning to fall into place for him. Was it the two generous helpings of stew and two glasses of Merlot that he had enjoyed as the perfect accompaniment that were weighing him down, making him sleepy, unable to fully concentrate? After thirty minutes of putting numbers by names, scratching through them, printing new names in all caps, and numbering those all over again, he wondered if he should just give up, get some sleep, and tackle it again in the morning. There was still plenty of time to let people know before Saturday rolled around. Plenty of time for them to make other plans or get used to what he had to tell them. If they possibly could.

Frustrated, he crumpled the sheet of paper he had been scribbling on into a ball and dropped it into the trash can by his feet underneath his desk. It was nearly full, as he had not let Wyvonne in to empty it all afternoon. But instead of heading off to bed, he decided to give it one more try. With a fresh sheet, he listed everyone in all caps once more:

MOM AND POP (Together? Separately? Last? First?)
BELLA (Before Patrice? After?)
PATRICE (Same as above)
WENDY RIERSON (Last of all?)
WYVONNE (?)—When? She'll have to know. Sooner rather than later?
MARCUS SILVERTREE (?)—Option? Does he even need to know? Do I even owe him?
VERA MALONEY—When she comes back from vacation, obviously. She will do as she is told.

Then, an additional scribble:

HOUSE OR OFFICE?

A couple of quick knocks at the doorframe of the den startled him, and he looked up from his paper to see Wyvonne smiling his way.

"I've put all the dishes in the dishwasher, so I'm heading home."

King managed to return her smile, but he was not feeling it at all. "Great." He gave her a thumbs-up. "Primo stew, as usual."

"Thanks." There was a pause, during which she worked her fingers together nervously. "Oh, you be sure and leave the shopping list for the party on the counter so I can go to the grocery store for you tomorrow afternoon."

Her words sounded like she was a recording on the wrong, slow speed. They crawled along in his brain and refused to stop.

Well, there it was—out in the open. Should he tell her now or wait? It was all a matter of timing for what lay ahead of him.

"About the list and the party Saturday," he began at last. "I've decided to call it off. You don't have to come in or prepare anything." He faked a couple of coughs for effect. "I think . . . I think I may be coming down with something. I've had the sniffles all day . . . and sneezing, too."

Wyvonne looked and sounded startled. "Really? I didn't hear any of that from you today. You must have been covering it up awfully well."

"I kinda suppressed it, but yes, I've got that scratchy throat feeling I always get when I'm getting a cold," he continued.

"I know that feeling. I hate it. But this isn't flu season."

"It's just now coming to a head, and people can get the flu in May."

She was still glancing at him sideways. "But you may be better by Saturday. Are you sure you wanna call the party off now? You could always wait and see how you feel tomorrow. To tell the truth, I was looking forward to putting together another of your parties for you. We've got quite the track record, you and I."

He coughed again, this time adding a sniffle or two. "I'm sure you were. But it wouldn't do either of us any good to have it while I'm sick, now, would it?"

She didn't answer immediately but finally gave in. "No, I guess not. Are you gonna go to the doctor tomorrow?"

"I never like to go unless I have to. I have a thing about that. I'd rather not hear bad news if there is any."

"You men are all alike," she told him with a wry grin. "You wait until things get out of hand before you do anything about 'em. Then, when it's too late and you do get really sick, you act like the biggest babies. I don't know how those of you who don't have wives to look after you get by."

King recognized himself in her sentiments and allowed himself to smile, holding up his right hand. "Guilty."

The conversation seemed to lapse at that point. Nonetheless, he wondered if he should leave it at that. She would have to be told sooner rather than later, even if he had taken care of the matter of the party. At least he had done that much. Should she now be his trial run? Would he learn anything at all from her reaction? And then beyond all that, could he trust her? What if he told her part of his decision but not all of it? Maybe that was the way to go.

CHAPTER 2

On Friday morning, a little before 9 a.m., Wendy received a text on her cell as she sat in her cubicle at the *Citizen* and focused. The message from King Kohl was more than surprising. Furthermore, her investigative instincts were fully aroused, alerting her to the probability that something unexpected was hunkering down just below the horizon.

Canceling the party tomorrow; need to explain in detail; come to my house; is 10 AM doable?

Wendy didn't have to check her schedule. There was nothing urgent that had to be composed that day, and she had just tied a ribbon neatly around the piece Lyndell had assigned her about whose bones those were that had been found in the basement of Lacework House on Broad Street during a recent renovation. In an unsensational manner, it was revealed that they had belonged to a carpenter named Billy Caspian, who had gone missing seventy-five years ago. Rosalie's longest missing person case was now solved, thanks to Wendy's superb "poking around" skills. Mind you, what had caused his death had not been determined, nor did it seem likely that it would ever be, given the three-quarters of a century that had elapsed. But her reputation as the town's greatest amateur sleuth—one who simultaneously held down her paying job— would only be further enhanced by the episode. "Billy Caspian's Bones" would be yet another notch on her gun.

10 is fine, came the reply from her deft fingers.

please don't be late; tight schedule; come right on in.

She texted back: *I understand; see you soon.*

What was up with King? Why go to all the trouble of is- suing expensive invitations to one of his events and then can- celing it at the last minute? Rosalie people in the social swim of things were experts at coordinating their events, always making sure they did not conflict with something else going on at the same time; unless there was an unexpected death and subsequent funeral to attend. No one could ever foresee something like that, of course. King surely could not have been guilty of committing such a grievous error. No, some- thing else was in the works, and Wendy could hardly contain her curiosity. But first, she needed to drop in on Lyndell and let her know about the curious development. It was always protocol to go through channels at the *Citizen.*

"In the couple of years I've been living here in Rosalie, I've become more than familiar with the Kohls and their in- fluence," Lyndell said, after Wendy had explained everything in a concise manner. Then she leaned forward in her leather chair behind her desk, looking every inch the professional ed- itor she was: her streaked hair in the flattering, short style she preferred; her mustard-colored business suit making her pop in an office featuring nondescript beige walls decorated with numerous journalistic award plaques.

"So you think something strange might be going on?" Lyndell continued.

"You know all about me and my instincts," Wendy said. "The text was so matter-of-fact. Not an atom of flirting, which he's always doing. I think there may be a scoop for the paper that comes out of this meeting."

"But you have no inkling as to what that scoop might be?"

Wendy hesitated at first, then thought better of her reluctance. "He's Rosalie's most eligible bachelor. So if I had to guess, I'd say maybe some sort of wedding announcement was intended with the bridge party in the first place. I have to admit, it seems like the ideal way to spring that on people. As I don't have to tell you, Rosalie loves its weddings."

"Your father went all out for ours, I know that much," Lyndell said, her long, angular face lighting up with what were obviously her many cherished memories of the occasion.

Wendy smiled back and nodded. "Agreed. Daddy did both mine and yours up right. But if I had to second-guess myself, I'd say that maybe King Kohl's wedding plans with a certain someone fell through at the last minute, and he figures the one-on-one approach is the best to let everyone know. Maybe less humiliating."

Lyndell was shaking her head emphatically. "Doesn't sound right, though. I predict that this is about something else. You said the text was out of character."

"Yeah, I wouldn't be surprised if I were entirely mistaken. But neither of us has long to wait. I'm heading over there in less than an hour, and I'll be back with the real story in all its gossipy, Rosalie essence."

"Have fun," Lyndell told her, as Wendy rose from her chair and headed to the door.

"Depends upon what you mean by *fun*," Wendy said without turning around.

Lyndell got in the last word. "It's been my experience that you always end up making your own, my dear stepdaughter."

* * *

Wendy was excellent at time management, having an unerring sense of the distance to be traveled to reach any particular destination. It wasn't a matter of familiarity, either. She
was almost never late for any appointment anywhere, even for
the first time. Her predilection for higher math, her college
minor, always kicked in and served her well; and King Kohl's
home on Minor Street was one of her favorite destinations because of all the fun she'd had there previously. She'd even
pulled off a grand slam at the very first party King had
thrown—7 spades bid and made, as a matter of fact. Doubled
and vulnerable. What a Fort Knox of points that was, and she
thought the celebration would never end. Cocktails were
raised high, and rims clinked.

As Wendy turned onto Minor Street, she was still trying to
figure out what King was going to tell her in no uncertain
terms. It had to be of a serious nature in order to postpone one
of his legendary social gatherings featuring unlimited food,
drink, and game playing; there was also the matter of request-
ing such a private audience with her. Mental snippets swirled
around her brain, at times seeming to escape into the intimate
space inside the car itself. She found herself almost wanting to
snatch them out of the air to examine them closely in the
palm of her hand. Suddenly, nothing was off limits:

a wedding or engagement called off?
a medical diagnosis?
a crime revealed?
something completely out of left field?

Her wild speculation, unfortunately, was resolving nothing as she pulled up in front of Kohl Place, as the family had
decided to call it, and parked the car. Her cell phone showed
9:58, so she was a bit early. She took a deep breath and psy-
ched herself up for whatever was going to take place. But no

sooner had she done so and stepped out of the front seat than a swarthy man with a great handlebar mustache charged out the front door as if he had been set on fire, cell phone in hand. He didn't even bother to close the door behind him. The look on his face was crazed, his eyes seeming to move in all directions at once. Then he caught sight of Wendy emerging from her car. He stopped as if he had run into an invisible wall. His words came in spurts, and he was in a visibly confused state.

"I . . . I just called . . . I just . . . 9-1-1 . . . they're . . . they're coming. I wasn't running away . . . I just wanted to get outta there . . ."

Whatever it was that had the man in his constrictor-like grip reached out and engulfed Wendy, as well. She had no idea what he was talking about, but she immediately felt alarmed, even terrified, and could not move. She was certain there were molecules of fear in the air. She had long suspected that crisis could sometimes become a tangible thing.

"What . . . are you talking about? What's going on? Has something happened to Mr. Kohl?"

The man did a half-turn and pointed back to the door. "He's . . . he's dead . . . long live the King—King Kohl is dead."

Now, Wendy was right up in front of the man, and she could easily see the rapid rise and fall of his chest underneath his white shirt. "Are you sure?"

"Sure, I'm sure," the man told her. "Anyone could tell. His head, the side of his head . . . and as I said, I've called 9-1-1."

Almost as a reflex, Wendy said, "Who are you?"

"I'm . . . Marcus Silvertree," came the reply. "But . . . I swear he was dead when I got here just a few minutes ago."

Being the investigative reporter that she was, Wendy frowned at his choice of words. There was some sort of guilt implied in them. She hadn't accused him of anything, yet he had obviously been concerned about appearances. Or was he just in shock and couldn't think straight? And what about that phrase—*long live the King?* There was almost a mockery implied.

"And . . . and I wouldn't go in there if I were you," Marcus continued, his eyes still refusing to light anywhere. "It's . . . not a pretty sight. His temple's been bashed in. It's brutal."

Wendy would not allow herself to conjure up any sort of image and said, "I'll take your advice. But you did say you called 9-1-1?"

He nodded emphatically.

"I'll text my husband. He's a detective," she told him, and then proceeded to do so.

you're kidding? came Ross's nearly immediate reply after she'd condensed the news.

no

on the way; I'll tell your daddy, too.

"My husband's coming," Wendy said, looking up from the phone. "He'll probably get here about the same time as the first responders."

Marcus Silvertree's response again struck Wendy as overly emphatic. "I didn't do it . . . you have to believe me . . . he was already dead when I arrived."

It was a trite expression that occurred to Wendy, but it was amazing how often it turned out to be true: *Methinks he doth protest too much.*

Kohl Place had been turned into a crime scene with breathtaking speed. Sirens and flashing lights alerted the entire Minor Street neighborhood that a crisis was in their midst, and spectators began to emerge from their houses onto their porches or out onto the sidewalks to gawk at the proceedings. First, the paramedics; then the coroner, the scrawny Tommy

Cantwell; then Ross and his father-in-law, Captain Bax, along with a couple of criminologists, all arrived within a few minutes of each other. In a small town like Rosalie, where no destination was more than twenty minutes or so away, it was SOP that such situations were tended to quickly. Ross and Bax made a quick, preliminary foray inside and emerged shaking their heads. But it mostly fell to Wendy to try and comfort Jackson and Ethel, still in their bathrobes, when all the noise and commotion roused them from the slave quarters, and Ross gave them the terrible news as gently as he could.

"I'm so sorry to have to tell you that your son has been killed."

"What? How?" Jackson said, his voice high-pitched and stressed.

"It appears he was attacked with one of his awards plaques. There were fatal blows to the temple area. Again, I'm very sorry for your loss."

Ethel was unable to say anything, nearly collapsing and then dissolving into tears in her husband's arms while he stroked her graying hair gently. Jackson, however, was not at a loss for words, his eyes frantically scanning the sidewalk as if trying to find someone to blame. "I can't believe it. How could this have happened? He was busy preparing for one of his big bridge parties Saturday. Everything was just fine." Then, he lighted on Marcus. "What the hell are you doing here? Did you do this to our son, you scum?"

Ross wedged himself quickly between Jackson and Marcus to avoid a possible physical confrontation. "Mr. Silvertree was the one who discovered the body. That's all we know right now. Everyone must remain calm."

But Jackson ignored the comment. "What the hell were you doing here anyway, Marcus? I thought we'd seen the last of you."

"King texted me to come. He said he had something important to tell me. He practically begged me to come. I assure you that I didn't want to."

"Sure you didn't," Jackson continued with great intensity. "What would he have to say to you? You're finished in this town."

Captain Bax now decided to intervene, thrusting out his strong jaw and impressive chest while conjuring up his most paternal demeanor. "I know how traumatic this must be for you both. But we've just this minute started our investigation. We intend to follow the evidence. Meanwhile, if there's anything you or Miz Kohl think would help us with our investigation, we welcome you down at the station. Mr. Silvertree will be doing his part, I assure you."

Jackson's tone softened a bit. "After we . . . I take care of a few things. The funeral home, you know. The arrangements . . ." Suddenly, his emotions matched those of his wife, and tears welled in his eyes. "This is . . . such a blow. He was our only child."

"Again, we're all so sorry for your loss," Wendy said, reaching out to touch Ethel's sleeve. She could feel the woman trembling.

Once the entire house had been encircled with crime scene tape, both Ross and Bax went in again to do more work. Wendy, the Kohls, and Marcus Silvertree were not allowed inside. Of course, Wendy had not wanted to enter from the beginning. She only had Marcus's frantic, heavy-breathing account of everything, and the stroking of Ethel's arm every now and then, to occupy herself until the criminologists and coroner completed their work. When that was finally accomplished, and King's body had been conveyed on a gurney to the ambulance in a body bag to the accompaniment of his wailing mother, Ross and Bax at last emerged from the house.

Ethel broke away from her husband and reached out for the gurney, shouting defiantly. "No, no, you can't take him away from me just yet. I must see him. He's my son."

"Dear, no, no, we have to . . . let him go," Jackson told her, pulling her back. "We'll have services and visitation and all the rest and send him on his way as we should. Neither of us wants to remember him the way he is now, I'm sure."

Ross addressed the entire group. "This is a terrible tragedy for Rosalie. We'll all want closure." Then he took his wife aside and said in nearly whispering tones, "As I told the Kohls, it was blunt force trauma to the head with one of his real estate plaques, which was on the floor beside his body. You could see where it had been ripped off the wall from the lack of discoloration on the wallpaper behind it. Looks like someone was full of rage, to me."

Marcus continued his robust objections, even though he could not make out everything Ross was saying. "All I did was discover the body, though. He texted me to meet him in his den and just to come on in, I swear and . . ."

Ross held up his hand, signaling that he wanted Marcus to stop talking. "You'll have plenty of time to tell us everything down at headquarters, sir. The report from the crime lab will tell us the rest of the story about prints and DNA. We'll want you to get in the squad car, of course, since you are a person of interest."

Marcus's voice was still raw with emotion. "Yes, but . . . I didn't do this . . . he was already dead when I walked in. He was already slumped over his desk."

Ross put on his best professional smile. "You'll be treated fairly, Mr. Silvertree. Just tell us the truth as you know it." Then he turned to Jackson. "I know this is traumatic for you and your wife, but if you can come down to the station later today, it would be appreciated."

Ethel finally managed to speak through her sobs. "Does it

have to be today? I don't see how I can do that. My son is dead. Have you no sense of my grief?"

"When you're up to it, Miz Kohl," Bax butted in. "We completely understand how upset you are."

Then Ross patted his wife's shoulder gently. "You come on down, too, sweetheart. Looks like you've stepped into the middle of one again, and you need to tell us what you know."

Wendy knew he meant nothing smart-alecky by the remark, but she couldn't help but wince a bit. Not that long ago, on the day she had received the invitation from King himself, in fact, Ross had been joking about how long it had been since she'd had her hand in a genuine murder mystery. And now, here she was again, involved from the beginning; no secondhand accounts for her. There was still much to learn about the apparent murder: the TOD, if any witnesses had seen anyone besides Marcus Silvertree coming and going, and the universe of facts and speculations to blend together until someone—perhaps the Rosalie Police Department, or herself, or some combination of the two—discovered the *who* and the *why,* because the *when* and the *where* had already been determined. Or so it seemed at this early stage of the case.

But more than once in Wendy's career as an amateur sleuth and investigate reporter, what appeared to be obvious and taken for granted was *anything but.*

CHAPTER 3

Down at headquarters, in the cozy interview room with its institutional green walls and camera rolling high up in one corner, Wendy had just shown Ross and her father the text that she had received from King earlier that morning and had also let Lyndell in on a few minutes later. Both men could only shrug at the evidence, which seemed entirely unremarkable and straightforward.

"And there's nothing further you can add personally to this message?" Ross said, sitting across from her with Bax by his side. "No inkling of what he was getting ready to tell you?"

Wendy put the palm of her hand to the right side of her face and leaned on her elbow. "Nope. None whatsoever. Lyndell and I did discuss it a bit before I left, and I theorized that he might be ready to cancel wedding plans that he had intended to announce in the first place at the bridge party. I thought perhaps something drastic of a romantic nature had happened at the last minute, but Lyndell had a different idea."

"And that idea was?" Ross said.

Wendy shook her head. "No, there wasn't anything definite that she mentioned. It was just that she seemed to be betting against the wedding scenario. Rosalie being the social town it is, I agree that it's hard to keep wedding rumors from climbing the grapevine."

Bax chimed in agreeably. "That's true. People thrive on weddings and wedding news in this town. I believe the slightest little hint of tying the knot sparks the fires of gossip, if I do say so myself." He paused, and his pleasant features were suddenly creased with lines. "And I hate to say it, but Rosalieans feel the same way about funerals. In fact, I know one grande dame, who shall remain nameless out of respect for her privacy, who confided to me once that if it weren't for funerals, she would never get to see anyone socially. She said she actually looked forward to them."

Wendy had a look of resignation on her face. "I can well imagine. And I think I know who you're talking about, but I won't say her name, either."

Bax asked his daughter to summarize again the sequence that she had previously described as Marcus Silvertree barreling out of Kohl Place onto the sidewalk just as she was emerging from her car. That testimony, too, seemed unremarkable.

"So, we've done our legal duty, daughter a' mine, and gotten all outta you there is to get," he concluded, looking supremely satisfied. "You can get back to the newspaper now, and we'll see what Mr. Silvertree has to say for himself. My sense of this is that he really did walk in on what looks for all the world like a murder—after the fact. Just my detective intuition."

Wendy slowly rose from the table. "I don't have to tell you that Lyndell will want me to do a piece on this. This has happened to one of Rosalie's most prominent families, and everyone will be shocked to hear it."

"What else is new?" Ross said with a smirk. "You know the rules by now. We won't be able to share much of our official investigation with you, but you can certainly share anything you come across with us in your research for your newspaper article."

"Seems to have worked for us in the past. Among the three of us, we seem to get at the heart of these crimes rather quickly."

Ross continued to look pleased. "Then let's keep our string going."

Ross knew very little about Marcus Silvertree except that he was stubbornly single, his real estate company had recently folded, and Jackson and King Kohl were the reason. He did know from the town scuttlebutt that there was no love lost between the two firms. He had never met Marcus socially, which was the officially approved way of getting ahead in Rosalie, under any circumstances. There were so many different opportunities to enter the mainstream and make good— Pilgrimage parties; Mardi Gras parades and balls; celebrations like the Food and Wine Festival, the Literary and Cinema Festival, and the Music and Opera Festival. There were committees galore to join and people to impress as a result. Ross had essentially achieved that without trying when he married into the well-connected Winchester family, headed by Captain Bax, and thus didn't have to worry about such things. Not that he ever had, really. He was a detective through and through, not a dandy with a penchant for small talk and getting a buzz on.

At the moment, Ross was sitting across from Marcus, studying his body language and facial expressions and hoping to glean information from those observations. A detective worth his or her salt could often zero in on certain things before the first words were spoken. It was clear that Marcus was nervous. There were beads of sweat across his broad forehead, and his lips were drawn back in a grim slash. All of it was inconsistent with his swarthy complexion, dark hair, and handlebar mustache, which suggested a most imposing personality.

The first order of business was the text that King had sent

Marcus, inviting him to come to Kohl Place for reasons unknown. King's phone, which was found on the desk next to
his slumping body, was confiscated as evidence and had already been examined for prints and DNA. Texts to Marcus
and Wendy had been made on the phone at the times both
said they were. The crime lab's timely report showed that only
King's prints were found—a fact that Ross chose not to reveal
to Marcus for the time being. He did, however, mention that
Marcus's prints were found on the doorknob—no big surprise—and that King had been dead less than an hour, according to the coroner's report. That put Marcus in the right place
and within the right time frame. Was this a slam dunk?

"So, why do you think King wanted you to come to his
house this morning?" Ross began. "Was there some unfinished business the two of you had to discuss?"

Marcus frowned but did not answer.

"We need you to be completely open with us, Mr. Silvertree. Tell us the truth, as you know it."

"I suppose you're referring to the fact that my firm recently went out of business. Everyone around town knows
about it, so that's no secret."

"Yes, it's not a secret," Ross continued. "But why do you
think Mr. Kohl wanted to talk to you at this point in time? Do
you think it had to do with your business or something entirely different?"

Marcus seemed to relax slightly, and his tone became
softer. "I don't see what he could possibly have had to say to
me. I'll tell it like it is. He and I had it out in his office a while
back when I said my final piece to him about his ethics—or
rather, his lack of them. About the way he and his parents always attended everybody's funeral in hopes of finding out
what was going to happen to the houses in question and
schmoozing the hell outta people to try and get their business
if they intended to sell. They shed many a crocodile tear, be-

lieve me. And it wasn't just that. Sometimes, they stole clients from me at the last minute before they'd signed on the dotted line, offering this and that incentive, offering to taking less commission than I would, that sort of thing. There was also gossip spread about me, which I did not appreciate."

"I can well understand that you wouldn't appreciate that," Ross said as evenly as possible.

"They already had the advantage in this town. They were the established firm. I had to work twice as hard just to keep my head above water. The Kohls got away with things because they could. You have no idea."

"Sounds like you had a tough row to hoe," Ross continued, trying to sound sympathetic but wondering at this point if the formidable-looking Mr. Silvertree lacked the toughness to prevail in a monopoly market like Rosalie.

"At any rate, I have no idea why King wanted to talk to me. But he texted it so urgently, I decided to take the bait, if you'll allow me to use that phrase. So I headed over, making sure I was on time. He emphasized that I must not be late, and he said just to come on in, that he'd be waiting for me in the den. I thought that was peculiar. Why wouldn't he just greet me at the door?"

Ross sat up a bit. "What time did he ask you to arrive?"

"A little before ten. He said come five minutes early. I was already wary of the invitation. I guess I didn't expect things to be so casual, since the last words we'd had were pretty angry. I was expecting some stiff greeting from him at the front door. Anything was possible. Maybe he was gonna punch me in the face for old time's sake?"

"That's a peculiar way of putting it. Did you make any threats to him that first time?"

"No." There was a brief pause. "Well, not anything specific, anyway. I was just spouting off at the mouth, I was so angry. People make angry threats all the time on the spur of

the moment. I had no intention of following through on anything but leaving this snobby town."

"And I assume from what you are telling us that no threats
were made this time as well."

Marcus looked exasperated. "If that was supposed to be a
trap, it didn't work. How could there be any threats? I'm telling
you, when I entered the front door into the foyer, I called out
his name. When there was no answer, I headed toward the den,
where he said he'd be waiting for me. I have to say that the second I entered the house, something felt wrong to me."

"How so?"

"Just a feeling I had. Something in the air. Do you suppose
there are such things as molecules of death that are actually given
off when someone leaves this earth? I can't explain it. Haven't
you ever had sensations like that as a detective? That something
bad was looming ahead or surrounding you, and you just
couldn't shake it? You could almost reach out and touch it."

Ross managed a hint of a smile. He had indeed encoun-
tered such circumstances and had always come away from
them alive, without a bullet wound or worse, despite his mis-
givings going in. "I know what you mean. Please, go ahead
with your story."

"There's not much more to tell. I saw King slumped over
the desk with his head bleeding and that plaque on the floor,
and then I called 9-1-1 and got outta there as fast I could." He
paused to swallow. "And then, when I got outside, there was
your wife waiting, and all I could think of was to tell her that
King was dead. I know I must've sounded crazy and off my
rocker, but I wasn't thinking straight after the shock."

"You realize, of course, that you are a person of interest
and must remain here in Rosalie during this investigation."

Marcus shrugged and tried to sound disinterested. "I have
nowhere else to go. I've been trying to decide what to do next
since the business went under. I grew up in Greenwood.

Maybe I'll move back there and try to start over. People said to me before I moved down here, 'Don't go to Rosalie. It's so closed off and full of layers, and nobody plays by ordinary rules. You'll never make it there.' Well, they were right, as far as I'm concerned."

"Then you have to understand why you remain a suspect in this case," Ross said. "You had motive and opportunity, and you admit you were there this morning."

"Yes, I understand all that. But you should talk to King's parents and find out what was going on in his life, if you want my opinion. The three of them, they were all intertwined— and maybe in not such a healthy way."

"We intend to do that," Ross told him. "This investigation has just begun, and we'll get in touch if we need to run something else by you."

Marcus exhaled noisily. "I assure you, I'll cooperate. I did resent King and his parents, but I wouldn't even think of bashing their heads in. Hey, they might not have a moral code worth a hoot, but I assure you that I do."

Not long after Marcus had left, Bax came into the interview room and took a seat next to his son-in-law. "Jackson Kohl is here, but without his wife, and he wants to speak to both of us now. I told him I'd check and see if you were free."

"Yep. Might as well show him in. I just hope he and Marcus Silvertree don't meet up on the way in and out."

Fortuitously, that did not happen, and soon, both Ross and Bax were sitting across from Jackson Kohl, who seemed in control of his emotions for the time being and immediately handed over a piece of paper. "That was King's original guest list for the bridge party he was supposed to have tomorrow. He and his mother sat down at one point and drew it up, and she even designed the invitations for him using this as her guide. Your wife is on there, as you know, Mr. Rierson. Oh, and I've taken the liberty of adding in my own handwriting someone who wasn't on the original list—Miss Wyvonne Sidley. You'll note the way I pronounced it with a *Y*. It's one of those peculiar names we insist on inventing down here in the Deep South. This is the young lady that came in several times a week to cook and clean for our son. Very admirable of her to put herself through college that way, she told us. She was also planning the refreshments end of the party with King. I'm sure you'll want to question her, because she might know something the rest of us don't know."

Ross nodded agreeably. "Thanks for the addition. And yes, my wife was very excited to receive her invitation as we sat down to breakfast last weekend, as I recall. She was looking forward to the event very much. As you probably know, she is quite the bridge player after years of fine-tuning."

Jackson took a deep breath and said, "No matter who else you interview, my money's still on Marcus Silvertree as his way to get revenge on us—he gives the impression of being strong and sturdy, but I assure you, he's not. He can even be a bit soft and flighty at times, if you catch my drift. It was almost like he expected us to do him favors and let him move in on our territory. The real estate business doesn't work that way. No, we didn't drive him out of business, as he might insist. He just wasn't up to the challenge, that's all. Still, it might help to interview the others to see if you can get to the bottom of my son's dreadful murder. Rosalie will never be the same."

Jackson suddenly paused and looked down into his lap, while sighing yet another time. "I don't see how we'll ever get over this. It's taking a terrible toll on us. I've got Ethel well-sedated at home, and I don't know how she'll get through the visitation and the requiem Mass. Everything she did revolved around our son, you know. If you don't mind, it might be better for you to come to our house if you need to collect anything like prints and DNA from her. She can hardly keep her legs underneath herself. I'm very concerned about her at this point."

Ross scanned the list and then handed it over to Bax. "Both my father-in-law and I again want to express our sorrow at your loss. We can't imagine your pain, and we'll be happy to make arrangements to come see her when she's up to it."

Jackson recovered his composure somewhat and said, "Thanks. I don't know if any of those other people on the list have any answers for you, but as you can see, Ethel and I are on the list, and I'll be happy to cooperate with you and tell you what I can."

Ross nodded, and then his demeanor changed substantially. "So, let's get to that. Can you tell me more about these other two people besides yourselves and my wife? I do know the Compton family, of course."

"Yes," Jackson began. "Bella Compton and my son had been seeing each other off and on for a while. When Ethel saw that Bella was on the list, she thought maybe that King was ready to propose to her at long last, and that maybe the party was to announce their engagement. At least, that's what she would speculate to me every five waking minutes. She certainly couldn't get it out of King. She thought he was set on surprising us and everyone else. But she's always been crazy about the idea of having Bella as a daughter-in-law. You know how certain families in Rosalie are about passing on their genes."

Jackson paused to gather his thoughts, which brought a troubled look to his face. "As for Patrice Leyton, Ethel and I never understood King's relationship with her. He never would discuss it with us during the time they were together and even after they broke up a while back, so Ethel was particularly surprised to see her name on the list. In the end, King had us guessing as to what he was really up to with this particular party and this particular list of guests. His attitude toward it seemed different than to the other bridge extravaganzas he's hosted."

"So you definitely don't think it was simply to play bridge and have a good time?" Bax said, stepping in.

There was a hitch in Jackson's throat. "I don't think so now. I'm convinced our son's murder and that party have something to do with each other, but will we ever know? Personally, I think you only have to look as far as that pathetic Marcus Silvertree. He was quite bitter about his business going under. My son told me they had angry words. Just the image of him tearing that plaque off the wall and hitting King over the head with it makes my blood boil."

Ross and Bax quickly exchanged glances, and Bax said, "You leave that up to us to find out if that's the truth or not, Mr. Kohl. I had another point I wanted you to clear up for us, by the way. I'm assuming from the reaction of you and your wife when you were told about your son this morning out on the sidewalk that you were not in the house during the time the coroner ruled your son had been killed. If that's so, where were you? And why did you not come out through the front door when you arrived?"

Jackson's tone had a note of relief in it. "Ah, I see why you're confused. A little while back, we turned over the house to our son, and we moved to the slave quarters in back. There's a pathway from the backyard that goes along the side of the house to the sidewalk. It's lined with crepe myrtles and caladiums and flower beds that Ethel planted all by herself. She's quite the gardener, you know. Loves working her hands in the soil. That way, we don't have to enter the house to get to the mailbox in front of the house, although we're in and out all the time. When we heard all the commotion and the sirens while we were still at breakfast, we hurried along the pathway to see what was going on, and our hearts were in our throats when we were told what had happened."

"Thank you," Bax said. "That clears that up nicely."

Almost as an afterthought, Jackson said, "I don't know

how I got through it all, but I talked to the funeral home before I came down here, and also to Father LeBlanc, and we'll have visitation and the requiem Mass day after tomorrow at the basilica and the Family Life Center. We'd appreciate it if you could come."

Ross stepped in. "Of course, the three of us will come—my wife included. She was certainly fond of your son. She enjoyed his bridge playing and hosting very much. This is a great loss for everyone in Rosalie."

Jackson rose from the table, nearly executing a bow as he did so. "Well, I just wanted to do my part while I still had my wits about me. Naturally, my wife and I want justice for my son. Is there anything else you need from me right now?"

"We need your prints and DNA, please. Just as a formality, you understand."

"I'll be happy to cooperate, but I can save you the trouble if you wanna know if you'll find our prints all over the house—because you will. We were always visiting and taking meals there with King. We were a tight-knit family—the three of us."

"That's very evident," Ross said, getting to his feet along with Bax. "And we will do our very best for you to bring this to a close as quickly as possible."

To the extent they could, Wendy and Ross were comparing notes on the Kohl case that evening around the dinner table. It had become commonplace for Ross to share details here and there with his wife on certain cases, even though he knew he ought to keep everything to himself according to regulations. In this instance, Wendy was already involved, and he knew she would eventually find a way to weasel things out of him as time went on. And if she couldn't get what she wanted out of him, there was always her father as a backup.

Furthermore, because of the hectic work schedules that

both had to manage, she had become quite the expert at making things that could be stored in the freezer and then heated up at the last minute. These included casseroles of every known variety, quick breads, and walnut brownies for dessert; since Ross was no stranger to sophisticated salad-making from his bachelor days, they could usually whip up an evening meal together when the opportunity arose. On this occasion, caprese salad and chicken cacciatore, along with a glass or two of Merlot, comprised the bill of fare, leaving just enough room for one of Wendy's desserts.

"What I find curious," Ross was saying, after he had downed the last bite of his brownie, "is the time frame of these texts to both you and Marcus Silvertree. He asks you to arrive on time around ten a.m. and asks Marcus Silvertree to drop by about five minutes earlier. That appears to be a transparent calculation to me. If his intention was to talk to the both of you together, why not just ask you both to arrive at the same time? Why this minute differentiation?"

Wendy leaned back in her wicker chair and considered. "I agree. It's only a matter of a few minutes, but perhaps the intention was for me to catch Marcus after he'd discovered the body, setting me up as a witness to at least that part of it. Which would mean that someone else sent those texts using King's phone. The killer, I suppose. Do you think I'm too far ahead of myself, or do I make any sense to you?"

"My thought processes are going into overdrive because of this sugar high from your insanely good brownie," Ross continued. "But a case could indeed be made that King wasn't the one who sent those texts. Perhaps he was already dead, as you suggest. Perhaps his murderer did that to set Marcus up, and then set you up as the witness after the discovery. We seem to be on the same page. I'm seeing it the way you're seeing it at the moment."

Wendy reached over in an attempt to retrieve Ross's

dessert plate, but he waved her off. "No, I'll clear later. My turn. But I feel like a hot slot machine, and I need to keep playing my hunch here until I get the payoff."

Wendy smiled at the analogy and said, "Didn't you mention that the only prints found on King's cell were his and nobody else's?"

"I did."

"Then maybe you're right. Whoever killed King sent those texts to me and Marcus, then wiped the cell clean and put it back in King's hand to maneuver a fresh set of his prints. Could certainly have been done easily enough with gloves on. Is that forensic enough for you?"

"Perfectly." Ross shoved away from the table slightly but did not make a move to rise. "Of course, we're assuming that Marcus is telling the truth that he didn't do it. His prints weren't on the plaque, either. It must have been wiped down, as well. Marcus could be too clever by one half."

"Do you see this as being premeditated, with all the maneuvering you're bringing up?"

Ross winced so dramatically that an observer might have interpreted it as pain. "My instincts tell me otherwise. My experience suggests that this was a crime of passion. Tommy Cantwell says those were multiple, well-aimed blows to the temple, and that the wounds match using the corner of the plaque as a weapon. Whoever did this was going for a quick and definite kill. And to your point—it also means that it could have been both premeditated and a crime of passion when it came to the execution—no pun intended."

Wendy didn't bother to disguise her discomfort. "Is there going to be an autopsy, or are King's parents going to accept Tommy Cantwell's verdict?"

"Jackson Kohl told us he saw no reason not to accept the verdict. He said they wanted to get to the peace of mind that comes with services as fast as possible and try to pick up their

lives from there," Ross said. "I understood completely where
he was coming from. When I lost both my parents in the car
wreck when I was in college, I thought I'd never recover, as
you know. But when my grandparents took care of everything, took me under their wing as my guardians, and everyone came to the visitation and funeral service, it really did
help. I felt better just knowing that so many people had
known and loved my parents. Closure means different things
for different people, but we all need it."

Ross rose, picking up both dessert plates as he had
promised to do, and headed toward the sink. "So what angle
does Lyndell want you to pursue for your piece?"

"The family angle, of course," Wendy said, remaining
seated. "What the Kohl family meant to Rosalie, their background, their achievements, that sort of thing. I always start
out with that approach in these cases. Rosalie always wants to
know who all was related."

Ross ran the faucet water briefly over the plates, wiped his
hands on a paper towel, and then turned around, folding his
arms. "And what about what happens after that, once you start
poking around?"

"Yes, things do start evolving, and I generally don't fall
down the rabbit holes. I am not an Alice."

"You're good at avoiding them."

"I suppose I am. I seem to reach these junctions in my
brain, and then, depending upon the road I take, I adjust my
goals and expectations. At this point, I'm particularly curious
about the women in King's life—Bella Compton and Patrice
Leyton, and any others that might emerge, for that matter.
When were you planning to interview them down at the station?"

Ross moved to the table and sat down beside her again. "I
thought maybe a day after the services. That'll at least give 'em
time to catch their breath."

Wendy sighed. "Yes, there's all that to get through. I imagine there will be quite a turnout, since it's the Kohls. The last time we had this much excitement in Rosalie over foul play was when the four Gin Girls were poisoned a few years ago. My very first case."

He leaned over and kissed her gently on the cheek. "A case you solved beautifully with your knowledge of cards."

Wendy drew back smiling, but suddenly looked lost in thought.

"What is it?" Ross said after more silence ensued.

"I was just thinking about when King first joined the Bridge Bunch out at the country club some time ago. He wanted to get back in the swing of things and just asked me for a brief refresher course before his first game with us and the parties he intended to throw, and, of course, I gave him one. We were going over point count—which, as you know, is pretty basic: four points for an ace, three for a king, two for a queen, and one for a jack. But we were reviewing exceptions to the rules. For instance, if the king is a singleton—all by his lonesome—you can't assign full value to him. His stock plummets drastically. I mean, he's next to useless in a good many cases."

"Remind me again."

"It's just that the first time the king's suit is played, he will fall, because he is not protected. There's not even one other card to follow suit with and save him. If someone leads an ace by chance, the king becomes worthless. So a king by itself—or himself, if you will—is not nearly as valuable as a king protected by one or two other cards." Wendy's tone changed to one of sadness. "So, here we are. The king falls all by himself, out there on a limb, and applying this to our current reality, somebody took advantage of that with fatal results."

"So, are you telling me you're getting one of your brilliant ideas?"

She shook her head. "Not yet. But something tells me that this case will be one for the books for all time here in Rosalie." Then she smiled and snapped her fingers. "I almost forgot. Merleece is coming to clean tomorrow. We switched days this week because of a glitch in her schedule."

Ross matched her smile and leaned back in his chair. "So, do I take it that the two of you are gonna come up with the solution to King's murder already and beat the police department to the punch? This wouldn't be the first time."

"You always underestimate our friendship," Wendy said, briefly pointing her finger at him. "You know as well as I do how often she gives me just the right inspiration in these investigations of mine. She'll say some little something that will trigger the right synapse in my brain, and then I'm on my way. It may sound crazy, but it's the truth."

"I thought it was due to her applesauce pie," Ross said. "I know one slice will light up my day. I hope she'll be bringing a fresh one, since we're down to one slice on the last one. I wouldn't mind if she'd fix us a hundred a' those."

Wendy eyed him intently. "No thanks to you. Every time I check on it in the fridge, I see you've been picking at it with a fork. Don't think I can't tell that you shave off a sliver and hope I won't notice."

"Why should I deny it? Merleece is one helluva housekeeper, and she can whip up one helluva pie. She's worth every penny we pay her. And your daddy feels the same way."

"I promise I'll tell you about any sensational conclusions we reach tomorrow," she told him.

CHAPTER 4

The next morning, at the kitchen table over coffee and blueberry muffins, it did not take long for Merleece Maxique to contribute to Wendy's cause. Ross had left early for the station but reminded his wife to ask about the possibility of another applesauce pie, if Merleece indeed did not show up with one. But Merleece had not forgotten how much her employers craved them, and Wendy had popped the fresh pie into the fridge as the two of them got down to the business of catching up before any cleaning got started. It wasn't exactly a gossip session—more like two old friends shooting the breeze that blew in off the Mississippi River up from Under-the-Hill. Plus, Wendy always looked forward to hearing the name Strawberry bandied about—Merleece's nickname for her, because of her luscious red hair.

"Such wickedness here in Rosalie," Merleece was saying while patting her close-cropped hair. A network of lines creased her rich, brown skin.

Wendy had just outlined her part in the discovery of King Kohl's body. "We seem to have more than our share of chicanery now and then."

"Sometimes, I think the older the town, the more wicked the number of people that live in it."

After a sip of coffee, Wendy said, "Do tell. And why do you think that is?"

Merleece leaned in and lowered her voice. "I think it's 'cause you got more generations to bring the bad genes to the surface. They bound to be some of 'em floatin' around in there, and if any family lasts long enough, the bad things'll show up sooner or later. Just the odds, the way I figure. My Hiram, he's the perfect example. I made him go to church all the time as a boy, but later on, somethin' bad came out, and he got into all that trouble up there in Chicago with drugs. So, if you did errything you could to bring him up right, you gotta believe somethin' else was goin' on that you couldn't control. You can try best you can when you have any influence in the young days, but you can't make people do the right thing once they get out on their own in that big world out there. That's on them—and maybe a bad gene or two?"

"But he's okay now, still working for the fire department down here, right?"

Merleece gave a hearty sigh of relief. "And I thank God erry day for that. It's a good, honest job for once in his life. No more a' that sneakin' around, up to no good."

"I never would have thought about that bad gene angle in a million years. You really are an insightful person."

Merleece lowered her voice even further and said, "And furthermore to that about the genes, I also think that when you dealin' with a man like this Mr. Kohl, you gotta think about a woman scorned. You say he was a player, and you saw it at the bridge games out at the country club all the time. Maybe he can't help his bad self."

"He was pretty much on the make. There was no way around it."

"Strawberry, there is such a thing as too many irons in the fire, know what I'm sayin'?"

Wendy pretended to be putting on airs as she struck a dramatic pose with her coffee cup. "You are talking to a happily married woman, and neither Ross nor I have any irons out there anymore."

Both women laughed, and Merleece said, "I heard that. No more marshmallows to roast around the campfire."

"But about the 'woman scorned' angle," Wendy continued, "I have to tell you that Ross says he thinks this was a crime of passion. I didn't actually see Mr. Kohl with his head bashed in before they took him to the ambulance in the body bag, but I was certainly willing to take my husband's word for it. He seems to think that the nature of the wounds suggests a man's rage."

Here, Merleece drew herself up with the authority of an oracle. "Lemme tell you this much, Strawberry. The angriest person I ever did witness in all my entire life was a woman. I tell you, the Devil was shootin' outta her eyes. And she was goin' after another woman for the same man, and that was what it was all about. I say either one of 'em that day could've grinded the other one into the good earth with the heel of her shoe as easy as they could've breathed the air. You coudda sold tickets to it and made a lotta money."

"I believe you," Wendy said. "Maybe one of his many female friends did take him out. I'll be talking to some of them for the article I'm doing about the Kohl family in general."

The conversation lapsed, and Merleece seemed to start fidgeting, putting down her coffee cup and catching Wendy's gaze. "Speakin' of family, I know it's been a while since we talked about it last, but . . . any change in the plans you had, Strawberry?"

Wendy looked resigned and averted her eyes briefly. "No. We had some tests run, and there doesn't seem to be any reason we can't conceive. We just haven't been able to so far. We've tried, as I told you before. The doctor did say that sometimes stress can get in the way. Of course, Ross is always under a lot of stress with his job as a detective, and that causes me to worry because he's always potentially in harm's way. You'd think I'd be used to it by now, growing up as the daughter of a police chief, but now that I'm married, I seem to have kicked into another gear emotionally. I have my deadlines for the paper, too, but I consider it to be my dream job. There are times when I don't even think of it as work. Not many people get to say that."

"So, I guess you gone get pregnant when you gone get pregnant, then."

The mood at the table lightened, and Wendy found her smile. "I guess so. Daddy is so impatient all the time. 'When is my grandchild comin'?' he's always saying to me. Even Lyndell sniffs around the subject at the paper now and then. She thinks she's being subtle about it, but she's not. That would officially make her a step-grandmother. There is such a thing, right?"

"Yes, indeed. Got many a lady at my church with a step-grandchild or two in the house. Or three, maybe more. I always say they's not just one definition of what a family is. All it takes is some love, and it'll fall into place the way God intended. But I always say you gotta have the wisdom to realize it, too."

"I wish more people thought the way you do," Wendy said. "Because if it turns out that Ross and I can't have children of our own, I think we'd consider adopting and making a family for ourselves that way. I've always admired people who take children not of their own making into their hearts."

Merleece got in the final word, reaching over to grasp Wendy's hand warmly. "The way I see it, erry one of us is related, whether we think so or not. Gettin' along with each other is the reason we get born in the first place. And as for Mr. Kohl and what's happened, the last thing we should ever be doin' is committing murder. Somebody's just not right in the head."

Father Emile LeBlanc sat at his office desk in the Rectory, sipping his Earl Grey tea and then writing down the last paragraph of his eulogy for King Kohl. He must, of course, travel the straight and narrow and emphasize all the positive things that King and his family had done for Rosalie over several generations. He knew that was what his congregation was expecting to hear, and he had no intention of veering off course.

Yet, he had heard confession from King and his father and mother many times over and was privy to information practically no one else knew about their family. Because he must never break the seal of the confessional, those insights would forever remain a secret. If they somehow ever emerged, it would not be because of him. Perhaps the town gossips? He had been shocked to his core at the news of King's murder and had found himself in a thoroughly untenable position. Did the things King had confessed to him, particularly, have a bearing on his death? Would they be helpful to the Rosalie Police Department? Perhaps. Perhaps not. It was possible that King had been killed for reasons other than the contents of his confessions. And then there was the matter of King's decision that he had intended to reveal, first at the party and then changed to one-on-one.

Above all, Father knew he dare not break the seal of the confessional. Everything was so interconnected. How could he reveal one part without all the rest? Was there, however, something along the lines of a hint that he might mention to Detective Rierson? Just a comment that there was one person he might be sure to pay particular attention to, and nothing more revealing than that. Surely that would do no harm, because that same person would be interviewed, anyway. On the other hand, perhaps it would be best if he just stayed out of it and let the police do their jobs. It was their mission to deal with crimes; it was his to deal with souls. Both were urgent missions that would never disappear.

Father sat back and read the last paragraph of his eulogy aloud. As he held the page in his hands, the incoming light from the stained glass window struck it at just the right angle, giving it a rose-colored hue and making him smirk. He had indeed painted a very rosy picture of the Kohl family:

> *Above all, let us not forget that the Kohls helped the citizens of Rosalie not only find houses but make homes for themselves. Homes are what this country was built upon, because they shelter families. We pass down our wisdom and love from generation to generation, and the proper environment makes that possible. King treasured his mission in life and took pride in the results. Sometimes, we take professions like his for granted, that there's nothing to matching these properties with the proper people. But only when we find ourselves content within the confines of our daily living environment do we realize what a gift this truly is. Let us keep all that in mind as we say goodbye to him and entrust him to Our Lord and Savior.*

Father frowned at the last sentence. Did that imply that King was especially in need of help, more so than anyone else, or was he overthinking it too much? After all, the congregation would not know what he knew. They would likely think of those last words as the typical sign-off, bowing their heads and crossing themselves in contented fashion *in the name of the Father, the Son, and the Holy Ghost.* Yet it fell to a priest to encounter the worst from his parishioners. For instance, the gist of that one particular confession from Jackson that stood out from an assortment:

"Forgive me, Father, for I have sinned. It's been six months since my last confession. I slept with the wife of one of my clients in order to get their listing, and then I kept seeing her after that. Her husband did not know what was going on, only that his wife kept putting pressure on him to list with me. My wife, Ethel, does not know it happened, but I have finally broken it off. I did it because our competition, Marcus Silvertree, looked like he was gonna get the listing, and I was bound and determined not to let him get it. I did not like the fact that he was trying to butt in on the business I've worked hard to establish here in Rosalie. It is my life's work and my legacy. That was my motivation, not the fact that I was particularly attracted to this woman."

"Then why did you continue seeing the woman after you obtained the listing?"

"I don't know. Maybe because I enjoy winning and the feeling that comes with it. I got a high off of it."

"You surely knew how wrong all of that was."

"Yes, I suppose I did. But it didn't seem to matter to me."

"You need to find a way in your heart to make it matter."

So the truth was there was nothing that Jackson Kohl would not do to promote his business, even at the expense of his marriage. Father had advised him not to tell Ethel about the affair, reasoning that there likely had been others, even though Jackson had not revealed them in confession.

On the other hand, Ethel's confessions had been of the mild, garden variety—literally. She had once lamented that she had let the ficus in her parlor die and wanted to know if that qualified as a sin. She admitted that she had given it the right amount of water—not too little, not too much—but wondered if the fatal blow had been dealt by too much light or not enough. She was, of course, told not to fret about such things if that was all she had to confess, that she no longer had to concern herself with maintaining the lives of plants as the path to Heaven. That doing her dead-level best to keep them alive needed no absolution. Then recently, Father had noticed a subtle change in Ethel's demeanor, something he could not quite put his finger on. Had she stumbled onto the truth about her husband's adultery, and was she in some sort of shock or denial? Or was there something else going on?

Father finished off his tea and sat with the eulogy for a minute or two more. He was not all that happy with it, but it would have to do. It would give King a proper farewell, and none would be the wiser that the truth about him and his parents would be buried deeply within the protections of the church. At least, for the time being.

Wendy and Ross stood in the long line outside on the sidewalk, waiting to enter the Family Life Center across from the basilica as King's visitation got underway. The turnout for the event was impressive, so it was fortunate that the May weather was cooperating, with a late spring breeze mitigating the humidity that was increasing day by day until summer made things unbearable. They had both steeled themselves for the process of paying their respects to Jackson and Ethel Kohl, who stood beside Father LeBlanc at the end of the line, bearing up as bravely as they could while receiving cliched best wishes and condolences from Rosalieans who knew them anywhere from casually to intimately. Meanwhile, the Riersons busied themselves with their phones as the line inched along in imitation of a glacier.

"I'll have to leave as soon as we make our manners," Ross was saying. "I just got a text from Bax that something has come up regarding the case."

Wendy knew better than to ask if he could share the news, but she also knew that she would eventually find out what was going on. She had her ways of sweet-talking either her husband or her father, even though neither was supposed to let much of anything leak from their official investigations. Wendy had become a force to be reckoned with regarding these cases, since they usually involved her own journalistic pieces for the paper.

Another ten minutes passed, during which the line moved along enough for Wendy to catch a glimpse of Jackson and Ethel holding court, in a manner of speaking. She noticed that while Jackson seemed game enough, with his perfunctory smiles, hand-shaking, and head-nodding, Ethel appeared to be nothing less than washed-out. She had not applied makeup for the occasion, her skin presenting as especially pale against her black dress—essentially, a ghost in mourning. Furthermore, she was unable to muster a smile as people passed by. In fact, Jackson had his arm around her waist, not so much as a display of affection, Wendy imagined, but more as a method to keep her standing. She looked as if her knees might buckle, and she might collapse at any moment.

When the time finally came for the exchange, Wendy said to the couple, "I'm so very sorry for your loss. King was so much fun to be around when he came to play bridge with us out at the country club, and his parties were delightful. I hope you both will find some peace of mind in the coming days. You'll be in my thoughts and prayers."

Ross settled for something more succinct as he shook Jackson's hand. "Please accept my sincerest condolences."

And then it was done. Ross gave his wife a peck on the cheek and headed for the station, while Wendy decided to linger and perhaps gather some material of an anecdotal nature for her forthcoming piece on the Kohl family. At the busy refreshments table, she helped herself to a cup of fruit punch and then surveyed the small clusters chatting around the room. It had always amazed her how sociable people were at funerals, and King's visitation was no exception. There were flashes of smiles here and there, along with a polite chuckle or two, though the overall effect was a low and respectful hum throughout the spacious building, designed to complement the magnificent Gothic basilica across the street.

Then, out of nowhere, Wendy was approached by a young woman with rainbow-colored hair, wide brown eyes, and a breathless quality to her voice.

"I hope you don't mind my intruding, Miz Rierson. I recognized you across the room from your column picture in the paper. I'm Wyvonne Sidley, Mr. Kohl's part-time housekeeper and cook. Before I came to the visitation, I talked to your father on my cell and told him I wanted to come down to the station to reveal a few things I think he ought to know." Her voice began trembling, and she briefly shut her eyes, as if to summon strength. "I'm having a very hard time with this, but I think I might have a very good idea who did this to my King—" She paused and then added quickly, "To Mr. Kohl, my employer, I meant."

"So you're the new development my father texted my husband about not long ago?"

"I suppose I must be."

Wendy's interest ratcheted up a notch. "It so happens that my editor wants me to do a feature on the Kohl family. Perhaps after you've finished being interrogated at the station, you can drop by my office at the paper."

"I don't see why not. I could tell you a few things now, if you wanted."

Wendy made a mental note that Wyvonne sounded a bit too eager to talk. She was rarely mistaken about her instincts. "Perhaps this isn't the ideal place, though. I think we'd both be more comfortable in one of the meeting rooms at the paper."

"That would be fine. Doing it today would be best. I worked my schedule for Mr. Kohl around my classes out at the college, you know. I'm bound and determined to get my degree, and I think I'd like to go on and teach."

Wendy took a sip of her punch and smiled. "Very admirable of you to be working your way through college like that. I've heard nothing but nightmare stories about student loans these days. And we certainly need more good teachers. Sometimes it seems it's becoming a thankless profession, but we still need dedication and persistence. Good for you."

"Tell me about those student loans. Anyhow, I know things," Wyvonne continued, ignoring Wendy's advice to save their interview for the paper later. "Sometimes, King . . . umm . . . Mr. Kohl and I would have a drink before I served him his dinner. And once in a while, he would drink a lot more than he ate, even though I'm a great cook and he loved my food, I can promise you that. So, he would let me in on a thing or two regarding his personal life, and he swore me to secrecy. But now that he's dead, well . . ." She could not seem to finish her sentence.

"I can see how fond you were of Mr. Kohl," Wendy said.

"Yes, I was. I don't mind admitting it. He was a very likable man, charming to a fault, most of the time. But he . . . he made his mistakes, and I guess he didn't want to keep one or two to himself. That's what I'd like to talk to you about—your husband, too. Because I'm convinced I know who did this, and why."

Wendy again surveyed the room, noting the number of people within earshot. "Well, why don't we save something for later?"

"I'll text you as soon as I finish at the station and then come by the paper."

"I'll keep my desk cleared for that, and I look forward to hearing from you."

Wendy squinted as Wyvonne turned her back and headed into the crowd. She had the distinct sensation of being stalked. Nonetheless, she shrugged it off and circulated with a smile to get anecdotal material for her upcoming article. There were more than a few willing to say good things and share pleasant memories about the Kohl family. By being especially diligent, Wendy was also able to introduce herself to both Bella Compton and Patrice Leyton, who both promised to cooperate with her on the Kohl family feature article. She was pleased with herself. All of her journalistic boxes were being properly checked.

Wendy and Wyvonne had settled in across from each other in one of the *Citizen*'s small meeting rooms, but Wendy was having trouble maintaining control of the interview. Wyvonne kept insisting that they start off with her theory on King's murder, something she had practically bragged about at the Family Life Center. All sorts of alarms were going off in Wendy's head.

"I appreciate your dropping by to talk to me, but you understand that my assignment is primarily to get information on the Kohl family's contributions to Rosalie. I got off to a good start at the visitation, with all the comments friends made to me right and left. I'd like to concentrate on that first, if you don't mind."

Wyvonne looked annoyed, making the face of a spoiled child. "But I want you to let me tell you everything I told your husband and your father down at the station. You see, King . . . er . . . Mr. Kohl, was carrying around a bad secret that was weighing him down, and he said I was the first he'd ever told about it, except his priest. Other than that, only one other person knew, and she was involved in it with him."

"We can get to that," Wendy told her, still intent on running the show. "But first, I'd like you to tell me how you came to work for Mr. Kohl and what that experience was like."

Wyvonne finally drew back with a sigh and then started reeling off words in a monotone. "I answered an ad in the *Cit-*

izen, and then I had an interview. Not with Mr. Kohl, though. It was with his mother, Ethel. I'm just glad I didn't have to work for her. She was so prissy and fussy about everything, and her questions were over the top. She even asked me how many times a week I bathed. Can you believe that? If you ask me, I think there's something seriously wrong with her. She's missing something, and I'm not sure I want to find out what it is. And anyway, what's a grown man doing letting his mother control things like that? Maybe a bit of a mama's boy in him, if you ask me. I know he never came off that way in public, but that's my two cents."

Wendy made notes, even though she knew she would not be able to use that particular bit of information in her piece. "Well, no, I can't believe the question about bathing. That's downright bizarre. But please, continue with your views of Mr. Kohl and his parents, if you would."

Wyvonne's comments had a perfunctory aura about them. She spoke without conviction and gave the overall impression that she was just getting something over with as fast as she could. "So," she concluded, after disclosing bland details about holiday celebrations such as Thanksgiving and Christmas, "is that enough, or do you need more?"

Wendy saw clearly that she would not be able to get much more of what she needed, so she steeled herself and said, "Go on, then, about your theory, I mean."

Wyvonne leaned in, running her tongue across her lips, her tone almost gossipy yet triumphant at the same time. "It was that Patrice Leyton, you see. King got her in trouble, if you know what I mean."

"As in pregnant?"

Wyvonne worked the corners of her mouth into something resembling a smile, but it seemed forced. "Exactly."

"Go on, please."

"I'll admit that when Mr. Kohl told me this a while back,

he had a buzz on from several neat bourbons. He knew how to tie one on, believe me. But anyway, he told me that when that Miz Leyton came to him with the news that she was expecting . . . well, you know, he said at first, he didn't believe her. I mean, why shouldn't he be skeptical?"

Wendy sounded resigned. "Most men would be."

"Right. But he said she wouldn't let him off the hook as easy as that. The bottom line here is that he eventually talked her into letting him . . . make arrangements for her."

Wendy stopped writing with a quizzical look on her face. "I take it that you mean by that, he—"

"Yes, he paid for an abortion," she interrupted. "Might as well say the word. One of those out-of-state things so it couldn't be easily traced."

"Do you have proof of this?"

Squirming slightly, Wyvonne said, "No. But why would a man admit to something like that if he hadn't done it? He might have been a little drunk, but I just knew he was telling me the truth. Women can sense such things, you know. It's not something to brag about, the way I see it."

Wendy put her notepad in her lap and sat back. "So, are you also telling me that you think it was Patrice Leyton who killed him? How long ago was this abortion supposed to have happened, by the way?"

"King said about two years ago. He said they were having a casual fling. He said Patrice told him she was on the pill, but she got pregnant anyway. Women can lie about such things. Of course, men lie too, and don't ask me to count the ways. This was probably two people lying to each other. It was one big mess."

The comment found its way into the pit of Wendy's stomach as it instantly brought back her inability to conceive. She tried to keep it all bottled up, but she couldn't. "Yes, sometimes women get pregnant . . . and sometimes they don't."

After a pause, and exhaling for good measure, she continued. "But why would Patrice Leyton wait three years to get her revenge on Mr. Kohl? That doesn't make much sense to me."

"I've been thinking about that very thing," Wyvonne began. "And it's my opinion that she was just waiting for the right moment. I think some people can go along suffering for years and then strike when you'd least expect it. Bad memories never go away. They settle in deep down and won't ever let you rest."

"Speaking of timing," Wendy said, "I find it interesting that you tracked me down at the visitation. You seem to be covering all your bases."

"Are you implying I had something to do with King's death?"

Wendy's instincts were now fully engaged. She knew where to go next. "I didn't say that at all. I was just making an observation."

"Well, I can assure you there was nothing complicated about it. As I said, I just happened to spot you at the Family Life Center once I got there. I was not about to miss paying my respects to King. It was a very emotional thing for me, but I knew I had to get it over with if I'm to get on with my life. This is almost as much a shock to me as I'm sure it is to his parents. I suppose I knew nothing would ever come of the crush I had on King."

"I understand, but it also seems clear to me that you were in love with him. The question is: How far were you willing to go because of that?"

Something caught in Wyvonne's throat, and she took a moment to clear it before speaking. "I have my limits. And I want to see justice done. I feel it is my duty to help."

Feeling completely in command, Wendy said, "Let my husband, my father, and the police department do that, then. They work from the evidence, but I'm sure they will take all your input into account. Meanwhile, I appreciate your backstory about working for Mr. Kohl. I'm sure you realize you must remain here in Rosalie during the investigation."

Wyvonne straightened her posture and sounded almost threatening. Indeed, there was something unsettling about the glint in her eye. "I wouldn't even dream of leaving until justice is done. There's somebody out there that is beyond evil, and I wanna do everything I can to help you find them."

Wendy and Ross were sitting at the dinner table that evening, just beginning their appetizer course of tomato-basil soup with baguettes, with grilled chicken to follow. So far, the subject of Wyvonne Sidley had not come up. After lightly buttering a chunk of bread and dipping it into the bowl ever so gently for that sublime touch, however, Wendy decided to break the silence and pressure her husband as usual.

"What was your opinion of Miz Sidley today? She came off to me like a woman scorned. She was trying way too hard, I thought."

Ross swallowed a sip of his Merlot and said, "Same as you. Your daddy thought the same thing. She ended up making herself a person of interest with the way she presented herself. We certainly would've gotten around to interrogating her, but she definitely didn't let any moss grow under her feet and made that quite easy for us."

"Are you able to share anything with me right now?"

Ross winked, which Wendy recognized as a sure sign he intended to cooperate with her. He knew by now her discretion could be trusted. "Yes, but you first. I'll allow comparing notes, because it won't do me any good not to include you. Even though you aren't on our payroll, your daddy and I agree that you're worth your weight in gold when it comes to solving certain cases."

"Thanks," she said. "I assume she told you about Patrice Leyton's abortion?"

"Check. She was most emphatic about it being a key element in the case. She was extremely helpful, if you want to put it that way."

"I'm wondering if Miz Leyton will confirm or deny that. It can't be an easy thing for any woman to admit. Or to go through, for that matter."

"That's why we bring 'em in. That's why the camera rolls, and then we study their body language and listen to their words carefully."

Wendy paused for a generous swig of her wine and said, "Well, I did get some backstory about how Wyvonne came to work for King, and she explained that she answered an ad in the paper. But she did say she had to suffer through a bizarre interview with Ethel Kohl for the job. Did you get into any of that with her?"

Ross broke off a piece of his baguette over his bowl so any crumbs that fell would soften in the soup and said, "Nope. We quizzed her about the crime lab report on prints and DNA. Hers, of course, were all over the place, and she brought up the perfectly reasonable point that since she cooked and cleaned, it would be hard for traces of her not to show up. She said that King had told her he was calling off the party on Saturday and that she didn't need to come in on Friday. She says she didn't come in as a result, and heard about King's death through the grapevine, but didn't volunteer exactly how. That strikes me as being almost too convenient."

Wendy seemed amused. "Perhaps it speaks to her qualifications as a housekeeper. Maybe she wasn't all that great, which means there's some evidence left behind to help you out."

"That's a reasonable point, but we asked her when she had cleaned the house last," Ross began, "and she admitted it had been the day before. She doesn't come in every day anyway, she explained. Nevertheless, Marcus Silvertree's prints were on the doorknob, but not on the desk. King's prints were on his cell and on his desk, and Jackson's were here and there, but not on the desk or on the plaque. In fact, there were no prints of any kind on the plaque, but there were traces of bleach. So obviously, someone cleaned the plaque to remove them—and the blood. Of course, there were other prints that we have yet to identify. I'd hope she was a better cook than she was a housekeeper, therefore. Or perhaps she was a good house-keeper in specific areas of the house when it suited her."

"I see what you mean about Wyvonne Sidley ending up making herself a person of interest by volunteering informa-tion to all of us so eagerly," Wendy said. "But I also think you could explain it another way. She admitted to me that she was in love with King and also told me that she would not be sat-isfied until justice was done. She thinks Patrice Leyton was the murderer, but I don't suppose you've had a chance to interro-gate her yet?"

"Everyone on the invitation list, which Jackson gave us, will be interrogated and printed, swabbed, and such. We've got most of our work ahead of us—with Jackson, Marcus, and our woman scorned done first."

"Merleece," Wendy said, cracking a devious smile.

Ross stilled his spoonful on the way to his mouth. "What about her? She can't possibly be a suspect in this case."

Wendy raised her left eyebrow by itself, something she had inherited from her late mother, Valerie. "No, I meant that Merleece suggested that the murder was the work of a woman scorned. It's always amazing to me how often she finds the bud that flowers into a solution for me."

"Hold your floral work right now, because we're certainly not there yet," Ross said in between spoonfuls of his soup. "We have Patrice Leyton and Bella Compton to get to, as well as Ethel Kohl. Jackson has asked us to wait just a little longer to question her, because she's taking King's death really hard, as you can imagine. What mother wouldn't, but you know as well as I do that we can't overlook anyone."

Wendy's gasp was on the quiet side but still audible. "Wait . . . you're not suggesting that King's own mother could have killed him, are you?"

"I didn't say that. But we do need to get her prints and DNA to match up with the crime lab's report of what was found here and there in the house. She and Jackson spent a lot of time there with King, so we're just going by the book."

Wendy returned to her soup while trying to envision the alternate universe in which any mother might be driven to do away with her son. Or daughter, for that matter. Try as she might, she was unable to fathom it. Yet she remembered that Wyvonne had mentioned that she thought something was definitely "not right" with Ethel Kohl these days. Was that just more of Wyvonne's apparent maneuvering? Or was there actually something substantive to it?

CHAPTER 5

The slave quarters behind Kohl Place lacked nothing in the way of luxurious decorative touches. Ethel Kohl had spent nearly as much money on the project as she had in restoring the main house decades ago; the only thing she and Jackson had given up when they had moved in several years back to accommodate King was space. The two-story brick outbuilding was a bit on the cozy side, as Ross discovered when he entered for his "kid gloves" interview with Ethel.

"Please, come on in," Jackson told him at the red door with the impeccable fanlight above it. He gestured toward Ethel, who was seated on the Belter sofa in the middle of the living room with its sumptuous Persian rug and Zuber wallpaper panorama of myriad frigates in a harbor somewhere for a background. The air was also laden with the essence of furniture polish. "I've just given my wife something to calm her down, since she's been so inconsolable. I'm sure you understand, detective. Please forgive her if she's a little groggy. We'll get through this somehow."

Ross bowed his head slightly. "Of course. I will be as brief as possible."

"Dear," Jackson said, approaching his wife, "you remember Detective Rierson, don't you? He just wants to ask you a few questions and do a bit of forensics."

"What?" Ethel said, gesturing toward her ear as if she were hard of hearing. "For-rest-tics?"

Jackson reached down and patted her shoulder gently. "He wants to take your fingerprints and that sorta thing, like I told you. It won't take long."

Ethel was dressed in her pink bathrobe and white fuzzy slippers, and her half-lidded eyes suggested that she might have just been roused from bed, although it was nearly ten-thirty in the morning. Then again, the sedative that Jackson said he'd given her might have kicked in, as well. Nonetheless, she finally patted a spot on the sofa and managed a smile. "Come, sit next to me, young man."

"If you don't mind, I'd prefer to stand," he told her, matching her smile. "I'll need to get your prints and swab the inside of your mouth, Miz Kohl. Just standard procedure, you understand. You probably know your husband has already co-operated with us. And let me again express my sorrow for the loss of your son."

"It has devastated us," she said, pointing across the room with a sigh. "There's his portrait over there on the wall. We had it painted when he graduated from college. But now I'm thinking of taking it down and putting it in storage, because every time I walk past it, the tears come out. If we did, though, I might miss it, and that would be even worse."

Having settled into his favorite armchair nearby, Jackson said, "I told you we can do that if you want, dear. You just tell me what you prefer to do."

"If you could just stop me from dreaming," she said, look-ing over at her husband with a doleful expression. "King's still alive in these dreams I'm having, and when I wake up, I remember that he's gone. My husband seems to have a pill for all my aches and pains and so forth, but not for that. I know something like that doesn't exist."

Ross steeled himself, hoping to strike the right tone. "I can imagine how difficult that is for you. I lost my parents in a car wreck when I was in college, and it was very difficult for me to get through. Dreams have a way of either soothing or disturbing you."

Then came Ross's forensic duties, which he performed quickly, and he was somewhat surprised when Ethel seemed to spring to life with a little giggle, her sadness suddenly vanquished. "Goodness, that Q-Tippy thing tickled. I enjoyed that."

"Glad to hear it," Ross said, relaxing somewhat himself. Then he began his questions with his pen at the ready.

"Miz Kohl, to the best of your ability, can you tell me what you think your son was up to with this party he was planning? We have reason to believe it was not primarily to play bridge. Did he give you any inkling?"

Ethel became even more sanguine, her eyes opening wide. "I like to think he was going to make an engagement announcement to all of us. He invited the two girls he'd been seeing the most of in recent years, and he was someone who liked his drama."

Ross scanned his notepad. "That would be Miz Bella Compton and Miz Patrice Leyton, right?"

"Yes, that's them," she said, but there was an uncomfortable edge to her voice. "You see, I helped him design the invitations, but I'm fairly sure that the Leyton girl did not play bridge. Her type wouldn't have, you know. Bella did, of course. The Comptons are quite social, in case you don't know that. At least they were before Peter died. Since then, not so much. Greta keeps to herself more."

"I believe I'm aware of that," Ross said. "Being social in this town is a prerequisite for becoming a true Rosaliean, and I've learned a lot more about that since I married my Wendy. Before, I was just your everyday policeman type."

"Yes, I've adored that pretty, redheaded wife of yours since she started writing her social column a few years back. It's not even worth reading anymore. That girl they have now is just a waste of copy. She gets her descriptions wrong."

Ross brightened. "Lotsa people liked the job she did back then, with all the wedding write-ups and baby showers and things like that, but I'm sure you know she's an investigative reporter now."

"Is she?"

Ross fought back a frown, observing Ethel's sudden befuddled expression. It was accompanied by a return to the profound sense of sadness that had enveloped her demeanor a minute or two earlier. "Yes, but her assignment at the moment is to do an in-depth feature on what the Kohl family has meant to Rosalie all these years. All those people who showed up at your son's services proved that all of you mean a great deal. They're a testament to your status in Rosalie."

"That's nice to hear."

"If I may ask you just a couple more questions, then." He paused to look down at his notepad once again. "What is your opinion of Miz Sidley?"

"Who?"

"Miz Wyvonne Sidley."

Ethel shot a bewildered glance at her husband first, then turned to Ross. "I don't believe . . . I know her."

Jackson quickly intervened, leaning in her direction. "King's housekeeper, dear."

"Still not ringing a bell," she said, turning both hands palms up. "Did she just start?"

"Miz Sidley told me that you were the one who inter-viewed her for her job and hired her for her position," Ross said.

Ethel shook her head emphatically.

"I'm afraid she's been deeply affected by the tragedy that's befallen us," Jackson said. "You'll just have to forgive my wife. This continues to be quite a burden for her to bear—for both of us, you understand. She may not be able to give you much that's helpful to you. We've been broken in two, and there's no putting us back together."

"Humpty Dumpty," Ethel said under her breath. "Jackson told me to say that if I couldn't think of anything else to say. He told me not to strain. He's always reminding me of things. He says one thing, then he says another. But all I seem to re-member is 'Humpty Dumpty'."

Jackson rose from his armchair. "Detective, I don't believe my wife will be able to tell you much more. If you don't mind, could we bring this to a close?"

"Of course," Ross said. "I understand. And I want to thank you both for your cooperation. We will keep in touch with you as our investigation proceeds." At the door, Ross continued, "My thoughts and prayers are with you. And those of my wife's, too."

"And we sincerely thank you for that," Jackson said with a gentle wave of his hand before closing the door.

In the background, Ethel could be heard saying, "Humpty Dumpty," again.

Once outside, Ross began walking down the path leading past the main house to the sidewalk that Ethel had landscaped so expertly, so lovingly. The crepe myrtles lining both sides were getting ready to bloom, and the pea gravel crunched under his feet, a surprisingly pleasant sensation. Flower beds filled with pansies seemed to be smiling at him as he made his short trek, as if he were in the midst of an ongoing garden party.

It was only after he had slid into the front seat of his car that a phrase came to mind, and he couldn't exactly figure out why: *being led down the garden path.*

Was he beginning to develop the sort of special instincts that his wife had become famous for? Beyond those he had acquired in his years of police detective, of course. He decided he was going to bounce that particular sensation off Wendy that evening and see what she had to say about it all.

Because the weather was mild and sun-splashed on this late May afternoon, Wendy and Bella Compton were sitting out on the commanding veranda of Bella's Victorian raised cottage on Lambert Street, sipping coffee under the ceiling fan and engaging in small talk at first. Wendy had already observed, however, that Bella's cheerfulness seemed decidedly forced—too many smiles where none were required, too many averted glances when nothing much of consequence was being said. It was almost as if Bella didn't want to acknowledge that Wendy was there. Yet, it was quite evident why King had taken an interest in the young woman. Even in this cautious mood of hers, she was quite the dazzling blonde specimen, and the sunflower-print dress she was wearing spoke both to her sense of fashion and her accompanying fitness.

"I know this is difficult for you to talk about," Wendy began, intent on leaving behind all the casual pleasantries and getting to the point of her visit, "but I would like some background on your relationship with the Kohl family. As I told you, my editor wants me to do an in-depth feature on them in light of this terrible tragedy. It's to be something in the way of a tribute so that people can get closure. It won't be an exposé or anything like that, I can assure you."

That got Bella to face forward at last, and she quickly
dropped the perfunctory smile. "The Kohls and the Comptons have been close for generations. My family, being in
banking the way they are, and theirs first got connected because real estate firms need their bankers to seal the deals, of
course. It was a good partnership over the years. I'm sure you
know how successful the Kohls have been in business. There
have been the occasional soirées, cocktail parties, and picnics
that both families have enjoyed together. My mother Greta
and Ethel Kohl have been great friends for at least thirty-five
years and belong to hundreds of planning committees in this
town. And then it was Ethel and my mother who picked out
this cottage for me after I graduated from Ole Miss. Mother
let Ethel decorate it, because she didn't think she had Ethel's
taste. Once that got underway, Ethel even asked me which
fabric swatch I preferred—once in a while."

The sarcasm was not lost on Wendy. "Do you and Ethel
Kohl not see eye to eye on things?"

"That's in the past. The decorating thing, I mean. I trusted
her to do a job for me, and I'm mostly happy with the results.
It was clear to me that my mother and Ethel expected King
and me to get married eventually. You should have seen them
giggling together at times during that period when we were a
serious couple, and all of us were together at a party or something. But it's not worth dwelling on now." Bella twitched
her mouth to one side and then whispered, "Let's drop it."

Wendy changed the subject quickly. "So there were social
aspects to this, but the primary connection between the two
families was a business one."

"It certainly started that way, yes. But if you'd like more
details, I'd suggest you interview my mother, Greta. She'll
also have a million anecdotes for you about the Kohls and the
Comptons. I'm sure that's the sort of thing you'd want for

your feature article. I could text her and arrange a meeting for you, if you'd like?"

"Thanks. I'd appreciate that very much."

"I'll text her as soon as you're gone, and the two of you can nail something down."

Wendy scribbled something quickly in her notepad. Then she looked up, manufacturing one of Bella's forced smiles, and lowered her voice. "Is there anything else you wanted to add to any of this?"

"Such as?"

Wendy leaned forward and softened her tone further. "I don't want to intrude upon your grief, but would you mind telling me about your actual relationship with King, if it isn't too much of an invasion of privacy? You call the shots here."

Bella put her coffee cup down on the small wooden table between them, took a deep breath, and said, "Is this going to go into your article? You said you weren't doing some sort of exposé. You aren't the *Enquirer*, right?"

"No. If you don't want to answer, you don't have to. I'd just like to get a clear picture of the Kohl family from every angle. Again, I promise not to write anything that would be inappropriate. This will be a favorable snapshot in time."

It took Bella a while longer to gather herself, but she eventually said, "King and I had known each other from childhood. I had a crush on him since forever and used to chase after him at recess. But he could always outrun me. I hated that, even though I think he really liked me, too. It . . . well, it made me determined to catch him, no matter how long it took me."

"That's an interesting way to put it," Wendy said. "I remember having the same sort of crush in middle school on a boy named Rufus, even though he always seemed to be blowing his nose. He completely ignored me, and so to get back at him, I started calling him Rufus, the Red-Nosed Reindeer. Problem was, it stuck and followed him around the rest of his schooling. I'm sure he never forgave me for that, and I certainly didn't mean to cause all that trouble for him."

Both women laughed, and then Bella said, "I never had a nickname for King. Why would I need one? He got enough of 'Old King Kohl', as it was. Anyhow, eventually we went out now and then in high school, but nothing much ever came of it. King was quite the player. It was when he came home from college that we started seeing each other in earnest. I thought to myself, 'At last, we're on the same page.'"

"And were you?"

"Yes, and no."

"Could you explain further?"

Bella began tearing up and wiped at the corners of her eyes with her cloth napkin. "Just give me a minute, please."

"Of course. As I said, you call the shots here."

Finally, Bella opened up. "There was a period in there, not all that long ago, when I thought that King was going to ask me to marry him. He would hint around all the time, but he never proposed. I pressed him one summer about it, and he seemed to go off the rails. He mumbled something about not wanting to settle down and resenting having his life planned for him from cradle to grave. I swear I wasn't pressing him too hard, just a bit of casual, friendly persuasion with a kiss or two. Not long after that, I found out he was seeing Patrice Leyton. She has . . . a reputation, and I'm sure you know what I mean."

"I do," Wendy said, thinking to herself how harshly old Southern cities judged women compared to the way they judged the men who flitted around them and then flew away at a moment's notice without a care in the world.

"I'm leveling with you now—I was furious with him," Bella continued. "Why did he reject me at that point and settle for her? Do you understand how that made me feel? I could have killed him at that point—" She stopped suddenly, realizing what she'd just said.

The bitter undertone did not escape Wendy, and she said, "I think we've all felt that way about someone, but then regretted those feelings."

Bella conjured up more tears, dried them up again, and sniffled. "What I just said sorta slipped out. Then last week, I get this perfumed invitation from him for a bridge party, and I wonder what the hell is going on with this. Next thing I know, he's texting me that he wants to make things right with us once and for all, and I just have to come to his house for this to-do he's having. He says that I can't let him down. I had no idea what to make of it. Was he going to propose to me at last? Was that how he was going to make things right? But he didn't text that he wanted to make things right just with *me*. He said *us*. That put everything in a different context for me. I have to say, I wasn't looking forward to such a public proposal of marriage in front of everyone, if that's what he had in mind. Forget those Hollywood scenes where the man proposes to his girl in front of a multitude of people who applaud insanely. A woman wants her privacy for that. At least, I do."

"Do you actually think that he might have intended to propose to you finally, using that as his stage?"

Bella shook her head with her eyes cast downward. "Honestly, no. We just hadn't been having the kind of contact that would have justified that. Our relationship was . . . very intimate at one point. But that hadn't happened lately. I was planning to come to his party, or whatever it was. Maybe out of curiosity more than anything else. But then, the next thing I know is that he's been . . . well, you know . . . murdered. I can hardly wrap my brain around it. It's like I'm living in some sort of alternate reality."

"No one in Rosalie can understand it," Wendy told her.

"It's always much more shocking when someone from one of the elite families is involved in this kind of crime. It seems unthinkable, but then there was the case of the Gin Girls being poisoned at their bridge luncheon a few years back."

Bella did not bother to conceal her disdain. "Yes, I remember that you were involved in investigating that. But wealth is no guarantee of anything—not longevity, not happiness, not anything. Certainly not an early demise not taking place, as it turns out."

"Unfortunately, I agree with you there." Then Wendy decided to probe further, believing that Bella might be on the verge of revealing something important. "I hope you don't think it too forward of me, but do you have any theories about who might have killed Mr. Kohl?"

Bella's features hardened at the question, and everything about her sunny disposition turned dark. "Just one. I wouldn't have put it past Patrice Leyton, if you ask me. Something went on between the two of them after he dumped me and started seeing her on the rebound. There were all sorts of rumors about what it might have been—none of them flattering. Rosalie loves its gossip, as I don't have to tell you. But I've heard through the grapevine that King had invited Patrice to this party of his, too. I'm not sure how I would've handled myself seeing her there. I might have said hello but then torn her hair out."

Wendy let that sit for a few moments before speaking. "I received an invitation, as well. I was looking forward to going."

"Yes," Bella said. "If it was truly to be about playing bridge, I can see why. You're quite the player around town. I know just tons of people who swear by you. In fact, I wish you had taught me bridge when I was coming up. My mother oversaw that, and it just wasn't one of her gifts. She snapped at me all the time for making the least little mistake, and I resented it. I think I'd be a much better player now if I'd had someone like you. The buzz is that you have the patience of a saint."

Wendy hung her head and took the modesty route. "Thank you. I try my best and have helped quite a few people in Rosalie learn or better their game."

Surprisingly, it was Bella who decided to play detective with her speculation. "So then, from the texts King sent me and the fact that he invited Patrice and you, plus the fact that he made a big deal out of saying that he was determined to do right by everyone, what on earth was he going to say to all of us?"

"That would have included his parents, of course," Wendy added. "But when we find out what he was going to announce to everyone, I think we will likely know who killed him. I think my husband and my father are probably going to reach the same conclusion in their official investigation. By the way, when was the last time you saw King?"

"I can't really recall," Bella said, looking annoyed. "I get confused on the dates of my social calendar. Maybe sometime last year, at a Christmas party out at the country club where you have your bridge group. I spied him from across the room, and I didn't see him with anybody. Believe it or not, he seemed to be all alone with his eggnog in a corner of the great room. Then he waved at me as if he wanted me to come over, but I didn't wave back and walked into the crowd, where he couldn't see me anymore. I wasn't going to give him the satisfaction, and I think he knew it on some level."

"But you haven't seen him recently, then? You didn't go and see him in person after receiving the invitation?"

"No!" That one word was uttered more forcefully than Wendy thought it needed to be, and then Bella quickly switched subjects. "I wanted to say that I heard from your husband this morning, and I'm to be interrogated down at the station tomorrow. Should I be worried? I don't know anything about King's death, and I'm telling you the truth when I say that I haven't seen King recently. The invitation and the pleading texts were my only contacts."

Wendy's tone was somewhat maternal. "Don't be alarmed or feel threatened. Everyone connected to that party or King's life in general is being questioned. Just tell the truth as you know it, and you should be fine."

Bella picked up her cup again and sipped thoughtfully. "I'm beginning to wonder if I know what's true or what isn't anymore."

The idyllic weather they had been enjoying was suddenly interrupted by the low growling of storm clouds gathering on the Louisiana side of the Mississippi River some distance away, and Bella seemed to use it as her cue. "That'll be on its way over here in no time, so if you have no further questions of me . . ."

Wendy understood the meaning of the unfinished sentence and made her manners, ending the interview with more questions than answers. Sometimes, a reporter had to know when to quit.

Wendy and Ross were snuggling together on the living room sofa after a dinner of grilled salmon and green beans almandine, which she had purchased in the gourmet freezer section of the grocery store and heated up. If she was going to go the quick-and-easy route, she was going to spare no expense. It had been a long day for both of them, but they were reenergized by the tasty calories, so it did not take them long to bounce things off each other regarding the investigation.

"I saw a 'woman scorned' when I went to interview Bella Compton today," Wendy was saying. "The very concept that Merleece and I discussed the other day. You remember I told you that she thinks King's death was the work of a raging female."

"It was definitely a work of rage from King's wounds." Ross untangled himself from their affectionate postures, straightened up, and suddenly broke into a smile. "Ah, Merleece and her street smarts and intuition. I know better than to cross you regarding her insights. But from what I've seen, Wyvonne Sidley also fits that same pattern. So eager to help, so eager to point the finger at others. She's admitted to us that she was in love with Mr. Kohl. What if he said or did something that ticked her off in a way she couldn't handle? That could be a classic case of deflecting and leading us down the garden path."

"That doesn't sound implausible. I do admit there's something about Wyvonne Sidley that makes me uncomfortable. Of course, I consider myself a very inclusive, tolerant person, but that rainbow hair of hers . . ."

Ross's tone became more authoritative as he continued. "Personal grooming has occasionally led to the solution of a crime. Maybe not here, but I agree, I don't want to let this garden path idea go just yet. That was the very phrase that occurred to me today after I finished interviewing Ethel Kohl. She didn't even seem to know who Wyvonne Sidley was, though it's been acknowledged by everyone that she hired Miz Sidley as King's part-time housekeeper and cook. How could it be that she doesn't know anything about the woman now? The thought also occurred to me that she might be playing us. Maybe she and Jackson are both playing us."

"Acting, you mean. That isn't quite as surprising as it might be," Wendy said. "Seems everyone agrees that there's something not quite right with Ethel Kohl. I don't think what you just described could be attributed to a lapse of memory. Unless . . ."

Ross used her pause to complete her thought. Husband and wife had developed compatible wavelengths in their few short years of marriage. "Let's take it one step further, then. Unless she has a medical condition of some sort."

"Something cognitive, perhaps?"

"Bax and I discussed that possibility at the station when I got back from my interview, and we are wondering if Jackson Kohl would be willing to disclose such a thing to us. Of course, her doctor is bound by that oath they take to keep her medical records private."

Wendy's neurons went into overdrive as she stared at her husband and said, "If she did have one of those conditions, you'd think the Rosalie scuttlebutt would've nailed it by now. Do you think it's possible that . . . no, I'm driving off the cliff without a seat belt here . . . but could Ethel Kohl have possibly . . . ?" Wendy chose not to finish the sentence, shaking her head. She knew that even saying the words would give her the shivers.

"I've found that anything is possible in this detective business," Ross continued. "Even a mother killing her son. Parents have been known to kill their children, though it's rare."

Wendy turned away with a mournful expression. "I can't think of anything more despicable. How could any parent kill their own child? They say losing a child is the worst thing in the world to experience and try to recover from. I know it would be for me . . . for us."

Once again, the issue of not being able to conceive surged to the surface of Wendy's brain, but she fought it back and said nothing more.

Ross seemed less than confident as he said, "Perhaps it was a matter of self-defense? That's the only scenario I can dredge up."

"That seems equally bizarre. King attacking his own mother? How in the world would that ever happen, and why?"

There was silence for a while as they both contemplated further. Occasionally, they glanced at each other with quizzical expressions. "They were always known as such a tight family," Ross said. "Father and son, the most successful real estate firm that Rosalie has ever had. Also, we know that Ethel was devoted to her only child. I know that every family has its disagreements, but in what alternate universe would murder become an option for any of them? No, I think the answer lies elsewhere, and we have to dig it up."

"So, Merleece's theory of a woman scorned not named Ethel is beginning to sound better and better to you?"

Ross snickered. "I swear that you're not gonna be satisfied until Bax and I put Merleece on the payroll, are you?"

"I wouldn't go that far," Wendy told him, giving him a nudge with her elbow. "But perhaps the answer lies with the three other women that figured prominently in his life—Bella Compton, Patrice Leyton, and Wyvonne Sidley. At this point, I'm not saying that any of them did it, but Marcus Silvertree seems too obvious as the culprit. I believe him when he says he didn't do it. He was genuinely in shock when he bolted out the front door of Kohl Place and I confronted him. My impression of him was one of a man gripped by horror, not guilt. I think I can tell the difference. He literally didn't have a second to think on his feet. What gushed out of him was the truth, or my crime-solving instincts don't mean a thing."

"You know by now that I admire your instincts greatly." Ross put his arm around his wife once more. "Tomorrow is the day Bax and I interrogate Patrice Leyton. We've been anticipating this one, if what Wyvonne Sidley told us is true. She didn't sound at all uncooperative over the phone when I asked her to come down to the station. In fact, she came off at the other end like she was having one of those phone-sex calls."

"Really now?" But there was nothing but amusement in Wendy's voice. "So you think this scuttlebutt about her having an abortion might be saving the worst for last?"

"That could be the key to this whole thing, if it's true."

Wendy briefly squinted and said, "Suppose she denies it? We only have Wyvonne's word that it happened. If it becomes a 'she said, she said,' who do we believe? It wouldn't be unreasonable to picture one woman trying to smear the other in the arena of love and war."

Ross cocked his head and managed a smile. "That, my sweet wife, is what they pay me for."

CHAPTER 6

Down at headquarters, after the usual pleasantries and innocuous questions were out of the way, Captain Bax took the lead in the interrogation of Patrice Leyton, with his son-in-law by his side. He noted with some degree of curiosity how placid she appeared to be, dressed simply in a beige blouse and skirt. He even got the impression she was trying hard to downplay her noticeable curves, but her full-lipped pout worked against her. Succinctly put, it was practically impossible for this woman to come off as plain and unappealing. Perhaps his first question would shatter that carefully crafted image.

"Miz Leyton, let's get down to business here, and I don't mean to be rude or insulting. But we've heard something that we'd like to confirm with you, and we'd prefer that you be forthcoming about it, if you would. We need to find out if it has any bearing on this case or not."

"Go right ahead, then. I didn't come down here to lie. That's not my way," she said, stopping just short of her usual sultry smile. Instead, there was just the slightest uplifting of the corners of her mouth, not unlike that of a lizard cavorting on the leaves and stalks of outdoor plants in search of insects to ambush.

As a result, Bax could not escape the impression of something predatory about her as he spoke. "A Miz Wyvonne Sidley, who worked for Mr. King Kohl, has informed us that he confessed to her that he had paid for a certain procedure on your behalf in the fairly recent past. Do I need to get more specific?"

Patrice did not answer immediately, her dark eyes glaring at him with what looked like malevolence. Seconds later, however, something slightly more forgiving seemed to emerge as her brows lifted. "Ah, Little Miss Lysol has been doing some spring cleaning, I see. Bleach will cover a multitude of sins, you know. Yes, I'll insist that you spit out exactly what that woman told you, if you don't mind. She can't be trusted, although she comes off as such an earnest young thing with all her college courses squeezed into her daily routine."

"Okay, then," Bax added. "To be blunt, she claims that you got pregnant by Mr. Kohl and that he then paid for an abortion. Is that true?"

Patrice sat back in her chair and folded her arms defiantly. "No, it's not true. That . . . bitch! The part about me and King going out is true, but we broke up and never got back together."

"Then why do you think she would say something like that about you?"

Patrice looked down into her lap, her long, dark hair framing both sides of her face like window curtains. "Because that's who she is. That, and Rosalie's gossip mill that she bows down and worships. You do know about that, don't you?"

"Yes. The gossip mill part. I won't get into who I think pays attention to it and who doesn't. We don't go there in our line of work."

Patrice put a finger to her temple smartly. "Well, there's

your answer. Wyvonne believed anything she heard, being the gullible twentysomething she is. I can tell you she didn't know what she was talking about. Snippets here and snippets there is all she's about. I'd like to have it out with her face-to-face sometime if the opportunity ever arose."

Bax pressed on. "If you've never met, how is it you know so much about her then?"

"Word gets around," Patrice continued. "People knew she'd been hired to work for King. You can't keep much from not getting around Rosalie, you know. Plus, King and I kept in touch—we texted now and then, just to keep up with each other. He mentioned her every now and then in passing. He even said to me once that he thought she had a big crush on him. Men, being the narcissists that they are, can always tell who wants it. I'd keep that in mind if I were you. My opinion is that she would have given anything to have gone out with him. Maybe she was even jealous of me. I certainly wouldn't put it past her."

"I'm sure we will keep your ideas in mind, but why did you and Mr. Kohl keep in touch so frequently if you broke up?"

"Why not? We were friends. We'd gone out for a while there, as I said, and things were starting to get serious between us. It didn't work out for various reasons, but we've remained friends, no matter what anyone else may say."

Bax exchanged puzzled glances with Ross. "You say things didn't work out for various reasons, but you deny that one of those reasons was that you got pregnant and had an abortion."

"I didn't say that exactly."

Every line in Bax's rugged face appeared as he winced and set his jaw. "But you said Miz Wyvonne was lying, didn't you?"

"Yes, I did, and in a very real sense, she was."

"You're gonna have to clarify that, because we don't seem to be speaking the same language at the moment. Am I missing something?"

Patrice lifted her head, and there were elements both of defiance and triumph in the gesture. "The truth is that King wasn't the only man I was seeing when he and I were going out, and he knew that. We had no exclusive arrangement or anything like that. But King and I were careful and safe, if you know what I mean. There was this other guy I was seeing off and on—his name was Jimmers Tyson, and he's moved away with his tail between his legs—but we both got really drunk one night, and I don't recall him having protection when we . . . you know . . . did it. When I told him about my pregnancy, he got ugly and said he wasn't responsible, because I was the type who was always . . . well, I won't use the exact verb he used. I'll let you fill in the blanks. I have my dignity, despite what other people may say about me, even a rogue like Jimmers. Men get away with things that women are severely judged for."

Bax and Ross sat mesmerized next to each other until Bax broke their silence. "We've . . . filled in the blanks, and we understand your position. Please, go on."

"What it came down to was that when I told King about it, he had the same reaction as Jimmers did, except without the gutter language, and asked me how I knew the baby was Jimmers's. King even said to me, 'What if it's mine? Have you thought about that possibility?' "

"And what did you answer?" Bax added.

"I told him I was sure it wasn't, because we both took precautions, and I also asked him how he would feel if it was somehow his, and he said he'd have to think about it for a while. Now, how do you think that made me feel? Not good at all, I'll tell you. The next time we got together, he told me he'd thought about it every which way under the sun and wouldn't feel right about bringing up another man's child, if that was the truth of the matter, and he didn't think there was anything that could change his mind. So, I asked him if he would help me get an abortion, then, since I felt completely lost and wasn't receiving any support from anyone. You'd have to be a woman to understand about these things and how difficult the choices are. Men generally don't understand, because they can't get pregnant. It's easy for them to walk away and never look back. Way too many of them do just that."

"So he did pay for your abortion, after all?"

At last, Patrice showed some semblance of emotion, stuttering as she spoke. "He didn't agree . . . not at first. He said I could have the child . . . and I . . . uh, well, I asked him if he would support me if I did. He said no . . . why should he support another man's child? It's not like the Kohls didn't have the money. And then he said I could put it up for adoption, if I liked. But I told him I didn't want to go through all that. There are those who insist that it's not a woman's decision to make, that she should have the child no matter what. Like it's written in stone. How can you manage a stranger's life like that? So, you have to understand that . . . it wasn't as black and white as Wyvonne Sidley made it out to be. It was more complicated than that. King ended up paying for me to abort another man's child. It seems to me that he didn't tell Wyvonne the whole story, because what she said to you clearly shows she didn't know it. Now, I've told it all to the both of you, so you can take it from there."

Ross spoke up next. "We will do that, and we thank you for cooperating with our crime lab and giving us your prints and DNA."

"It's been a good while since I've been in Kohl's house, so I'd be surprised if you find any trace of me there."

"Someone did a bit of housecleaning, we've discovered."

Patrice wagged her finger energetically. "There you are. Remember what I said about bleach. I'd look to Little Miz Lysol with the kaleidoscope hair for that chore. She could certainly have removed some evidence and ignored the rest at her convenience. Just like the stage manager of a play, if you ask me. Placing and removing props as she saw fit."

Ross couldn't resist. "I do believe I'd buy tickets to a showdown between the two of you."

"Never mind that," Patrice said, not bothering to disguise her contempt for the remark. "Just take my word that she's not the goody-goody working her way through college that she pretends to be. King knew what she was up to—he was no fool. He knew his way around, all right. He had a way of knowing things but not letting on that he knew. He also kept a part of himself hidden from view. I can't explain exactly what I mean, but there were times when I felt he was gonna open up completely to me about his innermost thoughts, but changed his mind at the last minute."

"So you claim to be an open book, do you?" Ross said.

"I've never denied who I am. What's wrong with having a good time?"

"Nothing at all, unless someone gets murdered. We do place a limit on behavior in this country."

The comment appeared not to disturb Patrice in the least. "It may surprise you to hear that I completely agree with that, and I would never have touched a hair on King's head in a million years. Whether anyone approves of what he did or not—I guess what I did, too—he was there for me when I needed him, and I'll be forever grateful. People can throw judgment all over the place if they want to, but they weren't in my shoes, or in my maternity clothes, for that matter."

"No judgment here," Ross told her. "We're just about trying to find out who murdered Mr. Kohl, and no line of interrogation is off limits."

Patrice moderated her pout and said, "I've told you the truth as I know it."

"We'll get in touch if we need to see you again," Ross

said. "I'm sure you know we'd like for you to stay in Rosalie during our investigation."

Patrice then banished her pout. "I know the rules, gentlemen."

After she had left a few seconds later, Ross turned to Bax and said, "Well, that was a roller-coaster ride. She's a pretty cool number if I ever saw one."

"Well-rehearsed, I'd say. Reminded me of an audition for a play."

"She had an answer for everything," Ross added.

"Yes, she did."

Then Ross mumbled words under his breath.

Bax couldn't quite pick up on them. "What was that?"

This time, Ross spoke them evenly and audibly: "Bleach . . . will cover . . . a . . . multitude . . . of . . . sins."

It was later that afternoon that Bax settled in behind his cluttered office desk with Ross sitting across from him as they began discussing the latest update from the crime lab. "Well, there you have it," Bax was saying while thumping the paper for emphasis. "No apparent trace of Patrice Leyton in the Kohl house. She told us there wouldn't be. But there were either prints or DNA from Jackson and Ethel Kohl, Wyvonne Sidley, Marcus Silvertree, a couple of unidentified prints, and now, Bella Compton. One single blond hair of hers found on King's desk. That pretty much puts her there at the scene of the crime."

Ross cocked his head. "That hair is somewhat of a surprise, since Miz Compton told the two of us and Wendy that she had not visited King in quite a while. Wendy says she was quite emphatic about it. Yet, here we find that one of her blond hairs showed up on his desk, big as life. As you say, it becomes difficult to make the case that she was not there recently but was likely lying about it. She's put herself at the top of the list, and her explanation had better be a good one."

Bax took his time with a sharp intake of air just before he spoke. "Obviously, we'll have to get her back in here so she can explain. I'll admit that's not looking too good for her." Then he leaned way back in his chair and put his shiny black shoes up on his desk, his trademark ritual that heralded he was headed for some deep contemplation. "This is a strange case. Nothing feels right about it to me. The most obvious suspect, Marcus Silvertree, was witnessed fleeing from the scene of the crime by my own daughter, and we have motive, opportunity, and his prints on the doorknob—but not on the desk or the murder weapon—which were certainly tampered with, because the crime lab found traces of bleach. Back to the bleach again—and that statement from Miz Leyton, calling Wyvonne Sidley 'Miss Lysol.' Plus, we know the TOD and that Marcus was there within that time frame. Some people would say it's a slam dunk, but what we have on Silvertree is really more circumstantial than anything else. I smell a setup. I've come to the conclusion that the key to solving this case is to try our damnedest to discover what King was going to tell everybody at that party of his he had planned. No one who was close to him seems to have any idea what he was really going to say, not even his parents."

"Wendy and I have been speculating, of course," Ross added. "Was he going to announce an engagement to one of the ladies in his life? Wendy originally thought that might be the deal, but she says Lyndell convinced her otherwise."

Bax gave out a weak snort. "My wife never tells me anything about what goes down at her workplace, of course. But as you know, she and that daughter a' mine are thick as thieves at the *Citizen*. I guess that's to be expected between an editor and one of her best reporters. My Lyndell is her own woman, of course, and I like it that way."

Ross nodded agreeably and continued. "Anyway, Wendy has wondered as a backup theory if King was about to make an announcement about his health—a medical diagnosis, perhaps?"

"I suppose we could go really dark here and speculate that it was something terminal. We could get in touch with his lawyer and see if he would cooperate with us and HIPAA regulations to allow us access to King's medical records. Maybe something'll turn up there."

"If it turns out he was dying from something or other, that would have been a shocker to everybody." Ross paused and flexed his fingers for a second or two. "I mean, how do you tell anyone something like that and not shock them out of their socks? I would think it's impossible not to. Which reminds me of my visit with Ethel Kohl. Everyone seems to think that there's something not quite right about her—other than the shock of losing her son, I mean. She didn't appear to remember who Wyvonne Sidley was when the subject came up, and that is beyond odd, if she really couldn't recall. Could she have a medical condition, too? The more you delve into all of this, the more complicated and bizarre it becomes. What if we don't have any of this figured out right? It wouldn't be the first time."

Bax's frown was an epic one. Over the years, it had wilted many a suspect. "Then we figure it out another way. But no matter how we figure it, I still think the bottom line is that whatever he was about to announce got him killed."

"We're on the same page."

"On the other hand," Bax added, "in what alternate universe does someone get killed because they are going to announce they are dying? Seems redundant, doesn't it? Why not wait for nature to run its course instead of taking any sort of criminal risk?"

Ross resisted the smirk that was trying to emerge, but he

was determined to keep up. Such was the symbiosis between father-in-law and son-in-law. "Yep, why not, indeed? So, what other angles do we have available to explore?"

Bax sat up and then leaned forward with his hands on the table. That always meant he was onto something. "Here's an angle for you. I'm talking about aggression on King's part. Was he going to threaten someone about something? Did they then have no other choice but to stop him from exposure of some sort? Did someone have a dirty little secret hidden away?"

"Does that take us back to Marcus Silvertree and the bad blood between them? We already know that the Kohls drove him out of business," Ross added. "That's a given. Was there some unfinished little item that needed to be addressed between the two of them? Did King have something on Marcus that he wanted to rub in his face? In that case, I can see Marcus ripping that plaque off the wall and aiming it at King's temple a coupla times with those nasty blows."

But Bax waved off the suggestion, looking thoroughly disgruntled. "It's easy to go there, but think in terms of that party King was gonna throw. Why would you dredge up some business grudge and let all those people in on it? That might put you in a bad light as a businessman and community leader, and not the other fella. I just can't seem to get the right angle on this one."

"Okay, I'll get in touch with the Kohls' lawyer about King's medical records."

"Yep, they could give us some valuable info."

"Or not."

"Don't be a pessimist," Bax added. "You never know when the right clue is gonna land in your lap."

Wendy wasn't making much progress in her interview with Greta Compton in one of the *Citizen*'s meeting rooms, which her daughter, Bella, had arranged for her. The proverbial turnip was certainly not yielding much blood today. This tall, pleasant-looking, society matron, so smartly dressed and bejeweled, and so perfectly coiffed, with not a touch of gray—surely impossible for her age—maintained a smile and an agreeable demeanor while revealing nothing of much interest not known to the general public in gossipy old Rosalie.

Still, Wendy persisted. No reporter worth her font ever gave up easily. "Can't you think of some amusing little escapade that you and Ethel Kohl enjoyed together?"

Crickets followed, along with a shaking of Greta's head, and then the gratuitous smile returned after she'd taken a sip of her bottled water.

"Nothing at all?"

"It's just that dear Ethel is going through such pain right now. I can't even imagine what life is like for her. I'd be out of my mind if I ever lost Bella like that. Or any way at all. A parent doesn't expect to outlive a child, and I can't believe there are any exceptions to that. There's just a part of me that doesn't feel right being all lighthearted about such things. I feel like I'm somehow being disrespectful. Then there was the hope . . . and it seemed like it was about to happen at times . . . that King and Bella were going to become a permanent couple. At least that's what Ethel and I were always praying for—our families tied together through marriage, our genes intermingled. It was a thrilling prospect for the both of us, and now, well . . . it's going to be impossible."

Genes.

The word resonated with Wendy, and for a split second, she wondered why. Then she remembered that Merleece had brought up the subject of generation after generation of them; that eventually *bad genes* would emerge if given enough opportunities. Wendy was going to make a note to save that thought for later so she wouldn't forget it, but the sudden sound of rain on the *Citizen*'s metal roof distracted her, and the thought flew out of her mind. Time to resume the interview.

"I understand what you're saying about your two families, but think of it this way. This piece I'm doing is meant to be a tribute to the family, and you'd help make that happen."

Finally, there was a glimmer of hope. "Well . . . there was that time—"

"Yes, tell me about that time," Wendy quickly interrupted, desperate for copy.

Suddenly, Greta's frozen smile began to thaw, her words sounding more genuine, and Wendy couldn't help but pat herself on the back mentally. At the moment, she was falling back on her proven journalistic standby that even the oddest of ducks could be made to quack. Then, incredibly, serendipity fell into her lap. She must be living right.

"I call this the invention of duck spaghetti," Greta said, chuckling to herself.

"That sounds very amusing already," Wendy said, marveling at the *duck* delight going on inside her brain.

"It wasn't at the time, though," Greta continued. "I'd invited Ethel and Jackson over for dinner because Peter, my late husband, and I owed them one. We've always entertained each other as couples, and we do keep count. Anyhow, I'd found this elaborate recipe for orange duck that I'd been just dying to try to impress my crowd, you know, and I spent all day preparing it, hoping it would turn out well. I have to admit that I was very nervous about it from the start. So, about thirty minutes before serving it, I took it out of the oven and cut into it—just a little slice, you understand—for a taste, and it was so tough, I could barely chew it. They say duck can turn out that way if you aren't careful. I sometimes wonder why people bother with it in the first place. Same for quail—so little meat for all the trouble you go to. I was horrified about the tough duck, of course. If any of us had worn dentures, it would've taken them right out." Greta paused to tap her front teeth proudly with her index finger. "But all four of us have worshiped our dentists since forever, and by now, we all believe flossing is next to godliness. Goodness, that sounds like one of the commandments, doesn't it? Do you suppose Moses would approve?"

Wendy was writing fast now with a smile on her face. "It is a pretty funny line. So, tell me, what did you do next?"

There was a little giggle, and then Greta said, "Well, I'd taken it out of the oven on its platter and done the cutting over the sink. But when I tried to lift it again with my mittens, it slid off the platter and right into the disposal. Not the whole thing, mind you. It wasn't big enough to do that. But there it was—half in the dirty disposal and the other half—the hind end—sticking out. I could get a bit more graphic with my words, but I won't. Still, it was like the duck was giving me a sign, and it wasn't a polite one. I really don't think I need to elaborate further."

Now, both women were laughing freely, and then Wendy said, "Where does Ethel Kohl come into this misadventure?"

Greta leaned in and said in a conspiratorial tone, "That's the best part. I went into the living room where Jackson and Ethel and Peter were all waiting with their drinks and making the usual small talk that people do, and I whispered in Ethel's ear to come into the kitchen and help me. And for a while, we both just stood there in the kitchen, just laughing at that duck's behind. But Ethel told me not to panic, that she had a solution. She said she'd boil up some spaghetti real quick—everyone has those noodles in their pantry, you know—and I should cut up the duck from the part that hadn't been stuck in the disposal, and instead of chicken spaghetti, we'd have duck spaghetti."

"And did you?"

"We certainly did, and the men never knew what had really happened. Cutting the duck into really small bits made it much more edible. Really, it was even palatable. Although I'm sure they wondered why Ethel and I kept snickering at each other like girlfriends with a secret throughout the entire dinner. Of course, we never told them what went on behind the scenes. Most men don't care about what goes on in the kitchen anyway—not as long as they get fed properly, and we can fuss at them about suppressing their belches."

Then Wendy had a brainstorm. "This is a wonderful illustration of the kind of friendship you have. But would you mind if I packaged this as if it were an episode of *I Love Lucy*? You know—Greta and Ethel, instead of Lucy and Ethel? If I remember correctly, they were always messing up in the kitchen. Believe me, our readership will appreciate something like this to take their minds off the community's grief."

Greta clasped her hands together and rose up a bit in her chair. "That would be a scream. I don't mind one bit. I know all our friends will adore reading about it and why Ethel and I couldn't keep straight faces the rest of the evening. Really, the two of us were such silly gooses that evening. Or shall I say *ducks*?"

The dam had burst, and from that point forward, Wendy had no trouble extracting more entertaining tidbits from Greta, which would help bring her piece on the Kohl family to life with aplomb. Toward the end, however, the pall which previously had gripped Greta returned.

"Would you mind letting me read what you end up writing before it goes to print? I still feel so bad for Jackson and Ethel that I'd love to have a sneak preview."

"Of course I wouldn't," Wendy told her with a soothing smile. "And that way, you can rave about it to all your friends and let them know it's coming. There's no point in writing a feature if no one reads it. I'd welcome your help."

Greta took in a deep breath, looking like she'd just been appointed the Queen of the World. "You can count on me."

* * *

Wendy had just returned to her cubicle and entered her document to type in her notes from the interview with Greta Compton when her cell pinged. It was Ross texting her.

Just heard from Jackson Kohl; Ethel in hospital; suicide attempt; in waiting room now with Jackson
Should I come over? she texted back.
If schedule permits
The story is my schedule
C U soon

Wendy immediately headed to Lyndell's office with her phone in hand, but as soon as she walked in, her trusty editor gave her instructions, pointing at her vigorously with a look of satisfaction on her face. "I know, I know. Bax just texted me about Ethel Kohl. Go on over to the hospital right now and see what you can find out." Lyndell paused, with a sad narrowing of her eyes. "What that poor woman has been through. I just can't even imagine."

"Yes," Wendy said. "Looks like happy endings aren't in the future for the Kohls."

"In the space of a few days, they've gone from being on top of the world to falling completely apart," Lyndell added.

"So it seems."

Wendy wondered if it were actually as simple as that, however, as she made her way to the parking lot to head over to Rosalie General. Her instincts told her that lives couldn't unravel that fast unless they had already been severely compromised deep within the cores of where they nestled as unknowns; and something else told her that perhaps they had not seen the end of the tragedy of the Kohl family of Rosalie, Mississippi.

In the otherwise empty waiting room a few minutes later,

Wendy observed the contrast between her husband and Jackson Kohl. The former was his usual confident, sturdy self in his navy-blue uniform, perched on the edge of a long couch, with impeccable posture; while the latter seemed to have shrunk into an even smaller package of despair in wrinkled clothes, backed up against the cushions with his eyes affixed to the ceiling and a worn magazine in his lap.

Wendy feared the worst but managed the question anyway, addressing it to both of them as she took her seat in a nearby chair. "What's the latest update? I hope and pray it's good news, of course."

Ross spoke up quickly. "They're diluting the effects of the bleach that was in her stomach with an IV. Not to be indelicate, but she threw up some of it in the ambulance. They're working hard on reducing the damage to her esophagus. There could be long-term damage, or not."

"I should have seen this coming," Jackson said, his voice sounding small and frightened while he fidgeted constantly. "I should have known."

Both Wendy and Ross came to attention, and Ross said, "Tell my wife what you told me a few minutes ago."

Jackson took his time but finally said, "My wife . . . was diagnosed with Alzheimer's sometime last year, and it has progressed more quickly than the doctors thought it would. I've been trying to keep it hidden and keep Ethel safe at the same time, but I'm pretty sure people all over Rosalie were guessing what was going on. I should have known that our son's death might have triggered something like this. She was having a terrible time with acceptance, as you can imagine. As I said, I should have been more foresighted. She's been in quite a spiral for a while with the medications she's taking. Of course, she has her good and bad days. Sometimes, she gets these wild ideas, and there's no reasoning with her."

Wendy leaned in and lowered her voice to just above a

whisper. The great weight hanging over them all was nearly palpable. "It's a good thing you discovered her in time."

"Barely. I let her outta my sight for a while this morning. When I realized she wasn't in the slave quarters, I panicked and ran into the main house just in time to find her guzzling bleach straight from the gallon that Wyvonne used to clean with all the time. She kept it under the kitchen sink. I told Ethel to stick her finger down her throat, but she couldn't do it right. Not to be gross, but it wouldn't come up. I did get half a glass of milk down her before the first responders got there. Last time Dr. Grimes came out, he said he thought she was gonna make it. But no thanks to me. Well . . . he didn't say that . . . I'm saying that."

"It sounds like you did everything you could under the circumstances," Wendy said. "Try not to blame yourself."

"No . . . I . . . I never should have let her outta my sight. I told her to wait on the sofa while I went to brush my teeth. Just that small amount of time. She seemed drowsy, so I went ahead and did it. I've tried to be so careful up to now, practically every minute of every day and night. Believe me when I tell you that this is my fault. She may have even misinterpreted things I've said."

As Jackson seemed inconsolable, Wendy decided to let things lie. Perhaps the only thing that would cure his guilt would be a pronouncement from the doctor that his wife was out of the woods. Fifteen minutes later, the verdict was in: Ethel Kohl was going to survive her suicide attempt with some minor damage to her throat, but it was a close call.

"But we'd like to keep her overnight just the same," the very tall and lean physician in charge, Dr. Andrew Grimes, told them with authority. "We'd like our psychiatrist, Dr. Marlowe, to look in on her just to be on the safe side. It's in her best interests."

"If you think it's absolutely necessary," Jackson said, sounding a bit irritated. "I'd rather take her home with me now."

Dr. Grimes nodded with a hint of a patronizing smile. "We think it's best. You can visit her, Mr. Kohl, after we move her from triage, and she gets settled in her room."

Then he walked away, and the ugly little crisis was over.

After the initial sense of relief that washed over the three of them had subsided, Jackson spoke up. "How am I gonna manage keeping an eye on her round the clock? This is bound to happen again if I don't, but I'm not trained for this. I can only do so much."

"You could hire a nurse to help you," Wendy said quickly. "They're trained, and you'll be able to leave her when you need to."

Jackson's sigh was one for the ages. "This runs in her family, you know. Her aunt Phoebe is in a memory-care facility on the Coast. Has been for the last decade or so. We hear from her doctor every now and then, and there are never any complaints. She's a very good patient, but she was a handful to handle before her family put her in there. It can be like keeping an eye on a toddler at times. They get into everything."

"Do what's best for Ethel," Wendy said. "That's all that counts now."

Jackson did not sound convinced. "I suppose. But what a mess this all is, coming out of nowhere the way it did. Who would have thought that our son would get murdered?" Jackson clenched his fist as he finished speaking. "If only time could be reversed, and that awful act could be prevented."

Wendy glanced quickly at Ross and said, "We're both so sorry for all you're going through. It must be a nightmare."

"You have no idea."

Then Ross cleared his throat and said, "By the way, Jackson, did your son have any underlying medical conditions?"

Looking thoroughly surprised, Jackson said, "Do you mean mental, like Ethel?"

"Not necessarily. Just anything at all."

"Not that I'm aware of. He was in excellent shape. Of course, he was only in his late twenties, so he should have been. He took good care of himself, worked out, watched what he ate. He converted one of the bedrooms in the main house to a gym of sorts. I'd go over there every once in a while and work out myself. I will say that Ethel was furious with him for installing a gym in the house she'd decorated so properly. She insisted that gym equipment didn't belong there, but he was determined to stay in shape. On the other hand, Ethel just didn't want to let go of her disapproval."

Ross glanced quickly at Wendy, as she understood his line of questioning perfectly. "Youth isn't always a guarantee of good health. Some people are unlucky or just careless in that way."

Jackson's features hardened. "Not King. He was strong. He had no weaknesses, and never let it be said that he did. He inherited that strength from me, and I don't mean just physical strength. I also mean strength of purpose. Once he decided on something, nothing could stop him from trying for it. He was proud of the little empire we built together—every listing, every project, every contract signed. I better not hear of anyone saying that he wasn't."

"I'm sure he was all those things you said," Ross added. "As long as I've been aware of such things, the Kohls have been on top in the real estate business."

Jackson stared straight ahead with a discernible longing in his eyes. "And now, it appears I'm gonna have to go it alone."

Ethel Kohl recognized the man with the somewhat forced smile coming toward her bed. It was her husband of many long decades. Of that much, she was certain. She decided that he had the look of someone on a mission. But she had no idea why she was entangled in telemetry with an IV in her arm in the hospital. How had this come to pass? Nonetheless, she was glad to see a familiar face. She was sure he would explain things to her in just a minute or two.

"How are you feeling, dear?" Jackson said to her in soothing tones. "The doctor says you should recover completely."

For some reason, she decided not to tell him the truth. She felt awful and frightened at the same time. Sharp shards of recent memory surfaced here and there. They were painful, but she couldn't pin them down easily. Mostly they were something about *bleach*.

"I'm better, I think," Ethel told her husband in a raspy voice, but she thought the question from him was perfunctory.

"That's good. You gave us all quite a scare."

"Did I?"

"Yes."

Jackson gently touched her arm, trying to turn away from her face at the same time, but couldn't manage it. He was stuck with her confused expression, one he had seen far too much lately.

Then, Ethel remembered completely. "I tried to drink bleach, didn't I? I went into the kitchen of the big house and got it from under the sink. I don't think Wyvonne should have left it there within easy reach. They're always warning to keep such chemicals out of the reach of children. Why do you think she did that? I think she should be fired for such incompetence. Of course, I'm in no condition to do that. You'll have to do it. I suddenly recall that I hired her a while back, but I don't want to be saddled with firing her. Am I right? Was I the one who hired her?"

"Yes, you were."

"Then, you go right ahead and fire her, please. But I wish

I could keep track of things better. I don't know what to believe anymore."

Jackson managed to maintain his forced smile. "How could Wyvonne know you were going to do something like that? Anyhow, you did get some bleach down your throat, but I caught you in the nick of time. We rushed you to the hospital, and everything's gonna be okay."

More bubbled up in Ethel's brain. It caused her to shudder. "Did they ask you . . . and did you tell them everything? You remember what we've been talking about since it happened, don't you? I mean, since King's death."

Jackson shook his head slowly from side to side and said, "I remember everything you've said, and you've remembered some of what I've said to you, but don't worry about any of it."

"What does that mean? Did you keep your promise?"

"Yes, of course, dear. I would always keep a promise made to you."

"Do you think they'll find out?"

"No."

"Are you sure? It's a terrible secret to carry around." She focused on the IV going into her arm, frowning at it as if it were a poisonous snake. "Do you think this tube can absolve me? Is it cleansing me of my sins? Is it holy water they have going through me? Because, you know, I haven't said anything to Father LeBlanc about this. Not yet. I've been putting off my confession. I think I've been wrong to do that."

Jackson's head shaking became more emphatic as he changed the subject. "Dear, I want you to keep putting off that confession and forget about going to the basilica. God will forgive you, I'm sure. What would you think of a nice, long visit with your Aunt Phoebe? You said that you and she always got along famously while you were growing up."

Ethel considered and something lit up in her brain. "I haven't seen her in ages. She has to be pushing eighty by now.

She taught me how to sew and make lanyards and to style my hair in a French twist. Do you think she's still alive?"

"Very much so, she is. And that's right, you haven't seen her in years, and you're probably right about the age she's reached. You remember how much you like the palm trees down in Biloxi, where she stays? So many of them swaying in the breeze off the Gulf. Such a pretty and exotic picture."

Ethel actually smiled. She had adored palm trees since she was a little girl, thinking of them as exotic, sturdy sentinels that stood up to hurricanes well enough, even though a few trunks got bent and listed away from the water in their determined attempts to resist those howling winds. She had lost count of all the hurricanes that had hit South Louisiana and Mississippi through the years. She had ridden them out in partying style—every one of them and without damage to herself or her property. She considered herself fortunate. Others had not been so lucky.

"I like the palm trees here in Rosalie, too, even if they aren't exactly on a beach. I think Greta Compton has one in her backyard. It's one of those windmill palms that sticks its tongue out at the cold weather in winter. Do you think we could plant a palm tree in front of the slave quarters so I could see it every morning when I walk out?"

"We can think about it. And it's true enough. The palm trees here in Rosalie are on the river, which has its own charms. You just keep thinking about the serenity of palm trees."

"So when would I be visiting Aunt Phoebe?"

"Soon."

Then Ethel's mood changed quickly. "About my secret . . . are you sure you won't tell anyone? You've been so good to me about that."

"I wouldn't dream of it, dear. As I've told you over and over, your secret is perfectly safe with me."

"Because it's an awful thing that I don't want anyone else to know."

"They won't."

Ethel began to tear up. "There can't possibly be any greater sin in this world than for a mother to kill her own son."

Jackson nodded with an air of resignation but said nothing.

"Why did you have to walk in on me drinking the bleach? Why couldn't you have just done the right thing and let me go my way and face my fate?"

Jackson paused, moving his eyes from side to side, and said, "Because it wasn't meant to be that way. I mean, you leaving us that way. There are lots of things that were never meant to be, even though you can't understand at the moment. The world can be a confusing place, full of unpleasant surprises. Now. You've been thinking way too much. You must get some rest. The nurse said I wasn't to stay too long after what you've been through, but you'll be home soon. And then, we'll talk about that visit to Aunt Phoebe, okay? It'll be a nice change for you. Sometimes, I think it's too crowded in our slave quarters. We seem to be on top of each other all the time. Maybe we made a mistake in giving the big house to King, but we did what we thought was right at the time. He pressed for it, and we gave in, and now look what's happened."

Ethel shrugged but was surprised at how happy the mention of her aunt made her feel. She even started to say, "Then that's the answer to everything," but thought better of it. Some things were just too hard to figure out these days. Things had been difficult to figure out for a long time now. There were even times when she got her dreams and nightmares confused with waking life.

CHAPTER 7

This was the morning that Wendy would be turning in her feature on the Kohls to Lyndell, but she felt uneasy about the piece. Not the writing, of course. She was always secure in her craft. She had filled it with lightweight anecdotes such as the one she had coaxed out of Greta Compton, and there was nothing wrong with that. It all flowed beautifully. She had painted a picture of a family universally admired by Rosalieans, but it felt incomplete. How in the world could King have been murdered without something dark and fearful going on behind the scenes in his life?

No, it wasn't her job to solve the crime—that fell to her husband and father in the main. But her natural penchant for tackling puzzles successfully had kicked in once again. It was at times like these that she seriously considered taking her father up on his standing offer to train for and join the police force. Imagine that. A detective married to another detective. She was certain it had happened before in the great world of possibilities.

"I can get you in the academy anytime, you know," Bax had told her once again, right after a couple of men on the force had retired during the last year. There were openings just begging to be filled, and he just couldn't resist. "I'm sorry if I sound like a broken record."

But her response never changed. "You know I can't get past the gun thing. I don't even like the idea of target practice and having to wear earplugs. And do you know how mad at you Lyndell would be from taking me away from her? You don't want to get on the wrong side of your wife, do you? I'm serious about that, and you know it only too well."

Her predilection for the written word always swooped down to save her from even considering such a rash move. In real time, this was also the morning that Merleece came in to clean the house, which meant that Lyndell had continued to let Wendy arrive at a later hour for work; the two friends would catch up with each other over coffee and breakfast pastries, ignoring the rest of the world for a much-needed respite. Delivering the friendly feature on the Kohls to her editor would just have to wait a while longer.

"I keep thinking about what you said not that long ago about King Kohl's murder being a matter of a woman scorned," Wendy was saying as she sat at the kitchen table and spread a pat of butter atop one of her homemade blueberry muffins. She'd been a butter-spreader since toddler stage and couldn't be convinced there was anything unhealthy about it. "There was no lack of women scorned where the man was concerned. In fact, there were too many fighting over the same man, according to everything we've learned. I keep resisting one of my rogue instincts in the matter, and I wonder if I should."

Taking a sip of her coffee, Merleece said, "Care to tell me about this rogue instinct, then? I know you just dying to, else what am I really here for today? This house could practically clean itself. This is always about just you and me."

"I don't want you to think I haven't considered your theory seriously," Wendy continued. "Far from it. I shared it with my husband, and he filed it away for future reference, I assure you. Ross and Daddy will keep it in mind. They take nothing for granted, and neither do I."

Merleece smiled. "And I take no offense at what you just told me. Go on ahead and tell me this other thing you thought of."

"It's just that I keep thinking that with that many women upset with him for various reasons that—" Wendy took a deep breath and continued—"this might have been a very clever group effort. All of them playing different parts to get the job done. Does that make any sense to you?"

Merleece looked and sounded not the least bit surprised. "Far as I'm concerned, that's just an extension of what I said in the first place. I told you that the angriest I'd ever seen anybody was two women fightin' over the same man. They had they claws out, and they meant business. Do I think women can travel in packs and gangs now and again? Yes, ma'am, I do."

"And I certainly believe you," Wendy added. "So, if all that's true, it sorta implies that somebody might have been the ringleader of this fatal circus. Maybe one of those women came up with the idea and enlisted the help of the others. Of course, there are times that I think this is just too off the wall, and I put it away."

"Have you mentioned this to that handsome husband a' yours yet, Strawberry?"

"No. I wanted to run it past you first. You're my touchstone. I sorta never really proceed unless I give you a little taste."

Merleece enjoyed a good laugh. "I'm not somebody to worship thataway, but lemme give you some advice. Don't tell that husband a' yours you told me first. I don't think he'd like that much. Men always like to think they the first in just about errything." She finished with a quick wink.

Wendy joined her in brief laughter, but her solemnity soon returned. "Everything about all of this bothers me no end. I mean, besides the fact that someone was murdered. That's never easy to accept. Now, something else terrible has happened. Miz Ethel Kohl apparently tried to commit suicide by drinking bleach. She ended up in the hospital emergency room, of course. It appears she will recover, though."

Merleece made the sourest face possible and put down her cup. "That is some sad news. That is some nasty stuff, that bleach. I never can get it outta my head when Hiram, that son a' mine as a baby boy, went into the laundry room—he was about two years old—and he got into a bottle I had just lyin' around like nobody's business. Chirren will get into anything if you let 'em and leave whatever it is within reach. I had to rush him to the hospital. But that was uh accident. You say Miz Kohl did it on purpose?"

"That's what they say."

Merleece drew back in her chair and eyed her friend intently. "And this is where I'm s'pose to give you advice as usual on the whole thing?"

Wendy's smile was sly as she glanced at Merleece sideways. "Bingo."

"So now the deal is that one a' Mr. Kohl's girlfriends is a ringleader?"

"Now that I've put it out there, yes. What I really need from you is just a big slice a' your common sense. It'll do me good, just like a slice of your applesauce pie always does. So, what's your take?"

Merleece thought briefly and said, "I guess what you gotta do is look for the one that has the least amount a' forgiveness in her heart. Grudges, they can kill people in a lotta different ways. Once they kill a person's soul, anything can happen. If I never got anything else outta my church, it'd be that. You cain't walk through life with a weapon aimed straight at it. Sooner or later, somethin'll fall down dead."

Wendy immediately thought of Patrice's remorseless abortion story. Had Patrice fallen off a cliff as a result? Was she totally broken as a result? "There was a rage aspect to Mr. Kohl's murder. He was bludgeoned with one of his own real estate plaques that was torn off the wall. It's not what most people would consider a murder weapon, but it got the job done in this case. I keep wondering if there was any significance to the choice of weapon. That keeps bringing me back to a man—Marcus Silvertree, not a woman or a ringleader of women. I keep going round and round. Unlike whoever killed King. They went straight for the kill, believe me."

Merleece shuddered. "That's hard for a gentle soul like me to hear."

"I don't doubt that for a second. Join the club," Wendy said, raising her hand briefly.

Merleece looked dissatisfied. "But now, if you think you barkin' up the wrong tree with the girlfriend ringleader theory, you could always fall back on the fact that people in business can sometimes make some bad enemies."

"Yes. King and his father did just that. Specifically, Marcus Silvertree, the real estate wannabe that they drove out of business. And I caught Marcus rushing out of King's house the morning the murder took place. Of course, he swears that King was dead when he walked in a few minutes earlier, and all the evidence against him is purely circumstantial, particularly the lack of DNA anywhere in the house except on the doorknob."

Wendy suddenly paused and frowned. "Merleece . . . there was something else you said last time we talked about this, but it escapes me now. I've thought about it before, and it really grabbed me, but now I'm blocked. It's trying to bubble up to the surface because I think it's important. I know you can't recall our conversation verbatim or anything like that, but could you think back to anything you may have

brought up besides the woman scorned angle or even my latest ringleader theory? Am I asking too much?"

Merleece put her hands around her coffee cup, staring
down into it as if it contained tea leaves getting ready to speak
to her. "Right now, I think you might be. But l can think on
it some and get back to you. When you try too hard to remember things, they don't cooperate. Then, while you in the
middle of somethin' else, maybe even in bed in the middle of
the night, they pop up, and then you pop up and snap a finger
or two like you the dumbest person in the world."

"Isn't that the truth? You nailed it."

Both women went silent for a while with smiles on their
faces. Finally, Merleece said, "Maybe it'll come to me while I
clean this house a' yours. If I get a brainstorm, I'll write it
down and leave a note for you on this very kitchen table so
you can see it when you come home from work. How'd you
like that for a big slice a' applesauce pie?"

Wendy couldn't resist. "So, are you saying that Lysol and
furniture polish are brain food?"

They both snickered, and Merleece said, "If that's true, I'd
be a genius by now, Strawberry, and I'd be out at the college
as a professor."

"You'd be excellent at teaching Common Sense 101,"
Wendy added. "Just not a lot of it going around these days."

"Amen to that."

Ross had taken a reserved fancy to Wendy's "ringleader
theory," which she had outlined over a dinner of grilled
chicken and asparagus the evening Merleece had cleaned.

"That would be one helluva coordinating effort among
women who clearly did not get along with each other. I'd like
to have been a fly on the wall for that one. But, stranger things
have happened in the world of crime," he had said while
clearing the dishes.

"Worth looking into at least," Wendy had added. "Suppose King found a way to alienate everyone close to him? In that case, I think the king was destined to fall, if you'll forgive my bridge terminology."

"You wouldn't be you without your bridge terminology, but your daddy and I will give it the once-over, I promise."

"You know me, I practically live outside the box."

Ross was counting on his fingers and smirking. "So now, thanks to you and Merleece, I have two theories to consider: women scorned and a ringleader."

"Or both at once. One needn't exclude the other."

"You're so right."

The next morning at the station, Ross shared both ideas with Bax, thinking the timing was perfect. They were both interrogating Bella Compton again, this time concerning that single blond hair that had turned up on King's desk and been verified by the crime lab as hers. If the idea of a ringleader had any validity at all to it, they had to start somewhere. Was Bella Compton capable of such machinations?

"We have your previous recorded statement that you had not been in Kohl Place for quite a long time," Ross was saying to Bella across the table as they began. "Sometime the previous year, you said. I'm sure you recall that, don't you?"

Bella, who seemed overdressed and overperfumed for the occasion, with distracting, dangling earrings and too much jewelry on her fingers—including one ring so large that it suggested something Lucrezia Borgia might have utilized for dispatching poison in food and drink—remained nonchalant and said, "I do recall that, because I was telling you the absolute truth. I am always about the truth, even if it hurts. And believe me, it does hurt sometimes."

Ross dangled a small plastic bag in front of his face. "Then how do you explain this single hair of yours we found on Mr. Kohl's desk? How did one single hair survive housecleaning after housecleaning in the interim? Does it make sense to you that one, brave little hair could hang out all that time and escape the attention of a diligent housekeeper?"

Bella suddenly looked triumphant. "That's your answer."

Ross and Bax exchanged puzzled glances, and Ross said, "What's my answer?"

"Sloppy housekeeping from a college student, shall we say?" But there was an insolence about her inflection that did not go unnoticed.

Then Bax took over from his son-in-law. "I'm sure you don't even believe that. She would have been fired if she wasn't getting the job done. The Kohls are very exacting people. Ethel Kohl, in particular, has the reputation of being persnickety, if you'll allow the word, about everything under the sun. She would have given such a housekeeper notice immediately and with great delight."

Bella leaned in with a smirk on her face, pointing at them both with a bejeweled finger. "You're overlooking something important, though. I believe that that Wyvonne Sidley is not what she appears to be. Believe me, I know what I'm talking about."

"Meaning?" Bax continued.

"Word got around that she had a crush on King. You know how Rosalie is. Someone drops a hint over cocktails, and then the rumor spreads like a brush fire. It doesn't take much to get something started in this town. People do everything but pay for gossip on billboards."

"We already know that about the crush. Miz Sidley told us that herself."

"Did she now? I wouldn't trust her, you know. My opinion is that she volunteers too much, too often. Whenever I think of the phrase 'ulterior motive,' I think of her."

Bax said nothing.

"She's quite the cooperative little doobie, isn't she?"

Bax again was silent, although he nodded his head.

"Well, I hate to disappoint you both, but I've got this thing all figured out. I was playing games with you when I suggested sloppy housekeeping just to get your reaction. When you called me up and told me about the hair, I immediately knew what was going on. It absolves me completely, so that's why I suggest you look elsewhere for the solution to King's hideous murder. It's right under your noses."

It was clear that Bella had the undivided attention of both men now, and Bax said, "So tell us what you've figured out. It couldn't hurt us to hear a different angle."

She removed the oversized ring from her finger and, exactly in Lucretia Borgia fashion, manipulated it so that the top of it opened up in imitation of the hatch of a submarine. Then she handed it over to Bax. "That, gentlemen, is the other half of the equation. Handle it carefully and look closely, and all will become apparent. I am handing over to you a once-cherished part of my life."

Bax brought the ring to eye level, as Ross leaned over to examine it himself. "Are we looking for some sort of poison inside? Perhaps a residue?" Bax said. "I don't see anything."

"No, no poison, not at all. And I'm happy to tell you that I am not a witch. You'll notice that there is a single hair," Bella added. "That belongs to King. At one point, when we both thought we were deeply in love and were going to be united in holy matrimony forever, we decided to exchange with one another a single strand of hair for safekeeping. Or as a keepsake, whichever way you want to look at it. We had a romantic little pluck-fest, if you will. We laughed ourselves silly. I admit it was corny and makes us appear like a couple of teenagers, but there it is. Make of it what you will."

The faces of both men registered genuine surprise, and Ross said, "So you're saying that that single strand of your hair was something Ross was holding onto for sentimental reasons?"

"Exactly. And I did the same."

Ross took back the floor. "We have run across such things before. But why would he take it out from wherever he was keeping it and put it on the table?"

"I don't believe he did," Bella said. "I believe someone else did, and that someone was his killer. If you ask me, my money's on Wyvonne Sidley. I think she was trying to frame me."

"But why would she do that by killing the man she had a crush on? It doesn't make much sense."

"Do things have to make sense if you're not right in the head? I'm convinced that's what we're dealing with here."

Ross looked sideways, his face breaking into frown lines. "Let's move on. May I ask you, who knew about this exchange of hairs besides you and King? I'm assuming it wasn't written up in the *Citizen*'s society column."

Bella flashed an obsequious smile. "Just the two of us, as far as I know. But that doesn't mean that Wyvonne couldn't have found out somehow. She was all up in the family's business, believe me. King did discuss her with me a while back, and that's how I know what I know. He was given to having a few drinks now and then and spilling his beans all over the place. Who better to spill them to than Wyvonne? You might get her back in here and surprise her with that question and see what happens. She might just lose her cool and give the whole thing up. It would make your jobs a lot easier."

"I wish it was that easy, but I assure you, we'll question Miz Sidley again," Ross told her. Then he relinquished his frown to one of his best interrogation smiles. "On the other hand, you could be too clever by one half. Suppose you were the one who put that hair on the desk."

"That would be another thing that wouldn't make any sense. Why would I want to implicate myself? I assure you I am incapable of murdering someone who was once very close to me. Or anyone, for that matter. That's all you need to know about me."

"That may very well be, but of course you have no alibi for the morning of King's murder," Ross said. "We have that on record. In fact, none of you do, except Jackson and Ethel Kohl vouching for each other in the slave quarters that morning. We have no idea where any of the rest of you were."

Bella straightened up in her chair a bit and gathered herself. "Yes, I admit that no one can vouch for me. I was rambling around my house with my thoughts that morning. For some reason, I had a feeling that something bad was going to happen."

"Why do you think that was? Are you psychic?"

Bella made a face like she was about to spit something out. "No, I'm not. At least I don't think I am. Haven't you ever gotten out of bed and felt that it was not going to be your best day? Just one of those anecdotal things. All that aside, I'd still put my money on Wyvonne Sidley up to no good. Meanwhile, you are more than welcome to give that hair to your crime lab to have it checked out that it really belongs to King. I can't pretend I'm all healed up inside and that I'm truly over him, but in turning that hair over to you, I feel I am at least trying to put that part of my life behind me. It was all clearly not meant to work out for me and King. Now, get out there and go find his killer."

"Offhand, something went very wrong in King's life, I'd say," Ross added, slightly surprised at the authority in Bella's tone. It almost reminded him of his earliest days at the police academy, when he was ordered around by those who were training him to see if he was tough enough to make the cut. "And whatever it was cost him his life."

Bella softened her tone and said, "It's still hard for me to wrap my brain around. To some extent, I'm still in shock, though I try my best not to show it. A woman is always better off not to tip her hand too much."

After she had been dismissed and left, Ross turned to Bax and said, "My impression is that Bella Compton was very well-rehearsed in everything she just told us. She even brought props. This might be a first—a single prop consisting of a single hair. Do you believe her story?"

Bax, who had gently closed the ring which Bella had let him keep quite willingly without much emotion, said, "Let's admit that it was quite a surprise. But as you say, there was something very theatrical about it. I don't think we can dismiss this idea that Wendy brought up of a ringleader in all of this."

He paused for a chuckle. "Ringleader. We even have a ring to go with it now."

"That didn't occur to me, but you're right."

"Next move—we get Wyvonne Sidley in here and see what she has to say about this latest development," Bax said. "It's all beginning to remind me of a script executed down to the last word."

Ross looked incredulous. "A murder play, cast and directed? Could King Kohl have really made that many enemies? Particularly the kind that wanted him dead? He gave the impression of having the world at his beck and call."

"Which obviously was not the case," Bax said, shaking his head. "It occurs to me that he and the moon had their dark sides in common."

It wasn't that Patrice was paranoid by nature. Although she was cautious, she never cottoned to conspiracy theories, and she had no use for people who espoused them. They took the fun out of the ebb and flow of relationships. Yet, she had developed a sixth sense about certain things because of her status as a "good-time girl." It was unwise to take people, particularly men, at their word. For instance, she could always tell if a man was too dangerous to fool around with and therefore should be avoided at all costs; by the same token, if a man was an easy mark, akin to a puppy with its tongue hanging out, eager to fetch the ball, that scenario generally fell into her lap effortlessly. Often, a lap dance soon followed, and the rest would become history.

She just knew that something was going on around her. She felt it. This morning, she had walked down to Bluff Park because one of the Viking Cruise Line ships was in, and she always enjoyed watching the passengers disembark several hundred feet below. She liked to wave at them, welcoming them to Rosalie officially for their brief visit ashore. Nearly all of them waved back with delight, and it made her feel like a goodwill ambassador. In fact, she wasn't looking at it from a clientele point of view, for the most part; it had been her experience that these Mississippi River cruises appealed to a large percentage of couples, some retired, and not likely to be in the market for her charms. True, a stray single occasionally wandered away from the herd, and she had been known to meet up with him at one of the local watering holes and take it from there. It almost always worked out, as the stay in Rosalie was a matter of hours, and no strings attached was the perfect, uncomplicated accompaniment.

Now, it was time to walk away from the edge of the bluff. She had things to do on this sunny day in May—a trip to the bank, some last-minute groceries to shop for, and some dry cleaning to pick up with the money from the ATM—and then home to fix a light lunch of soup and some kind of sandwich, probably tuna fish. No, it would be grilled cheese this time. She was consummately bored with tuna. She had parked the car on Broad Street some distance away, since she was not the only one who liked to witness a Viking Cruise Line dock-ing. Spaces were at a premium, and the usual crowd had gathered to rubberneck all the way over to the pedestrian Bridge of Sighs, which afforded the most breathtaking view of them all.

As she reached the car door, Patrice particularly felt it again. Someone was stalking her. She had been stalked before for various reasons during her young life, and the sensation was back. Quickly, she whirled around, but the sight that greeted her was nothing out of the ordinary. In the distance was a young mother wearing a large picture hat and crossing the street while holding the hand of her little girl, who had a pretty pink bow in her hair. She knew they could not be the ones, either of them. There was still that group of people at the edge of the bluff watching the passengers disembark, all of them focused on what was going on far beneath them at one of the docks. If whoever was doing the stalking was among them, they had embedded themselves well. Didn't blending in and stalking go together as a subtle performance art form? Perhaps she had been standing next to them, or just a few people away.

Patrice unlocked the car with the key remote and slid into the front seat. Sitting at the wheel, she decided to remain still and observe for a while. Still, nothing out of the ordinary appeared during all that time. A couple of gawkers, teenage boys, pulled away from the edge of the bluff and raced each other across the great expanse of grass to destinations unknown. She could tell by their demeanor that they were happy and full of energy and certainly not up to anything nefarious. True, she had been followed by hormonal young boys before, but this didn't fit the bill.

Patrice took a deep breath and thought back to what had happened the day before yesterday. She had been coming out of Strands of Glory, where she had just had her hair streaked, and had glanced down the sidewalk to her right without thinking about it. Because her mind was on the expert job that her long-time stylist and girlfriend, Hommajean Edwards, had done as usual, whatever she'd seen didn't register with her at first. She was just feeling too proud of her new look, as women frequently allow themselves to feel.

Later, when she had returned to her apartment and settled in with her latest copy of *People* magazine and a bag of unshelled pistachio nuts, the little sliver of memory popped up like a creepy jack-in-the-box. Had there been someone ducking into a doorway almost subliminally during that glance of hers? That was the nature of stalking, of course—a suggestion of something wrong at first, and then, snowballing until something got dangerously out of hand. It was nothing to fool around with, but she had chosen not to walk down the street in that direction to pursue her curiosity. Apparently, pistachio nuts and *People* had dragged it out of her.

Then yesterday, she could have sworn someone was following her in traffic, a white car making every turn she made downtown as she was on her way to the dry cleaners with some of her most provocative outfits that needed tidying up; and because of the one-way-street setup of Rosalie, those turns were complicated, if inevitable. She was the sort of person who always focused on what was going on in her rearview mirror—call it an OCD holdover from driver's training—and that was how she picked up on it. Yes, it was possible that someone could have been making all those turns for legitimate reasons, and it was all just coincidence; but when she had dropped the clothes off at the drive-through, her jaw dropped when she noticed that the white car was now parked across the street, having pulled out of traffic as if waiting for her to resume her journey. Yet the car, which she did not recognize as belonging to anyone she knew, did not wait for her to do so, pulling back into traffic as soon as she quit the drive-through. Whoever was behind the wheel also had the visor pulled down across the driver's-side window so they could not be observed. Patrice was unable to merge into traffic fast enough to get the license plate. She was left only with the color of the car, which had seen better days, and the impression of an unnerving interest in her daily routine by a person of unknown gender or any other distinguishing characteristic.

She decided that if things persisted and developed further, she would go down to the station and ask Detective Rierson if it would be remotely possible to put a tail on her as she went about the daily rituals of her life—which she did not want to have to cash in early. Perhaps whoever it was had no such intentions, and it was all very above board, but she did not want to take any chances.

Then, suddenly, an epiphany caused her to press against the car horn, startling her at the hiccup honk it produced, followed by chuckling at herself out loud: Of course someone was stalking her. The Rosalie Police Department obviously still regarded her as a suspect in King's murder. They were likely tailing everyone involved in this manner, although she was disappointed that they hadn't accepted her backstory about the abortion. No one, it seemed, was comfortable talking about or accepting facts when it came to the issue. People went off on rampages pro and con, and there was no shutting them up. There was only black, and there was only white, and "n'er the twain should meet."

No matter. The net result was that she would no longer be paranoid about the stalking. What was there to fear when it came to law enforcement doing it? She had come clean with them about her big secret. She decided that she would let her guard down from here on in. Problem solved.

CHAPTER 8

It had fallen to Sergeant Ronald Pike, of the craggy features, burly arms, and buzz cut, with whom Ross had often paired for detective work, to keep an eye on Marcus Silvertree's comings and goings without being obvious about it; chiefly, to see that he did not leave town or do anything else untoward or suspicious during the course of the investigation. Marcus remained the department's main suspect in King Kohl's murder, but evidence also could only be characterized as circumstantial and hardly enough to warrant an arrest yet. A few prints on the doorknob just wouldn't do the trick. Marcus steadfastly admitted to only being at the scene of the crime, and whoever had texted him to come to Kohl Place was the real culprit. The general assumption had been made by now that King had not been alive when those texts were sent, but Pike had another theory, which he had shared rather vehemently with Ross and Captain Bax.

"What if Silvertree did do it after all, and he was the one who sent the texts?" Pike had begun in Bax's office one morning. "What if he killed Mr. Kohl in a fit of rage and then panicked, thinking the best he could do was set up a situation where he had a witness to his so-called innocent discovery of the body? Sounds a little desperate, I know, but why couldn't it have happened that way?"

Ross had not been impressed and shot Bax a glance with narrowed eyes. "You're overthinking this, Pike, my man. My wife is an excellent judge of character, and she testifies that what she witnessed in the way of behavior when she observed Silvertree rushing out of the house that morning was genuine and not staged. Wendy has superior instincts when it comes to that. She's helped us solve several major crimes these past few years, as you well know."

But the slightly patronizing tone had only annoyed Pike. "I respect your wife, of course. You and the captain keep thinking Silvertree is innocent, but I don't see it that way. After sending those texts, he could've been waiting at a window until your wife showed up and then busted outta the house at just that moment and gone into his spiel. He was plenty PO'd that the Kohls had put him outta bidness, so I can picture this happening in a bang-bang manner. He could have just lost it and acted out. I know everyone's giving him the benefit of the doubt right now, but people do dumb and crazy things when they're under that kinda pressure. I mean, you've just killed someone—maybe premeditated, maybe not—but your brain goes off the rails, and you do the best you can, even if it's not enough."

Ross continued to play devil's advocate. "But why wait around for anyone to show up? Why not just leave straight away? And why leave your prints on the doorknob?"

"Maybe Silvertree was the one who overthought it. Easy to overlook things."

Both Ross and the captain had granted Pike that much, but it hardly satisfied him. He remained convinced that the simple and obvious solution to the crime was the right one.

Furthermore, if the opportunity arose, he was going to prove it by catching Marcus Silvertree red-handed, making some move that gave him away.

Except that a little female voice intervened from time to time and told him that he shouldn't try to be judge and jury in any particular case. He knew where it came from, too. It was the voice of his girlfriend, Sarah Ann O'Rourke, whom he had been dating for a while now. During that period, this young, freckle-faced, former bridge student of Wendy Rierson's, fresh out of college, had worked hard to soften his edges, and he had welcomed it—so much so that he had begun to think of proposing marriage to her and settling down at last. He was tired of having only his career commendations and huzzahs to come home to, and envied the happiness his partner, Ross, had achieved since marrying Wendy Winchester. The only thing he wondered about was why they hadn't had any children yet, since Ross was always talking down at the station about how he couldn't wait to become a father.

Call it fate or timing or something else on this particular May morning, but as Pike was driving by the little raised cottage with dormer windows that Marcus rented—odd in itself, since here was a real estate agent who appeared to disdain home ownership for himself—he was treated to the sight of his favorite suspect hurriedly walking down the front porch steps, carrying a suitcase out to his car. That was reason enough to tuck quickly into a parking space and then walk crisply back down the crepe myrtle–lined sidewalk with an unerring sense of purpose.

"Going somewhere, Mr. Silvertree?" Pike said, sounding friendlier than he felt as he came to a sudden and rigid halt at some unheard military command. "I'm Sergeant Ronald Pike of the Rosalie Police Department." Then he peered through the backseat window and saw that there were a number of personal items stuffed inside.

"Open the trunk," he said next.

Marcus put down the suitcase with a frightened look on his face. "Wait. I haven't done anything wrong. Don't you need a warrant for that?"

"Nope. You're a suspect in a murder case, and you were distinctly told not to leave town, remember?"

Marcus pressed his remote key, and the trunk popped open with a sound not unlike tires going over a pothole. "But there was no warrant for my arrest. I wasn't charged with anything. My lawyer told me I'm free to travel. Anyway, rifle around in my trunk and see. I just have more of my personal stuff in there. No drugs, if that's what you were thinking. I don't do drugs. Is this supposed to be a drug bust?"

Pike walked around to the back of the car, lifted up the trunk farther, and examined everything closely. His voice was slightly muffled as he answered from behind the metal shield. "No, that's not what I'm doing at all. Unless you have something to hide. I was wondering where you were going and how long you intended to stay there. Looks like you pretty much cleaned out your closets to me." Pike slammed the trunk and walked back to join his suspect, his expression a perfect blank.

"Just . . . a visit to my old hometown in the Delta—Greenwood. You ever been there? It's pretty this time of year, with the azaleas and all."

"No, I've never been to Greenwood, but there are still plenty of azaleas to look at here, even if they are beyond peak bloom. But more to the point, you realize that by leaving town—or trying to—it looks like an admission of guilt, even if there wasn't a warrant for your arrest; and once we found out you were missing, we'd come looking for you with our guns a-blazin'. In your wildest dreams, did you think we wouldn't? Even if it wasn't Greenwood you were headed to, but some other place harder to track down. Just so happens you lucked out today before you crossed the line. City limits, county, state, or whatever."

Marcus exhaled. "I guess you covered all the bases."

"So, first thing. I want you to put everything back in that house. But before you do that, I want you to tell me where you were really going. No more stories about your hometown. I know better."

Marcus looked down at his shoes, clearly shamed. "I was—gonna catch a flight in Jackson."

"With all that loose stuff in the car? What were you gonna do with that? Leave it lying around in long-term parking?"

"I was gonna rent one of those storage units for a while and get back to it eventually. I was gonna worry about all my time here in Rosalie later on. It's been a total disaster for me."

"Where were you gonna fly to?"

"Chicago."

"Why Chicago?"

Marcus finally made eye contact. "Mostly 'cause it's close to Canada. I guess that was my next step. Canada—somewhere, anywhere up there. And then I'd become that old standby."

"I don't follow."

"You know—the 'man without a country' thing."

Pike took his time, but the look on his face was intense when he finally spoke. "Ever heard of extradition?"

"Yes."

"So, once and for all, did you kill Mr. Kohl? Is this what this is all about? You're acting for all the world like you did it. My money's been on you for a while."

"You just put it into words. Avoiding getting railroaded is what this is all about. I think some people in this town are gonna make me the fall guy, no matter what the truth is. I've been panicked since I walked into that room and found King with his head bashed in. It hit me even then that I had just been set up. Because that's what it was, you know. Ask me a million times, and my answer will still be the same. Somebody out there set me up."

That last sentence resonated immediately with Pike. Had he been one of those people who wanted Marcus to be the fall guy, no matter what? He could already picture what his Sarah Ann would say about all this, reminding him to be the "gentle giant" and not the menacing ogre while performing his duties.

"You need to have a little drawer in your brain," she had told him once on one of their dinner dates at the Toast of Rosalie. "Slip your work into it and keep it shut tight. Now, if it were me, I'd put some potpourri in there, too. You know, to make it smell good and keep me in the right frame of mind."

Pike remembered producing one monstrous frown. "Put some *what* in there?"

And she had gone on to explain and spell what she was talking about, leaving him still mystified but all the more attracted to her. She was indeed the perfect person to settle him down in life.

Returning to the task at hand with Marcus Silvertree, Pike said, "So you think if worse came to worst, you wouldn't get a fair trial in this town?"

"I'm afraid I do think that way. Rosalie hasn't been welcoming to me at all. I was told Rosalie treasured its pond of odd ducks, but it appears that you have to be an odd duck born here to make the final cut and stay out on the water."

Pike stopped short of laughing out loud. His family had not been to the manner born. Just working-class people who had abided by the rules, and he was proud of that. "That odd duck comment, that's true enough. But I have to tell you that I'm gonna report this to Captain Bax and my partner, Ross Rierson. Since you didn't actually leave town, they're not likely to take any action against you. But that's why I say you were lucky today. I stopped you from a likely arraignment. You know the rules well enough. Despite what I or anybody else thinks, you gotta play by 'em until this thing gets solved. Tell me you're willing to do that."

"I am," Marcus said, nodding his head enthusiastically.

"Guess you could say you were saved by my drive-by."

"Guess so."

Then Pike felt an infusion of his Sarah Ann's generosity of spirit and said, "Lemme give you some advice, sir. Never run away when you're involved with the police. Nothing good ever comes of it. It only makes things worse. You gotta stay here in Rosalie and stand your ground."

Marcus sighed. "I see that now. Thanks."

"Okay, then. I'll give you a hand with some a' your stuff."

"Isn't your feature on the Kohls about ready?" Lyndell said. She and Wendy were having lunch together at the Toast of Rosalie, since they had both had a hankering for shrimp and grits, which they likened to manna from heaven.

Wendy finished buttering a chunk of French bread and put it down on the edge of her plate. "Just about. But I'm sure Daddy has told you that I've gotten more than a little interested in the investigation, too."

"You always do where these crimes are concerned. A murder comes along, and you're practically in two places at once. You're a physiological, metaphysical wonder."

Wendy nodded, picked up her bread, and took a bite, chewing thoughtfully before speaking. "You and I have both agreed that Ethel Kohl's suicide attempt can't be a part of the feature, of course, and it does look like she'll make a complete recovery, thanks to Jackson's fast thinking. But there are so many things about this case that bother me. The way all the women in his life are so interconnected—and not in a good

way. When I went down to see the Viking Cruise ship dock-
ing yesterday morning, I noticed Patrice Leyton in the crowd,
but I didn't wave or call attention to myself. I'm a great be-
liever in observing people, particularly when they aren't aware
you're doing it. They can't hide their true nature from you
then."

Lyndell squeezed the slice of lemon hanging on the rim of
her glass into her ice water and said, "And did you observe
anything noteworthy about Patrice?"

"I did, actually. At one point, she broke away from the
crowd gawking at what was going on down below and
headed toward her car. But once she got there, she just sat behind the wheel, frozen in place as if she were part of a police
detail. That was beyond peculiar. For a second or two, I got
the impression that she may have spotted me, but I was far
from obvious, so I really don't think so."

Lyndell took a sip of her water. "And your conclusion?"

"She was acting suspiciously, guarded. Merleece put it
into my head that perhaps there was a ringleader among
King's girlfriends who thought up this murder scheme, and
I'm wondering if she doesn't fit the bill."

"Because of the abortion angle? Yes, I know. Bax shares
things he shouldn't with me, but he knows I can be trusted."

Wendy managed a wry chuckle. "Same with Ross. He
knows I'll keep nagging until he tells me what I want to
know."

"Ah, the special privileges of law enforcement spouses.
We keep their busy brains from exploding."

The side salads they had ordered arrived, and the two
women interrupted their conversation for a bite or two.

"Your daddy says the investigation is at something of a
standstill right now," Lyndell resumed. "Nothing new in the
way of evidence, even though nobody seems to have an alibi,

except for the Kohls themselves, vouching for each other. Bax is worried that the case may go cold if something doesn't turn up soon."

Wendy playfully stabbed a cherry tomato with her fork and popped it into her mouth. "I can't picture a case like this going cold. A brutal murder of a Rosalie scion? We'd never hear the end of it. More to the point, I think we've lost sight of the key to this. Somehow, some way, we have to find out what King was going to reveal to us all at that party he called off at the last minute. If someone knows, they're holding back, likely because it would incriminate them."

"And do you have a plan for discovering the truth? I mean, besides the one Bax and Ross have?"

Wendy cocked her head, her tone anything but forceful. "As a matter of fact, I had one of my rogue ideas earlier this morning."

"Care to share?"

"Yes." She paused to sit up a little straighter in her chair. "It has come to my attention that the Kohls were devout Catholics. Now, that isn't as obvious a statement as it seems. The services at the basilica were the obvious part. But when I say devout, I mean just that. The buzz at the visitation was that the Kohls took their beliefs seriously. There may be something to explore in that."

"Such as?"

"I was wondering whether Father LeBlanc might have something to share with me about the family dynamic."

Lyndell's expression was decidedly skeptical, and she drew back slightly. "You realize that priests are not supposed to reveal extremely personal things like that, particularly anything that takes place during confession. I'm not Catholic, but my roommate in college was—the very Irish, Bitsy O'Beirne, and a very dramatic theater major she was, always trying to convert me, filling in the theological blanks that she thought I just had to know. I did agree to go to Mass on campus with her one Sunday, and she was sure that would do the trick, that I would sign on the dotted line immediately. I didn't, but we were good roommates to each other. We didn't let religious differences come between us. Not that I officially had a religion even back then. I shed my fundamentalist, Protestant skin as soon I became a freshman. At last, I was free to think for myself. First elective I took was comparative religion, and I've been asking good questions of the universe ever since."

"You've been feisty for the longest time, haven't you?"

"Yep."

"So give me your feistiest opinion—do you think I should go and talk to Father LeBlanc?"

Lyndell made a brief, sweeping gesture. "Be my guest. Just don't expect anything more than general knowledge from him."

"I'll keep your advice in mind."

Then the young waiter with the man bun and a neatly trimmed mustache arrived with their shrimp and grits, and all serious conversation came to a halt as they began digging into their favorite Rosalie dish. Forget editor and reporter status. It was a girlfriend lunch for the ages.

Wendy's approach over the phone with Father LeBlanc was that she needed a bit more background information on the Kohls for her feature, and his tone had been welcoming as they set up an appointment. But now, as they sat across from each other in his cramped office with the stained glass window, his demeanor seemed to be a cross between businesslike and imperturbable. He had barely cracked a smile in her presence, and it was making her nervous.

"Yes, the Kohls all attended Mass regularly. Few could equal them in that respect," he was saying. "They were also no strangers to the collection plate. The church is always grateful for parishioners like that. They had done well in life and were willing to share with others. I'd be very grateful if everyone did just that much in their everyday lives. I seem to do homily after homily on the ripple effect of giving."

Remembering what Lyndell had told her, Wendy continued cautiously. "Yes, that would be a generous thing for people to do. Now, I wanted to ask you some questions about the late King Kohl, if you wouldn't mind."

Father's face was emotionless. "Yes?"

"I assume he confided in you."

"From time to time, yes, he did. Most of my parishioners do. That's part of my pastoral duties, of course. I came to the basilica shortly after he was born, and I presided at his first communion. He was a handful at catechism, always flirting with the girls in his class. They didn't seem to mind, but I did. It took their minds off my instruction. He needed correcting a good deal."

Wendy flashed a smile and added, "I can picture that so easily. Along those lines, I received an invitation to one of his elaborate bridge parties the week before he died, and I was very excited about attending. King spared no expense in putting these events together and making sure that everyone had a good time. Especially the ladies, of course."

There was a hint of emotion and softening in Father's voice. "Yes, well, I've witnessed it for myself. I have been to several Kohl to-dos over the years and have never been disappointed. If they knew how to do nothing else, they were great entertainers." He paused and blinked a couple of times. "Here I am talking about Jackson and Ethel as if they're no longer with us."

So far, so good, so Wendy proceeded. "What still puzzles me so is that King called off this latest party at the last minute and even summoned me to his house the next morning to explain why. Or at least, *someone* summoned me. I don't suppose you would have any idea why the party was called off, do you?"

Father's expression hardened. "There are things I am not at liberty to discuss."

"I understand."

"The seal of the confessional is never to be broken."

"But suppose it has a bearing on his murder?"

Father's brow became more deeply furrowed. "There are no circumstances under which it can be broken, and besides, I may not know what you think I know."

"Forgive me if I seem too forward, Father," Wendy added, "but do you think there is a possibility that you know the identity of King's murderer without knowing it?"

"Absolutely not," he said, morphing into anger. "If I can make any sense of what you just said, and if you intended this interview to reveal that to you, you are sadly mistaken. What I know about King and his parents is pastoral in nature and must remain so. Like all human beings, they weren't—or rather, aren't—perfect. But they looked to me for counsel to try and become better people. King especially wanted that for himself. I will always give him credit for that."

Wendy felt his discomfort alongside her own and moved quickly to dissipate it. "I'm quite sure you helped them all do just that. Just for the record and to clear the air a bit, I do know about the relationship King had with Patrice Leyton and the business about the abortion. Patrice has volunteered the information herself, and the police department knows, as well. I'm not asking you to comment on that further. I don't want to put you in an awkward position, but you can no longer protect that bit of information."

Looking somewhat surprised, Father said, "In that case, and since the information did not come from King himself, I know no more than you do. I do find that people rarely make things up during confession. Every now and then, I do catch a few of them embellishing, but that's human nature. At any rate, I know nothing about the details of what Patrice Leyton has told you, and if I did, I wouldn't reveal them to you. I only know that King sought absolution for all of his sins for as long as I knew him. It was genuine. I can tell you that much. He wanted to be a better person, he honestly did. But he was very conflicted in general about his life. That's about all I care to say in the matter. Anything else would be a breach of my mission."

"I can certainly appreciate that, and again, I hope I haven't offended you."

A genuine smile appeared for the first time. "No. I'm not offended. I must say that I am still somewhat in shock over King's death. Being born and dying are the natural cycle of life, but when something brutal like this happens, your faith is tested, no matter how strong you think it is. You wonder how such evil can exist in this world, ready to strike at a moment's notice without warning, and you can't completely pray the horror of it away. It sticks with you. I fervently wish it didn't, but it does."

"We're on the same page there," Wendy said. "It does seem like a nightmare."

Then, something peculiar happened. Father leaned forward in his chair a bit, looked like he was about to form a word and speak, but then apparently thought better of it and sank back down.

"Yes?" Wendy said. "Were you going to add something?"

His hesitation felt palpable to Wendy. That if she just reached out and politely shook him a bit, something meaningful would tumble out. Something that might bring the solution to King's murder closer at hand.

But in the end, Father said nothing more.

"I fully respect the boundaries of your position," Wendy said. "But if at any point you feel that you have anything you can rightly reveal about the Kohls that is not widely known,

you can always get in touch with me at the paper." She
handed over her card.

Father took it, rose, and offered his hand.

"Thank you for indulging me today," she said, and then
made her exit.

Outside, with the great, Gothic spire of the basilica next
door reaching for the sky, she paused briefly in front of the
rectory and took a deep breath. She was convinced that Father
LeBlanc knew something that had a bearing on this case, but
he chose not to reveal it. Of that much, she was certain. But
there also existed the possibility that he would never let it
come to light. And then there was this to consider: Father had
said that he *might not know what she thought he knew*. The silence and rigid posturing on his part might be evidence of a
rabbit hole she had created for herself. Down and deeper
down she might tumble.

Yet, he had left her with a pervasive image of King being
a player from a very young age. She started walking toward
her car, thinking that the "woman scorned" theory still had
legs.

CHAPTER 9

Ethel Kohl found it most peculiar that her long-time physician, Dr. Robert Pevey, was examining her elbow with such
intensity. She was sitting on the edge of the examining table in
a cozy room full of fluorescence and smelling strongly of rubbing alcohol and latex gloves, and while all she had been
telling him revolved around her inability to remember certain
important things in her life, all he wanted to do was examine
the crusty patch on her elbow. It was almost comical the way
he was squinting at it, as if he had discovered a new form of
life or evidence of the existence of aliens.

"I think you have psoriasis, dear," he finally told her. "It's
a classic case. Now, we can attack it two ways—systemically
or topically with a cream. Which do you prefer? I can pre-
scribe either for you."

Ethel remained thoroughly annoyed. What kind of visit
was this? "Wait a minute, I'm not the doctor, you are. You
tell me."

Dr. Pevey thought for a moment, looking ridiculous
while he did so. He had the type of old-fashioned bifocals that
made his eyes look huge. In fact, they dominated his long,

lean face so much that he came off mostly as an enormous pair of eyes, holding up his thin frame within a white lab coat. At times, Ethel thought it made him look downright creepy, even though she had trusted him with her health for years. He had also tended to Jackson as well, with commendable results. They had never gone to anyone else. All the more reason for her surprise at his peculiar behavior.

"I recommend systemic. Several injections throughout the year. I know it's a little more trouble than you'd want, but I think you'll get the best results."

"I don't like needles." She practically spat out the sentence. "You should know that by now and how I have to look the other way when they draw my blood, too."

"No, not a needle, dear. An IV."

"That amounts to the same thing, with the thumping and searching for a vein and then that awful sticking. The nurse never seems to find the vein fast enough. It all just creeps me out. Could we possibly go topical? I can smear something on my skin with the best of 'em."

"We could do that, of course," he told her. "But you asked for my recommendation, and I gave it to you. That's my job." Suddenly, he leaned in, getting inappropriately close to her face. So close that she could smell his garlicky breath.

"What did you have for lunch?" she said, drawing back.

"Spaghetti and meatballs. I love Italian food. I mean, real Italian."

Her face sagged into disgust. "Makes sense."

"Okay then, let's forget about the psoriasis for now. You are simply going to have to move away from Rosalie. You cannot stay here. I recommend the Coast. Jackson tells me you love palm trees and the beach. You could see them looking out your window every day."

Now Ethel was confused. "What window is that?"

"The window of your room, of course. They will try to put you next to your Aunt Phoebe, Jackson tells me. It'll be just a short hop and skip down the hall, in any case."

"But I don't want to be next to her. She might catch it."

Dr. Pevey moved in even closer, despite his breath. "Catch what?"

"Whatever it is I have. Don't you know by now?"

He finally backed away from her slightly, allowing her to escape the garlic. "I just told you, you had psoriasis."

She was becoming increasingly angry with his runaround. What was he up to with all of this? "But psoriasis doesn't make you forget things, does it? I have been getting worse and worse, and I can't go on this way. Please, give me some help."

"Aha!" He was actually pointing his finger at her as if she had done something wrong. "In some cases, psoriasis does make you forget. Especially if you have the wrong topical cream. Medical science hasn't been able to explain it yet, but there it is."

Ethel jumped off the table and stood her ground. She was actually taller than he was, and she believed she could take him in a fight. "But I thought you recommended one of those awful injections. Do you even know what you're doing?"

"I certainly think so. I've been practicing long enough. And I didn't give you permission to get off the table, did I?"

"No, but I did it anyway, as you can plainly see. You aren't the boss of me, though you apparently think you are."

Dr. Pevey flashed on her. "Listen to me, young lady, you get back up on that table this instant, or I will have my nurse come in here with a large needle and start poking around until she finds a vein large enough to stick but good."

Ethel felt cornered, and feelings of panic flooded her entire being. "Where is Jackson? I want outta here right now. You have become a bully after all these years. I'm gonna report you to the medical board or whatever group it is that hears about doctors abusing their patients. I know that there is such a thing. I know I read it in an article once."

Dr. Pevey grabbed her arm and started twisting it. "Your husband is out in the waiting room. I told him it was best for him not to come in this time. Now, get back up on that table right this minute, or there'll be hell to pay."

"I will not obey you," she cried out. Then she quickly surveyed the room, but Jackson was not there, as the doctor had said. "Jackson. I need you. Help me. Dr. Pevey has gone berserk!"

There was no cry from the other side of the door.

In response, he increased the pressure on her arm. It wasn't the pain so much as the indignity of it all. How could a doctor even think he could get away with this sort of behavior? It was beyond outrageous, and she envisioned a messy lawsuit in her future. She would sue for millions. Or at least thousands. But was she up to it? Getting before a judge and jury and accusing Dr. Pevey of sexual assault. Did this even qualify as sexual assault? Well, perhaps not. Perhaps just harassment of an elbow, and the elbow was not generally considered something sexual. Although she had gone to college with a girl named Poppie Greystone, who claimed that men dated her because of her beautiful elbows. Imagine that. Imagine . . .

Ethel awoke and found herself on the passenger side of the front seat of the black Buick SUV that she and Jackson drove around Rosalie. She cleared her throat and glanced over at the driver—it was her husband, taking his eyes off the road just long enough to flash her a smile.

"Did you have a nice nap?" he said.

Ethel frowned. She did not remember falling asleep in the first place. She did not remember getting into the car in the second place. But she was greatly relieved that the visit to Dr. Pevey's office had only been an outrageously bad dream.

"No, it was not a nice nap at all. I had something close to

a nightmare. Anyway, where on earth are we?" she said, looking at the thick stands of pine trees passing by in a virtual blur.
There was also a large billboard she glimpsed: CROCODILE-
REPTILE FARM AHEAD FIVE MILES, it read, in big, red
block letters. It seemed incredibly dated, the colors faded with
cartoonish images of the reptiles smiling, and an air balloon
coming out of one that was standing up on two feet as if it
were human. "See us and gigantic snakes, too!" the creature
was saying. At the very bottom of the billboard: CHILDREN
UNDER 12 ADMITTED FREE!

"Just outside Hattiesburg. Not far from the reptile zoo. I
hear it's about to go out of business after all these years."

"But why are we traveling at all? Did I miss something?"

"Because it's the shortest route to the Coast from Rosalie."

A female voice from the back seat said, "You were asleep
for nearly an hour, Miz Kohl. I'm sure you needed the rest. At
one point, you were talking a bit in your sleep. We heard you
say something about Dr. Pevey and elbows."

Ethel turned around as much as her seat belt would allow
and recognized the redheaded woman smiling at her. "Wendy
Winchester—what are you doing back there?"

"It's Wendy Rierson now, Miz Kohl. You remember.
Your husband thought I might be able to help out on your
trip, and anyway, I'm still working up an article on your family, and my editor thought my going along might tie things up
a bit." Wendy's tone was soft and solicitous.

Ethel suddenly did remember in quick flashes. At Jackson's
request, Dr. Pevey had gone to Captain Bax and Ross and
told them that she needed to be in memory care down at
Seabreeze Place. She was soon to be separated from Jackson
and the rest of Rosalie. That made her sad, but she understood
that she couldn't go on the way she was. The real conversation she had had with Dr. Pevey had been nearly as traumatic

as the one she had just dreamed—minus the physical stress and verbal abuse—and Jackson had been there by her side throughout that particular visit, not out in the waiting room reading a magazine or something where he couldn't protect her. He had told her over and over that his mission in life now was to see that no harm came to her.

"You see, Dr. Pevey," she had told him then, "I killed my son. I don't know what got into me. But I was out of control, and I will never forgive myself for what I did as long as I live. It was like something evil had taken control of my body. Do you think that's possible? Can a person be possessed? The church suggests that it might be possible. Of course, I haven't confessed this to Father LeBlanc. Jackson won't let me go to the basilica and do it."

At that point, Jackson had stepped in. "I can't talk her outta this, doctor, no matter how hard I try. I have no idea how she got it into her head, but she did. It's been a nightmare for me to handle, knowing that she is as innocent as the seasonal flowers she plants on our property. You know what a gentle soul she is better than anyone. She's out there all the time spraying our little gardens for aphids. She treats all our plants and bushes and trees like children, and they respond by blooming up so pretty every year."

And Ethel had gone vehement on them both. "It's the truth! I ought to know the truth when I speak it. Why don't you believe me? Could I be a better source of the truth?"

"I believe that you need a change of venue," Dr. Pevey had continued, as calmly as he knew how. "Somewhere that's usually sunny and warm where you can make new friends and see your Aunt Phoebe anytime you want. That's the ticket."

"Don't I get a say-so? I don't want to leave Rosalie. Why should I? I've lived there all my life. I don't want to go and live on the Coast. I only said I wanted to move there. I didn't mean it. There's no place like Rosalie. No place in the entire

world. Everyone knew it—the French, the Spanish, the British—
oh, and I'm leaving out the Indian tribe that lived there first.
They all knew a good thing when they saw it, but the French
killed them all off in a fit of rage, just like the one I had with
King. He simply didn't know what was best for him. I did."

But the inevitable had come to pass, as it must. It was
Dr. Pevey's intervention and professional input that caused Bax
and Ross to clear Ethel for transport to the Coast and into the
memory-care facility, which would become her new home. It
was his counsel that convinced them both beyond a shadow of
a doubt that Ethel Kohl could not possibly have killed her son
so brutally by pounding him with the edge of an awards plaque
she had ripped off the wall. It was all a figment of her rapidly
fading imagination, he had told them, and they did not want
to stand in the way of the humane option that was available to
her. Ethel, they concluded as law enforcement officers often
must to the best of their ability and experience, was not the
solution to her son's murder. They had further work to do to
unmask the real killer.

In the back seat, Wendy was reviewing the conversation
she and Lyndell had had about her going with Jackson on the
trip to take Ethel to her memory-care facility. Jackson himself
had come to the *Citizen* and made the request personally. The
last few sentences in his argument had been, "I think it'd not
only be good for your article, but I'd appreciate the company
on the way back after I've left her there. It will be a difficult
moment for me, losing another member of my family. You
have no idea how hard it was to lose King." And Lyndell had
said they would get back to him after discussing it thoroughly.

"Do you think I should go?" Wendy had said after Jackson
left.

Lyndell had shaken her head and pointed her finger. "I

have mixed feelings about it. More to the point, do you want to go?"

Wendy had a smirk on her face. Lyndell was very good at that. Never a micro-manager, she was skilled at hitting the ball back into the other fellow's court. She always trusted her charges to make the right decision, and because of that, she ran an unsinkable ship that continued to get press association awards.

Wendy did not have to think long about the proposition. "I know I want to go, yes. If we're going to depict the Kohls in the most sympathetic light in this time of tragedy for them, then I think this development should be a part of it. One chapter ends, another begins, even if both are sad. Many families never have this much trauma from birth to death, so I think I could bring an extra dimension to my piece by being a part of this difficult transition for Ethel."

And Lyndell had given her a wise, editorial wink. "We may have to revisit the inclusion of that transition at some point, but yes, go ahead and do the research, and we'll go from there. I think it may well be worth the trouble."

"I need to go to the little girl's room," Ethel said from the front seat, ripping Wendy out of her elaborate reverie.

"Next gas station I see, I'll stop," Jackson said. "Wendy, you don't mind going in with her, do you? In fact, I could use a stretch of the old legs and a pit stop myself. And maybe I'll buy a pack of spearmint gum. My mouth's a little dry."

"Got it covered. How much longer until we get to the Coast?"

"About forty minutes or so to get to Gulfport. Then, however long it takes to get to Seabreeze Place in traffic from there. It's one hot mess down there usually. The Coast is the Coast. Full of tourists making wrong turns and not bothering to ask for directions."

Ethel chimed in suddenly, sounding like a young girl in love. "I adore the beach. It's been such a long while since I've had the sand between my toes. I can't wait to build a sandcastle. Did we go to the Coast for our honeymoon, Jackson?"

He shook his head. "No, dear. We went to Yellowstone."

"I don't remember. Were there geysers?"

"Yes. In more ways than one."

Ethel giggled and put her hand over her mouth. "I get it. You naughty boy. I remember now. I was nervous and you eased me into everything slowly. Ease is the proper word, you know, because although I knew you were probably experienced, I definitely wasn't, and . . ."

"Dear, we have a passenger in the back seat, remember? I'm not sure she wants the details of our love life."

Ethel did another of her half-turns and smiled at Wendy. "Oh, yes. You *are* there, aren't you? Here to help us out."

Wendy's smile was genuinely affectionate. "Every step of the way."

"Are you still writing the social column for the *Citizen*?"

"No, ma'am. It's been several years since I stopped doing that. Now I do investigative pieces and features like the one I'm doing on you and your family. And I teach and play bridge in my spare time. That's how I first met your son. He wanted to brush up on his bridge so he could be more effective as a host . . . for his parties." Wendy came to an abrupt halt. Would these casual memories of her son upset Ethel?

"Really? I didn't know that. So, you and my son never dated?"

"No, ma'am, we didn't. We knew who each other was from afar, but that was about it."

Ethel chuckled and clasped her hands together, clearly not upset. "You described wedding dresses so well when you were writing that column, I thought. Speaking for myself, I love details when it comes to weddings. I want to know what all the women wore, you know, such as the mother of the bride and the mother of the groom. Their dress colors should never clash, you know. You don't want to get in-law relationships off to a bad start, and that would surely do it, I think."

Wendy continued her solicitous tone, greatly relieved she had not disturbed the peace with her previous comments. "That's a very good point. But I must tell you from my experience during that period of my journalistic career that the mothers often don't coordinate. I found that they like to make their own statements without any consultation with each other. It's a female thing, I believe, and they have every right."

A Shell gas station advertising decent prices and an accompanying convenience store came into view on the left just as Jackson had topped a hill on the undulating four-lane that snaked through the pine forests of Southeast Mississippi. "There we go, dear," he said, briefly turning his head. "Relief is at hand."

"And can I get some of that bottled water? My throat is dry. I think I must have napped with my mouth open. I'd be so embarrassed to hear that I did."

"No, you didn't, and don't worry, Miz Kohl," Wendy said, making light of everything. "We'll soon be taking care of all the water issues—intake and output."

From the outside, Seabreeze Place looked like a typical Coast hotel, four stories of metal, glass, and masonry. It was set back from the Gulf and its occasional hurricanes at a safe enough distance among the horizontally majestic live oaks and nosebleed palms surrounding it, and there was no indication that it meant so much to so many different people: an independent living facility; an assisted living complex; and its overriding function, a memory-care destination for those in the end stages of disease. In the main, it was quietly impressive, reassuring to both Jackson and Wendy.

As for Ethel, she was confused at first but eventually understood what was happening to her after a bit of solicitous orientation from a doctor and nurse team.

"You'll like it here, Miz Kohl. We have a good time together," the officious older nurse, whose nameplate identified her as Geneva, told her there at the end, leading the way to the memory-care wing.

"How often will you visit me?" Ethel said later to Jackson, once inside her cozy quarters. He and Wendy had just finished helping her put up a lifetime of memories in the form of framed pictures on the wall, hang clothes in the closets, and further arrange and personalize what would become her new home. It had taken some time, but Wendy had eventually stepped out to give the couple some privacy as the time for separation arrived.

"As often as I can, dear," Jackson told her. "The drive from Rosalie's not that bad. Four-lane all the way." He reached out to hold both of her hands and smiled. "Besides, I never get tired of gawking at crocodiles and huge snakes."

"Didn't you say the reptile farm was gonna close soon?"

"Oh, you remember that, do you?"

"Yes. Does that surprise you?"

"A bit, yes."

"Why?"

Ethel could see the confusion in her husband's eyes. They were moving from side to side, unable to settle.

"Never you mind," he told her. "Time for the biggest hug and kiss in the western world. And you know we can stay in touch all the time through cyberspace. I'm just a cell call or a text away anytime. And then there's Aunt Phoebe to visit with."

After Ethel had pulled away from the tightest hug and sweetest kiss she could manage, she said, "I don't think Aunt Phoebe looked too good a few minutes ago when we popped in on her. Don't they allow makeup? She looks really old. She was younger than Mama, of course, but still, she has to be way up there. Also, I don't think she's having her hair done regularly. She looked like she slept on it."

"Yes, she's up there in years, but the nurse says she's doing as well as could be expected these days. You haven't seen her in a while. People always look greatly changed when you don't see 'em on a regular basis."

Suddenly, the reality of Ethel's situation sunk in, and she burst into tears. "I don't want you to leave. Couldn't we share this room? The bed's big enough. Besides, we've shared beds smaller than that before. Remember after we were first married and rented that apartment on Lambert Street with that awful stove and practically no closet space?"

"The things you still remember," he told her. Then he gestured briefly toward the bed. "But there's even less space here than in our slave quarters in Rosalie."

"But you would be there for me."

"I'll always be there for you. I will always protect you. I will see that no harm comes to you. I made a promise to you, and I will keep it. Don't worry about a thing. You're in a safe place."

Ethel felt better now. "Do you think they will let me take walks on the beach?"

"I'm sure they will. I'm sure there will be many outings to breathe in the Gulf air and let the breezes hit your face."

"You are a poet," she said. Then she drew back, looking around the room. "Where is that woman who writes poems that came down with us in the car?"

"You mean Wendy Rierson?"

"Yes. Wasn't she here a minute or two ago?"

Ethel wondered why Jackson was wincing ever so slightly as he said, "She told us that she was gonna step out to give us some private time. Wendy writes articles, not poems, though."

"So she does. I just love her descriptions of wedding bouquets. I don't think it's a real wedding if there's no mention of baby's breath. I've always loved the sound of those two things, and it's true—there couldn't be anything purer than either one of those."

Jackson flirted with a smile. "Yes, bouquets and baby's breath. Those are two wonderful things, I agree."

"No, I meant baby's breath and puppy breath. To me, they're the same. As pure as the driven snow."

All Jackson could manage was, "Ah, I see."

"Baby's breath," Ethel repeated. "Why can't the world always be that sweet and delicate? And why can't dogs have puppy breath forever?"

"I wish they could. Unfortunately, they don't. And the world can be cruel and unforgiving, but I don't want you to think about that."

Ethel reached for his hand and held onto it firmly. "But you forgive me for killing King, don't you?"

"I've told you before—of course I do. You don't have to ask anymore, and you don't have to tell anybody else about it, either. They're liable to think you mean it."

Ethel's smile was all the way up to her eyes by then. "I do mean it, but I won't say anything then. I'll be too busy walking on the beach, and maybe I'll even build a sandcastle. Do you think they'll take us on a cruise to Ship Island? I haven't been out there since I was a little girl. Yes, I think it was the summer I turned ten. The water is so clear out that far, not like that muddy dishwater close to shore. I'm glad you brought me here. I think I'll like it. I really do."

Jackson leaned in and kissed her forehead. "That's what I'm counting on, dear."

* * *

There was a depth of sadness in Jackson's face that was mesmerizing Wendy during their drive back from the Coast to Rosalie. She had not been able to see it clearly from her vantage point in the back seat on the drive down. The backs of people's heads rarely revealed anything of consequence, except possibly how much money they spent on haircuts and styles. But now she was his passenger on the front seat, and the long silences between her conversations with him were awkward, to say the least. Should she continue to draw him out, or was always letting him be the one to initiate an exchange be the appropriate way to go? Her empathetic nature told her that he was likely agonizing over the mission he had just accomplished: physically removing his wife from his daily existence. What an agonizing one-two punch he had endured—losing first his son, then his wife, in a manner of speaking.

They were halfway between Hattiesburg and Rosalie when Jackson finally broke what had been the longest period of silence between them yet. The only activity had consisted of sips from their water bottles now and then as they stared straight ahead at the highway.

"I never expected to let Ethel go like that, you know. My plan was to hire someone to look after her right there in Rosalie after we got her initial diagnosis a while back. I saw no reason it wouldn't work out. But then, she got much worse quickly, and King's death changed things even more. I hadn't counted on Ethel going off the deep end to the point that she thought she actually killed our son. I tried my best to convince her that she did no such thing, but she wouldn't hear of it. She would stomp her feet at me, and sometimes she would even scream. My life has gone from anticipation of my golden years to entrance to the gates of Hell, and I have to accept part of the blame."

"Don't be so hard on yourself. I understand that this must

be awful for you to be going through," Wendy said, shooting him an understanding smile.

"What I can't understand is how she got the idea in the first place. The only thing I can think is that she felt terribly guilty about something that must have happened between them, and with her mind being the way it is, she made some sort of twisted leap in her head. Dr. Pevey says Alzheimer's is unpredictable and can cause everything from hallucinations to delusions to temper tantrums. I'm quite sure Ethel has experienced the former, and I've witnessed the latter in person. Maybe I shouldn't be so surprised."

"Sounds like Dr. Pevey had things pegged."

Jackson's face sagged even farther. "We were there together that morning in the slave quarters, having our breakfast while King was being murdered in the big house, until we heard the sirens and rushed out in our bathrobes to see what the commotion was all about. I know you've heard the story before, and you were there for part of it as well, but I can vouch for the fact that Ethel nearly fainted in my arms when we got the news, and it only got worse when they brought King out in the body bag. Our world came crashing in around us. You understand why I wanted Ethel to have the best care possible, and I just didn't think she would get it, even with a nurse coming in every day back in Rosalie. These memory-care places, they know how to keep their patients safe. Ethel won't be able to get into any bleach or anything else that would harm her down there. She'll only get the proper meds, along with the proper food, and that's the best we can do for her."

"Of course I understand. You don't have to justify anything to me."

Suddenly, the anger rose in Jackson's voice. "What really gets to me is why they haven't arrested Marcus Silvertree by now. They have everything for an arrest—motive, opportunity, and the fact that he was there on the spot, and you witnessed him coming through the front door all out of breath and panicky as all get-out. And I told your husband and your daddy that I could vouch for a showdown filled with nasty words that King had with Marcus not too long ago. My son gave me the details. What more do they need? What are they waiting on?"

Wendy realized she had to proceed carefully, since she was privy to more than she should know as a spouse of a detective; she was also more than aware of Jackson's precarious emotional state. And finally, he was the one at the wheel. She didn't want him getting to the point that he drove off the road or made some other mistake in traffic.

"I think what's happened is that there's an aspect of the proverbial setup here. Since I was involved by being summoned to Kohl Place, I know what I'm talking about. It's all too convenient, and I can tell you with certainty that those involved in investigating crimes never want to arrest the wrong person. Circumstantial is not good enough."

"But I know he did it," Jackson continued. "I feel it in my gut. There was no love lost between King, myself, and Marcus Silvertree. I admit that freely. But it's not our fault that he wasn't up to the task here in Rosalie. You trust me, he's your man; and when it's all over and done with, he's the one that'll be spending the rest of his life in prison."

"I just hope this can be solved soon for everyone's sake," Wendy said, trying her best not to aggravate the situation.

For some reason, Jackson calmed down, and the next five miles were spent in silence. Then he continued his previous narrative. "I feel bad about not protecting Ethel from that suicide attempt. That damned bleach bottle. It shouldn't have been so accessible. Ethel was right about that much. Wyvonne should have put it in a safer place. Suppose children had come to visit at some point? Some of our friends have grandchildren that they bring over from time to time. To show them off, if you ask me. Kinda gets on my nerves, since I don't have any. Guess I never will now."

Jackson exhaled, and his tone became softer, more somber. "That's what I was looking forward to the most in life. Becoming a grandparent, carrying on the family line. Doesn't everyone want grands? What's wrong with that?"

Jackson could have no way of knowing how his question resonated with Wendy in her quest for parenthood, but she nonetheless managed to answer him straightforwardly. "There's nothing wrong with it. You're absolutely right."

"Sure I am. Why wouldn't you want your children to give you grandchildren if they can? It's supposed to be the highlight of those golden years everyone talks about. Now, look where I am, where Ethel is.

"Not only that, I feel bad about a lot of other things that happened between me and my wife over the years, but they will forever remain private. I'll just have to deal with them in my head." He paused and seemed ready to say more, opening his mouth to form a word but then thinking better of it.

The gesture seemed familiar, and then Wendy was immediately struck by the comparison with Father LeBlanc backing off of something he wanted to reveal to her, but chose not to. Did they know the same thing, or did each know something different pertinent to the case? Perhaps Jackson knew more than he was willing to reveal about his son's death and Ethel's relationship to it. And was this rush to get Ethel settled at Seabreeze Place only about protecting her health? Did Jackson know more about the relationship between his wife and his son that was pertinent to the investigation? Had a heretofore unknown but critical incident occurred that no one else knew about?

Silence returned to the rest of the drive back to Rosalie, which was a relief to Wendy. It was hard to get reminders of her inability to conceive out of her head. There was a bit of small talk exchanged when Jackson made a pit stop because of their constant water consumption. In effect, they had used their sipping as a bit of business to relieve the tension that still permeated the car. But as they approached the city limits of Rosalie, Wendy decided to dismiss Marcus Silvertree as the culprit for reasons she had explained to Jackson. She just felt the solution was too easy—or that someone had gone out of their way to make it so.

Instead, she found the concept of a "woman scorned" at the forefront of her brain once again. Was there truly any way in hell that Ethel could possibly have been that woman, and if one existed, was Jackson covering up skillfully to *protect* her, a word he had used often of late? Was her suicide attempt not an expression of her Alzheimer's, but one generated by true guilt? And could Jackson not bear the consequences of what would happen to her if the truth came out?

Finally: Would Seabreeze Place keep her out of the spotlight permanently, allowing the case to go cold? Or was that the red herring of all time?

CHAPTER 10

When Wendy walked into the lobby of the *Citizen* after Jackson Kohl had let her off at the entrance, about thirty minutes before the office would close to the public, the receptionist, an empty nester with big hair and a nasal voice by the name of Sally Anne Simmons, said, "You have someone waiting for you over there—a Miz Sidley." She pointed to a somewhat plump woman sitting in the corner with her arms folded tightly around her; she wore way too much eye makeup and blush, both of which failed to disguise her sorrowful demeanor.

Wendy headed over and shook hands as the woman rose to meet her. "Miz Sidley, I'm Wendy Rierson."

"Yes, I recognize you from your column picture," she said. "I'm Odelia Sidley, and I apologize for just bargin' in like this without an appointment and all, although I didn't mind one bit waitin' here for you, but I needed to talk to you about my daughter, Wyvonne. Is there somewhere we could just sit and talk private-like?"

Wendy told her there was, and led the way down a long corridor with offices on either side to one of the paper's small meeting rooms. After they had both settled in, Wendy said, "Now, Miz Sidley, what can I do for you? I'm sure you know I've already interviewed your daughter for the feature I'm doing on the Kohl Family. She was very helpful."

Odelia sighed, looking even more downcast. "Yes, she mentioned to me that she liked you very much and could be trusted. That's why I've come to see you. Since Mr. Kohl's death—bless his soul—Wyvonne has become even more of a mess. She hardly eats anything, she doesn't sleep, she walks around the house crying and even misses her classes out at the college. She's gonna fail if she doesn't get back into her routine. She's just falling apart, and I don't know what to do about it."

"Have you consulted a doctor about this? Offhand, that would be my first suggestion to you," Wendy said.

Odelia shook her head emphatically, made a fist, and slammed it on the table. "This isn't physical. She doesn't have a disease or anything like that. I know it's mental. I think she's mixed up in all this more than she lets on. Of course, I don't wanna get my daughter in trouble, but I thought maybe you could give me some advice on how to deal with her."

Wendy began to wonder if she had missed her calling. She'd spent the better part of the day as a shoulder to cry on for Jackson Kohl—and Ethel, to a lesser extent—and now, Wyvonne Sidley's mother had come to her for counsel. Unbeknownst to her, was she listed as *Dr. Wendy W. Rierson* under "psychiatrists" in the Yellow Pages? Had she earned a degree somewhere during her spare time?

"What did you mean when you said that your daughter was mixed up in this more than she lets on? Do you think she knows something nobody else knows? I told her to share everything she could with me when I interviewed her," Wendy continued. Her instincts were telling her that this was something she should pursue indefinitely. Was Odelia Sidley coming forward to provide the break they needed to solve this case?

"The most my Wyvonne'll tell me is—and I quote—'I wish King hadn't told me that.' Told her what? She won't say what it was he told her, no matter how many times I ask. My take is that she knows something about his death that is driving her crazy. Now, I don't for a minute think that my little girl could ever murder someone. God forbid. No, that's not what bothers me. I don't think I could ever go on living if she did. It's just that I think she might know something the police should know, and I know you're married to a detective. Only thing is, I don't want Wyvonne to get mad at me for letting even this much leak out without her permission. She doesn't know I've come here, and I don't intend to tell her. Do you see where I'm comin' from?"

Wendy was beyond intrigued now. It seemed to her that there were several people who knew things but weren't willing to tell—Father LeBlanc, Jackson Kohl, and now Wyvonne Sidley—who had lost no time in tracking everyone down very early on to make sure the investigation moved into high gear. Why, then, was she reluctant to reveal whatever it was that King had told her shortly before his death? And was this secretive thing the same as what Kohl had intended to tell everyone at the so-called bridge party that was called off? Wendy was back to that again. Or, more properly put, she had never abandoned that as the key.

"I understand your concerns about your daughter completely," Wendy said. "They're perfectly reasonable. Do you think maybe we'd get somewhere if I talked to her again? The police have already questioned her, so anything more at this point on their part might be viewed as harassment without any new evidence. I would want to proceed carefully."

"I didn't know that," Odelia said, sounding as if she had

just been shamed. "If you did speak to her, I think it should be at our house, where she'd be more comfortable. Of course, I need to get her outta the house in the worst way, but in this case, I believe it's the best approach to take. I really can't stand one more day of her behavior."

Thinking on her feet, Wendy said, "You could tell her that I just need more background for my article on the Kohls."

"Even though you've already done that with her? She told me that you asked what seemed like a million questions."

Wendy gave her a reassuring smile. "Trust me. I've been a journalist long enough that I think I can handle this without upsetting her. Why don't you set up an appointment for me and then let me know? You can leave out your visit with me, of course. You find a way. I think your coming forward like this may be very important, and I want to thank you for doing it."

There was an unmistakable sigh of relief from Odelia. "I wanted to think I was doing the right thing. So, I'll go home and then get back to you as soon as I can."

After a dinner that evening with Ross consisting of turkey tenderloins, sweet potato mash, and some Darby's fudge for dessert, Wendy jumped into her car and headed toward the Sidley home across town. Odelia had told her that Wyvonne's demeanor had brightened somewhat at the prospect of doing more to improve the article on the Kohl family, so it was all set. Not only that, but Ross had also sent her off with a kiss for good luck. What could go wrong?

The Sidley home was located on an obscure side street; the address was hardly a fashionable one, and the house itself was a pedestrian bungalow with a screened front porch and a small yard featuring no trees, bushes, or flowering plants—just grass. Wendy was surprised when Wyvonne came to the front door, rather than her mother, but interpreted it as a good sign when she saw the pleasant expression on her face.

Equally as surprising was the disappearance of Wyvonne's rainbow-dyed hair. It had been replaced with some mousy shade of brown and made her look drab and colorless now. Wendy couldn't help but comment there in the doorway after opening pleasantries were exchanged.

"I see you have a brand-new look. We women know how to cheer ourselves up, don't we?"

In the small foyer, Wyvonne said, "Mother's greatly relieved. She's been on me for quite a while now to get rid of 'that leprechaun hair,' as she calls it. She keeps telling me that I look 'worse than that cereal.' But that's not why I did it. The rainbow streaks were impractical. Very hard to disguise the roots growing out, so I just did away with it. Now, I'm dull to go along with being down in the dumps. *Voilà!* The new me."

"Now, don't say that. A woman's entitled to do what suits her when it comes to her hair," Wendy said. "By the way, is your mother here?"

"Yes. She's back in the kitchen fixing us a little snack," she said, gesturing toward the cozy living room on the right, laden with family pictures hung on faded, floral wallpaper and featuring a small TV set that had seen better days snuggled in one corner.

"I appreciate that, but I couldn't eat another thing," Wendy told her while following behind. "I've just had the most enormous dinner, and I'm stuffed."

They sat beside each other on a sofa with a colorful collection of throw pillows, and Wyvonne said, "Then something to drink? She's also brewing some fresh coffee."

"That will be just fine. I think I can make room for that while we talk."

After Odelia had entered with a smile, set down a coffee service on the nearby table, and then left them to it, Wendy said, "I'm about to wrap up my piece on the Kohls, but you gave me such good backstory the first time, I thought maybe a few more little items might tie up my project neatly with a big ribbon. And then, I forgot to ask you last time if you minded being quoted directly in my article."

"I thought you did ask me that," Wyvonne said, while stirring cream into her coffee. "I seem to remember it. Are you sure?"

"Well, I didn't find it in my notes anywhere." Wendy quickly flipped through the pages of her notepad. "In any case, I wanted to make sure that I had you on record as being okay with being acknowledged as a source. Some people prefer to remain anonymous, and I always want to respect that."

"No, I'm fine with it. Whatever I told you was the truth."

Wendy took a sip of her coffee and then went for it. "The thing I hope you can help me with the most is this party that King called off. It so surprised me, since he was practically the best party-giver in Rosalie, and I know you were a big part of his success. I remember you being at his beck and call throughout the last one I attended. Of course, I intend to make an account of his entertaining faculties a highlight of my article. They were all really great fun."

Wyvonne's demeanor shifted slightly, the smile on her face not as broad. "I always looked forward to helping King put on a show. It wasn't like work at all to me, and I tried to vary his snacks and other things on the menu. Everyone always raved, and an invitation to one of his events was highly prized."

"You did a very good job. But no one seems to know why he called it off. Not a clue from anyone. Still, I can't help but think that someone might know something incidental, something that hasn't been mentioned because the significance of it hasn't been realized yet."

Wyvonne grew even more somber and leaned in farther. "And you think I might be that someone?"

"I'm asking everyone to think back and think carefully about the question. I realize how difficult this is, but I want to do the most objective job I can on this assignment."

There was an awkward silence. Both women sipped coffee to relieve the tension. Finally, Wyvonne spoke, her voice quavering. "I may know something that I didn't mention before. Maybe I should get it off my chest before it does me in."

Wendy felt a spurt of adrenaline behind her sternum. Was success near at hand? "If you'd care to share it with me, then."

Wyvonne's composure began to crumble further. "It's . . . it's been driving me crazy, really. I just didn't know if there was any significance to it or not. It's strange and disturbing. But this opportunity to get it out there will probably be the best thing I could do at this point. You will respect my privacy here, of course. I mean, I don't want you to write about it in your article, but maybe it'll help you and the police in other ways."

"Absolutely. I know how to do that as a professional journalist."

"It was something he told me that upset me greatly," she began, unable to make eye contact with Wendy. "It was the day before the party was to take place, and he told me that evening that he was calling off the party and that I could take the day off and didn't have to come in." Wyvonne looked sideways for a moment and sighed. "That, I've already told everyone. But I have to tell you, I was crushed by that alone. You have no idea. Beyond that, I've already told you that I was sweet on him."

"Yes. Please go on."

"He told me more, and that was when I felt my heart sink to the toes of my feet. He said that he knew I was sweet on him, but that I shouldn't waste my time, either. That he just wouldn't be around, *in a manner of speaking*. That *time was run-*

ning out, and he was very concerned about that. He was not going to continue with the status quo." Wyvonne began tearing up and took the time to dab at her eyes with the paper napkin in her lap.

"Take your time," Wendy said. "Take all the time you need."

"I was beside myself," Wyvonne continued finally. "What was I supposed to make of that? It was bad enough that he was telling me I had no future with him. But when he said that time was running out and that he wouldn't be around in the future, I thought maybe he was dying. 'Do you have a terminal disease?' I asked him. But he wouldn't say anything one way or another. He was just stone-faced from that point on. He just left it at that. In a horrible way, it lessened the blow slightly when he turned up murdered so brutally. But then, this whole thing began to torture me in a new way. Had he foreseen his own death? Did he know someone was coming for him and was going to take him out? I've been dealing with both the feelings I had for him and that odd confession, or whatever it was, about not being around. The whole thing just creeps me out."

"I can well imagine. It would me, too. But getting back to what he said, do you think by 'status quo' he meant everything about his life?"

"I don't know. That's why I didn't mention this to the police," she added. "I mean, that's all King said. He didn't mention a person, and he wouldn't clear up any further what he meant by it all. I can barely function these days. I have no appetite, I have trouble sleeping, I've been skipping classes, and I know I can't keep on doing that. My life is just completely out of control, but I'm helpless to straighten it out."

"No, you're not," Wendy said, rubbing her upper arm gently. "As horrible as all this is, you have to keep your goal in mind of becoming a teacher. That's such a worthy ambition, and you can't let it slide. I know how hard this is for you, because I lost my mother when I was just fifteen. I was in high school, of course, and I didn't see how on earth I was going to survive. But thanks to my daddy, I did. He helped me latch onto life again, and you've gotta try to do the same thing."

"Yes, I know that. I just have to bear down and do it."

"It would be entirely inappropriate for me to work what you've told me into my article. So let me reassure you about that. But I'm glad you leveled with me about what's been driving you crazy. Clearly, there's something none of us understands yet about what King intended to do or what was going to happen to him that caused him to call off that party. It seems he told you part of the story, but not the whole story."

Wyvonne cupped her hand over her mouth briefly. "And to be honest with you, I'm not sure I want to know the rest of the story. It could be perfectly horrifying to unravel. People are always raving about getting at the truth, but I'm thinking that sometimes it's better not to know. Does that make sense?"

"Yes, I understand what you're saying, but don't you also want justice for him?"

"Yes, of course. But I'm frightened to the core that the truth may be horrendous beyond words. As hard as his murder has been for me to get over, the solution may be even that much harder."

Wendy had to agree. And now she had some new words to contemplate: *time running out*. There was a finality to the phrase that could not be considered business as usual. King saying that he *wouldn't be around, in a manner of speaking*. Then where would he be going? Her instincts told her that King intended to tell everyone the rest of his story at the party that was canceled, then backed out of it. Did he intend to tell the important people in his life one by one, then? Although Wendy would not bring up the subject of Wyvonne's crush on King in her piece, along with the other comments, she did intend to pass them along to Ross when she got home. They might bring them one step closer to finding out who murdered King Kohl so cruelly and why.

When Wendy got home from her visit to the Sidley house, she found Ross in the living room in his recliner, watching a show about aliens being responsible for the extinction of the dinosaurs. Apparently, they had nuked them all, because their initial experiment with life on Earth had gotten totally out of control. She snickered and said, "Not that show again."

He craned his neck, and then she headed over and gave him a peck on the cheek as he said, "Yep, that show again. You should know by now that aliens are responsible for everything. Pike and I have made a list of the things they did and other salient facts about them. For instance, they have a permanent base under the ice in Antarctica, which they access via their flying saucers; then, they gave cavemen art lessons; they also live underground in cities on Mars so we can't detect them—even our land rovers are useless; and the ones that have gone rogue send ships and planes to their deaths on the bottom of the ocean in the Bermuda Triangle. That's the solution to that. Oh, and they very likely helped Michelangelo paint the Sistine Chapel."

Wendy sat next to him in her favorite armchair, unable to repress a giggle. "Is that all? I was wondering how he stayed up there without falling to his death."

"Obviously, they gave him an anti-gravity device."

"Are you quite through?"

"No, there's more. I just don't have time to go into it right now." Adopting a serious tone, he muted the TV with the remote and continued. "So how did the interview with Wyvonne Sidley go?"

"I may have something new for you. She revealed that King had told her that she shouldn't spend any more time thinking about him in a romantic way because—and these were the exact quotes in the notes I made that I can quote from memory—*time was running out* and *he wouldn't be around.* Both Wyvonne and I wondered if that meant he had some sort of terminal medical condition and was going to announce it to everyone at that party he canceled. Otherwise, it gets even creepier in that it might imply he knew someone was going to kill him. That just makes my skin crawl. What do you think?"

Ross operated the lever on his recliner so he could sit up straight. "I think one of those things you just said is a total dead end. Ben Profilet, the Kohls' lawyer, cooperated with us and let us have access to King's medical records. King had no terminal medical condition. In fact, he was in perfect health, according to the physical he had about three months ago. No blood pressure or cholesterol issues, not an ounce overweight; in fact, he took no medications of any sort. It seems highly unlikely, therefore, that what he was going to reveal had anything to do with his health. Something different was in play. Sorry."

Wendy was staring straight forward at the guy on the alien TV show with the ultra-high forehead and the electrocuted-looking hair, but she was not really seeing him. Instead, her mind was racing about Ross's deflating words, and that commanded her full attention. "Then what did King mean when he said he wasn't going to be around anymore, and that time was running out? The idea that he might have known he was going to die is beyond disturbing. I think I would absolutely lose it if I realized something like that. I'd be paranoid every waking second."

"But he may not have meant that at all. He may simply have been saying that he wasn't going to be in Rosalie anymore. He was going somewhere else."

"For what, though? If he wasn't sick and wasn't going off to be cured of something, then what was he going to do?"

Ross made a clicking noise, not unlike a rider giving a signal to a horse. "When we know that, we will likely know everything, and the case will be closed."

CHAPTER 11

Patrice knew she wasn't mistaken. The guy at the other end of the bar at Smoot's had been locking eyes with her for several minutes now. She knew the signs well, but even if she had been slow on the uptake, the fact that the man had raised his drink in a toast-like gesture removed all doubt. Her interest in him was immediate and undeniable. He had one of those mullet hairdos, a neatly trimmed mustache, and his features were craggy and yet handsome when admired together. She imagined that he would have a good-ole-boy speaking voice to go along with the rest of him, and she had already made up her mind that she would go home with him if he asked.

Then, right after the featured acoustic guitarist finished his set with his rendition of "Me and Bobby McGee," the flirtatious guy made his move. Picking up his drink, which appeared to be something amber-colored on ice, he headed toward her and said, "Mind if I sit here, ma'am?" The vernacular and his tone were exactly as she had expected them to be. He was, for all the world, exuding *cowboy* without the hat.

"Be my guest," she told him, gesturing briefly. Then she took a sip of her white wine and gave him one of her trademark, come-hither smiles. "Do you have a name?"

"Folks call me Beck. Short for Beckham. Family name, of course. But no, I wasn't named after the soccer player."

Patrice couldn't help but chuckle but said nothing.

"Are you laughin' at me?" he said, but he wasn't frowning. "I wasn't tryin' to be funny, ya know."

"To the contrary. I was just appreciating how accurate I was in sizing you up."

"And what did you decide about me?"

"That you were my type. Of course, I know that you aren't really a cowboy."

Now he was the one chuckling. "Is that what you thought? Do I really come off thataway?"

"Kinda. You seemed to be following a script in my head. I can't explain it any better than that."

He took a swig of his drink and said, "I'm a garage mechanic, actually." He put down his glass and displayed his hands. "Check out these callused babies. I did manage to clean all the grease off 'em, though."

Patrice leaned over to gawk, continuing to be highly amused. Then she actually touched one of his hands, verifying the roughness for herself. "So, you don't work with horses, just horsepower."

"That was a damned good line," he told her. "Pretty sharp, if I do say so. I'll have to try and use some version of it to my advantage. Now it's my turn to ask your name."

"Patrice," she said. "Patrice Leyton. Do you have a last name, too?"

"Landry. Beckham Landry. Born in Lafourche Parish, Louisiana. Cajun through and through by birth."

"Thibodaux?"

"Yep. How'd you know?"

"I have distant relatives who live there. On my mother's side. She was a Mayeaux. My dad was the white-bread Protestant by the name of Leyton. They were a match made in Hell and ended up divorced. At this point in my life, I don't claim either one of 'em."

Beck eyed her nearly empty wineglass and said, "You're about outta fuel. Want a fill-up?"

"That'd be nice, thanks."

After the bartender had complied, Patrice began more small talk to put herself at ease. "I don't think I've seen you here at Smoot's before, and I come here at lot. Are you up from Thibodaux?"

"Yep. Visiting an old friend for a day or two, and I'm stayin' at the Grand Hotel just down the street."

"Great views of the river. Best sunsets on the planet."

"And I'm on the top floor, where I can see the barge tows goin' downstream to the twin bridges. And you're right, that sunset here in Rosalie is somethin' else. I stayed at my window and watched it before I came over here for a snort or two."

"We're sure known for 'em up and down the river. Sunsets, I mean, not snorts."

He laughed heartily. "Never seen so much gold and orange and red on the horizon in my life. Just about blew my mind."

"You paint quite a picture for a mechanic. You're starting to sound like an artist now. Anyhow, the tourists who come here like to go up on the Bridge of Sighs and watch. That's the footbridge right across the street from the Grand. It's quite a romantic thing to do. Watch and smooch, and then when the sun's gone down, some more smooching."

He chugged the rest of his drink and then said, "Yeah, I know about it. Speakin' of romantic things, d'ya think that might possibly be in store for us?"

Never coy after being asked such a question, Patrice said, "I don't see why not. That acoustic guitarist is due out for another set real soon. Do you wanna wait for that, or call it a day here?"

Beck's grin was almost predatory. "I've heard guitar players before. He's okay, but they all sound the same to me. But every woman's a different tune for me to play."

"Sounds good to me," she said, lifting her wineglass and then draining it.

He settled up with the bartender and then gestured toward the door. "Shall we?"

Outside on the sidewalk, which was brightened by the string of colored lights around the tin roof, Patrice said, "Did you just walk down the street from the hotel? I mean, you'd hardly need a taxi. Not a big bruiser like you."

"I did walk down, and I thought we could just take a stroll thataway right now. Might as well get warmed up for the exercise to come. Whether you stay the night or not, I can walk you back to your car."

"A gentleman to boot, I see." She hooked her arm through his, and they headed toward the Grand, which was just a matter of a block or so down Broad Street.

In the ride up on the elevator, Beck said, "You know, I've always gotten lucky every time I come to Rosalie. It's that kinda town. Real laid-back, you know. I mean, almost no other Southern cities that I know of have a go-cup district like this one does. The French Quarter, sure. You can go anywhere you want to with a drink in your hand. I believe some people call Rosalie 'The Little Easy' because of its good-time, partying reputation. Any excuse to come up here, I always take, and I've never been disappointed."

"What you say is absolutely true," Patrice said. "There are teetotalers here, to be sure. But they don't run things. They're way in the minority."

They had reached the top floor, and the elevator doors opened. "After you, ma'am," Beck said, gesturing.

"More gentlemanly ways on display. Thank you, sir."

"I took a suite," he continued as they walked down the

carpeted hall. "Lotsa room, two TVs, a kitchenette, a wet bar, the works, fit for a king and his queen."

"Fancy."

"I spare no expense on these trips. If not on these occasions, then when?"

"I'm right there with you."

He swiped his room key in the lock, the green light flashed on after the clicking sound, and they walked in, one after the other. The room smelled of the aftershave he was wearing, and the window curtains overlooking the river were drawn back, evidence of the sunset-gawking he had described for her at Smoot's.

"Please, go ahead and fix yourself another drink. I ordered up some bourbon and gin, and there's some ice in the bucket. Coke and Sprite, if you like. And now, if you don't mind," he said, "I'm gonna go into the other room and slip into somethin' more comfortable. It won't take me long."

Patrice couldn't help but think that that particular statement sounded a bit off. It was the first thing he'd said that didn't come off as Hollywood-perfect and therefore out of character. Usually, it was the woman who said she was going to slip into something more comfortable and used that trite phrase as a prelude to the obvious.

"Don't be too long," she told him with a wink anyway.

"I won't. Be back in a jiff."

Although she preferred wine, Patrice ambled over to the wet bar and stared at the bottles, shaking her head. She and gin did not agree, even with an olive or an onion sunk to the bottom of the glass or tonic water poured and stirred into it. No, the juniper berry made her take leave of her senses. Bourbon on the rocks it was going to be, if she had to choose. A short one, diluted further by the ice. She always wanted to keep her wits about her in situations like this. Getting really drunk and abandoning all judgment had led to the most traumatic event in her young life—that unplanned pregnancy and subsequent abortion that continued to haunt her. She decided not to even take a sip until this cowboy-acting mechanic reappeared in whatever new getup he had chosen, so she set up shop in the middle of a small sofa, maneuvered a throw pillow behind the small of her back, and waited for him patiently with her legs crossed.

A few minutes later, the door to the other part of the suite opened, but it was not Beck Landry standing there. Patrice's jaw dropped, and she blurted out the words in knee-jerk fashion: "Oh, my God! Jimmers Tyson!"

Across town, Wendy and Ross were making an early evening of it, talking back and forth in bed with the lights already off.

"Do you think there's a possibility that this case will go cold?" Wendy was saying, snuggled up against him. He was facing away from her, hugging one of his pillows, his natural sleeping position since puberty.

She felt him making a shrugging gesture as he said, "My experience has been that just when you think a case might turn cold on you, something happens that sets off a ripple effect. Someone makes a mistake, and it changes everything. It might not even be the culprit who makes the mistake, but it's as if the universe wants justice to be served."

"I've never heard you sound so metaphysical about your job," she said, gently patting him on the back. "This might sound strange, but I've always thought of you as a 'meat and potatoes' police officer. Do you know what I mean?"

"I think so," he said, with a humorous little snort. "I've never taken any philosophy courses. Just not my style."

"But I've always believed in the ripple effect you mention," Wendy told him. "I don't think you can march through life without noticing it when it comes along. After I lost my mother when I was in high school, I didn't think I'd even graduate. Grades suddenly seemed so unimportant to me. Algebraic equations, particularly. I nearly failed that course because I suddenly thought to myself, 'Who the hell needs this? I don't want x and y, I want my mother back.' The gossip about 'who was going steady with who' also seemed even more ridiculous and beyond the pale. I wanted to shut out all that stuff, hide in my closet behind my shoeboxes, and deny reality. Until Daddy rescued me. I know I've told you all this before, but I think he dealt with his pain by helping me with mine. He gave me a purpose to go on. I was to honor my mother's memory by accomplishing great things in my life. So, we got through it together."

"I've understood for some time now why the two of you are so close. Bax is a good, family man," Ross said. "I couldn't have a better father-in-law."

"He thinks the world of you, too. You have no idea what all he says to me behind your back. But I'm not gonna tell you, because I don't want you to get the big head." There was a brief pause, followed by a sigh. "The only thing he doesn't understand is why we haven't gotten pregnant yet. His hints have become tiresome, but I don't blame him in a sense."

"I know," he said, turning over to face her, making all sorts of rustling sounds beneath the covers. "He'll bring the subject up every now and then down at the station. 'When am I gonna become a grandfather?' he'll say to me, and I haven't gone into the fertility tests with him yet. I figure that since we've determined that there's nothing to keep us from conceiving, that it'll happen one day—maybe when we least expect it—and then we can celebrate with him from there as if there never was any problem. So I say what he doesn't know at this point won't hurt him."

"'All good things in time,' my mother used to say. Or was

it, 'All things in good time'? Well, it doesn't matter. It'll happen for us when it's supposed to, when the gods of maternity smile down upon us."

"Now who's getting metaphysical?"

Wendy giggled, and they moved closer together for a lingering kiss. Afterward, she said, "As for King's murder, getting back to our original discussion, I'm more than ready for that something out of the ordinary to happen to create that ripple effect. For someone to make a mistake. Please, ripples, do your thing."

"Keep that thought," he told her. "Sometimes, you can only do so much with forensics. Sometimes the evidence falls short and has you running around in circles. At that point, you need a little luck. Then the ripples follow."

Patrice's adrenaline was coursing through her veins, her heart rate accelerating by the second, as Jimmers moved across the room and took his seat beside her on the sofa. He hadn't changed much. He had a slight sneer on his face, not because he was actually sneering, but because the right side of his mouth hitched up just a tad bit without his even trying. People had even told him over the years that he had a slight resemblance to Elvis, without the sideburns. His dark hair was still quite long and brushed back, pompadour-style, and he hadn't put any more weight on his tall, lean frame. He was essentially the same man who had impregnated her and left town, claiming no interest in helping her out one way or another. So why was he back in Rosalie, several years later? For some reason, it occurred to her that he might have returned to do her some sort of harm. Or to do harm in general.

Full of questions and slightly frightened, Patrice put her drink down on the nearby end table and said, "What's happened to Beck?"

Jimmers moved in closer and gestured with his thumb. "He's in the other room."

"I figured, but what is all this? A setup?"

"You could say that. Beck is the PI I hired to catch me up with you, and that's not his real name. He did an excellent job tailing you and finding out all about you, and here I am." He quickly grabbed her drink and said, "What are we having here? Bourbon on the rocks?"

"Yes," she said, as he took a sip and gave her a wink of approval.

"Seems your taste in liquor has improved. You were pretty much a bourbon and Coke girl when we went out. That's a high schooler's drink, guaranteed to make you hurl." Then he handed the glass back to her.

Patrice felt herself growing a bit calmer and said, "I never hurled around you. But I was right, you know."

"About what?"

"About that scene with Beck at Smoot's. Something about it felt very theatrical. You know, the cowboy/mechanic bit. It had a scripted quality to it. Not that I didn't enjoy it."

Jimmers drew back, squinting. "Whaddaya mean, 'cowboy'? We agreed that he'd come on to you as a mechanic."

"I added the cowboy element in my head. Women do that sort of thing, you know." She made searing eye contact with him. "So, I was also right about someone stalking me recently. I have eyes in the back of my head, you know. I have to, because I've had encounters with crazy men before. It's a hazard of the trade."

His squint morphed into wide-eyed puzzlement. "Are you talking about me? You think I'm crazy?"

"If the cowboy boot fits . . ."

"Enough with the cowboy bit."

She grabbed her drink and took a quick swig. "Why did you have whatever-his-name-is seduce me? Why didn't you just come up to me and say you were back, like a normal human being? Why all this silly game playing? It doesn't make you any more attractive."

"Because I thought you might just walk away if I did. I wanted to be sure we had the chance to talk. This way, I have a captive audience."

"What do you mean *captive*?"

"Just a phrase."

"A disturbing phrase. Anyway, what's there to talk about?" she said, folding her arms. Though she was no longer fearful, she was definitely annoyed about the stalking and the subterfuge.

"Randy—that's his real name—found out everything about you that he could. He did a good job for me. I paid him enough."

Patrice's mental alarm went off again. "Whaddaya mean, 'everything about me'?"

"What you and King did. It wasn't easy to track down, but he found out that you aborted my child. You know it had to be mine, not King's."

Patrice felt the anger rising in her blood. "Well, we'll never know that for certain, but wait just a minute. You ran out on me as fast as you could when I told you I was pregnant. You left skid marks in the pavement. You couldn't have cared less—at least, that's what you told me. And yes, it's true that King didn't want to help me raise that child any more than you did. Neither of you was my hero by any stretch of the imagination. The fact is that I only saw one way out, and King was willing to help me at least do that. I don't know why in hell you came back to Rosalie expecting anything of me. You are no sight for sore eyes."

Jimmers was staring down into his lap now. "I, uh, was hoping maybe I could make amends . . . for the past, you know."

"And how were you gonna do that? Do you have a time machine to whisk both of us back and change everything?"

He looked straight ahead, still avoiding eye contact. "By finding out if you were, you know, settled in life and by seeing if we could try again."

"You've got to be kidding me." She drew back as if he were a poisonous snake about to strike. "What we had back then was just sexual, nothing else. And even though we saw each other more than once, there was still a one-night-stand quality about the whole thing. Let's not pretend it was anything else. A great romance? Hell, no!"

"All of that may be true, but I've changed, I really have," he continued. "I have a good job over in Alexandria, Louisiana. I work at a car dealership in the service department. That's where I got the idea that Randy should say he was a mechanic. I mean, it seemed like a good idea to me."

"Big whoop. Are you even daring to suggest that I come live with you in Alexandria? Is that what this is all about?"

"Well . . . yes."

"Get a grip, Jimmers. I'm doing very well on my own, thank you. This idea of yours is way, way over the top."

Now he was the one who drew back. "So you're happy being on your own turning tricks? Don't you get tired of it?"

"It's really none of your business what I choose to do, or why I choose to do them. You can't be right in the head by thinking so."

His tone changed from snarky to hostile. "Why the hell not? And, by the way, I'd like to know if you and King aborted my son or my daughter."

"If you must know . . . the baby was a boy. At least that's what I was told. I . . . did really want to know, for some strange reason. I can't pretend it was the highlight of my life so far, though. It's taken its toll, and you were no help at all."

It was as if all the air in the world had been expelled from his body when Jimmers sighed and then said, "My son. I had a son." He covered his forehead with the palm of his hand and shook his head.

Unmoved, Patrice continued. "That certainly wasn't your attitude when I told you I was pregnant, and you know it. You're insane if you think there's any chance you and I could start over. You just wasted your time and money doing all this. It's hardly made you husband material in my eyes, if that was your goal."

"So you want to just stay stuck in this rut a' yours? Randy wasn't the only one tailing you. Once he confirmed you were still here, I took some time off to see for myself what you were up to. More than once, I saw you go into Smoot's, and so did Randy."

"As I said, you blew your chance several years ago to have any say-so in my life." Patrice could feel the fear creeping back into her mindset. "Exactly how long have you been here in Rosalie, ducking in and out of doorways? Because I was aware of something sinister going on, you know."

"Over a week."

"You were here when King was murdered?"

"So?"

"You don't know what I'm thinking?"

"Don't even go there."

She rose from the sofa deliberately, afraid to continue her train of thought with him. "So, I think it's time we ended this little play of yours. Find yourself some unwitting little number over there in Alexandria to settle down with, because it's no sale with me."

"You don't have to be so ugly about it." He rose as well and grasped both of her arms, facing her. "Why can't you believe I've changed? People can change for the better."

"Because that's your agenda, not mine. And why should I believe you? Your word means nothing to me, and I owe you nothing."

He began shaking her, gently at first, then with more urgency. "You don't have any moral high ground here. Don't be so stuck up. You are what you are."

"Let go of me," she cried out. "You're hurting me."

But he dug his fingers deeper into her flesh instead. "Not until you come to your senses about me."

"I said, let me go!"

'You think you're so much better than me, don'tcha? Living in some kinda alternate reality, you are. Well, I think it's time I shook that nonsense outta you."

This time, she let out a wordless scream, as he continued to shake her. It ran through her mind in a flash that Jimmers was exhibiting the sort of rage that could easily lead to further violence, even death. An image of him confronting King soon followed, terrifying her to the bone. Was his killer about to strike again?

"Stop that screaming!" Jimmers shouted, cupping one of his hands over her mouth. "You're hurting my damned ears!"

The last thing Patrice remembered was the door from the other room opening as she fainted dead away.

CHAPTER 12

Wendy and Ross were having roasted red peppers, fresh basil leaves, and mozzarella on ciabatta bread with a couple of bottled waters for lunch together on one of the benches near the south end of the sprawling Bluff Park. Another sleek Viking Cruise Line ship was in, this one on the Ferry Street dock, and the usual excitement of disembarking was going on two hundred feet below them—tourists sauntering down the ramp to the shuttle stop. Wendy had run by the Pearl Street Deli and picked up the sandwiches just after Ross had texted her with this intriguing message:

someone may have just made a mistake; let's have lunch breakthrough? She replied immediately.
possibly, was the return text.

Then they had decided on the place, the food, and the time to meet for further discussion in private, and now he was telling her all about Patrice Leyton's visit to the station earlier that morning.

"Then, Patrice said she just blacked out on the sofa for

what she believes was just a short amount of time," he continued, after describing everything that had been revealed to
him, starting with the flirtation at Smoot's. "And when she
came to, this Randy person had pulled Jimmers Tyson off of
her and was yelling at him to calm down and get it together.
So she thinks she couldn't have been out for long."

After Wendy had swallowed a bite of her sandwich, she
said, "And then what happened next?"

"Patrice says he apologized to her, although somewhat reluctantly, but she told him in no uncertain terms, 'I never
wanna see you again.' Then, something about a restraining
order if he wanted to keep hanging around Rosalie, spying on
her. She said he backed away and told her he wouldn't bother
her again, that he was leaving town for good."

Wendy rested her sandwich on the large paper napkin she
had balanced on her lap. "So, you think this Jimmers Tyson
might be the one you're looking for, since he admitted to
being in town when King was killed? Could it all be that convenient?"

"That's why she came to see your daddy and me—because
she says that in those moments of rage, during which he was
holding and shaking her like a rag doll, she could imagine him
acting out like that with King, only much, much worse. She
said she could see him ripping that plaque off the wall and
having at him with fatal results. If she's telling the truth about
all this, I can see her point."

"Do you and Daddy think she's telling the truth?"

Ross had just taken a bite and had to wait until he had finished chewing and swallowing. "It's certainly something we
wanna investigate. It turns out that Jimmers and his friend
checked outta the Grand early this morning, so we can't interview them right now. But Patrice did a nice job of thinking
on her feet there at the end. With a little sleight of hand, she
dropped her plastic drink cup into her purse and then handed

it over to us this morning. 'I thought your crime lab could give it the once-over and see if it matched any of the DNA found at the crime scene,' she told us. I have to give her credit for that. As I said, this could be the mistake falling into our lap that I mentioned to you last night. If his prints on that glass match anything found in that house, then we may very well have our man. It'll put him at the scene of the crime with motivation and a very bad temper to boot. After all, there were some unidentified prints found by the lab. They could be his."

They both continued enjoying their sandwiches as a shuttle bus headed down the steep incline of Silver Street, past the Under-the-Hill Saloon, and Silver Street Gifts; its ultimate destination was the Ferry Street dock to pick up the cruise passengers eager to wander all over Rosalie in their time ashore.

"I'm thinking that I might have to remove Patrice Leyton from my list of women scorned," Wendy said after a bit of contemplation. "What do you think?"

Ross managed a skeptical glance. "Never underestimate human nature, especially when it can think on its feet as fast as Patrice Leyton did. I'm certainly giving her the benefit of the doubt at the moment, but you have to admit that all suspicion in this case has suddenly been transferred from her to this Jimmers guy. It may have all gone down just the way she said it did, but I'm gonna wait to hear from the crime lab until I make any further judgments."

"Makes sense."

"Leaping to conclusions is all well and good," he added. "But the element of restraint is always a great idea during the course of any investigation."

"So, if the prints on the cup match any of those in the house, do you then issue a warrant for his arrest?"

Ross nodded emphatically. "We'll try to track him down and bring him in for questioning, if it comes to that. Then we go from there."

"Didn't Patrice say he said he had a job over in Alexandria?"

Ross wiped his mouth with his napkin and continued. "Yes, she did, and we got his driver's license and license plate from the hotel register. You don't need a warrant for that. His address checks out, and he doesn't have a record of any kind, not even recent traffic tickets. Same for the PI guy. Without DNA evidence, we just can't bring either of them in, so we have to wait. My sense is that this is a dead end—no more than a personal psychodrama for Patrice Leyton. The thing is, it's not a crime to hire a PI. Discreet stalking is part of the job."

"You are very good at what you do, husband," she told him, smiling affectionately his way. "I might just marry you."

"Ha, you already did." He nudged her gently with his elbow. "I saw where one of those *Thin Man* movies you introduced me to was coming on Turner Classic Movies tomorrow night. Is it wrong of me to think that you and I are becoming the Nick and Nora Charles of Rosalie? Updated by many, many decades, of course."

"We do make a good team. Daddy swears by us, you know."

"Wanna stay up late and watch the movie with me tomorrow night? I'm off duty the next day."

"Sure. We'll pop some popcorn."

When he had finished off his sandwich, Ross returned to the subject of evidence. "The crime lab should have a report on that glass from the hotel room by the time I get back. That could break the case wide open. If this Jimmers guy was in town when King was murdered, he could have gone over there and confronted King about Patrice and all that went down with their relationships with her. Maybe it got out of hand quickly, tempers flared, and Jimmers acted out of rage. It's that rage angle I can't dismiss, of course. Whoever it was went for the kill in no uncertain terms. The temple is one of the most vulnerable spots on the human body."

"I shudder to think," Wendy said, closing her eyes briefly. "Such a horrible visual."

"You got that right. It was a gruesome sight."

They both rose from the bench and discarded their napkins and plastic water bottles in a nearby metal trash can. "Hey, I'll text you *yea* or *nay* if the crime lab comes up with anything, and we can discuss it in detail tonight."

Merleece was winding up her long day, cleaning the imposing Old Concord Manor on Minor Street for her primary employer, the widowed Miz Crystal Forrest from *Al-benny*, Georgia. Fortunately, Crystal had allowed her to clean for the Riersons and Bax Winchester once a week, as well. By now—after several years of priming the pump of recognition by donating to local charities with her considerable, inherited fortune—Crystal was thoroughly established as a Rosalie social fixture, like her or not. It was difficult to say what percentage regarded her as a paragon of virtue and which as a pain in the rear, but there was no one in Rosalie without an opinion. Some thought *Divisive* was Crystal's middle name.

"Don't toodle off just yet, *dahling*," Crystal said in that faux British accent of hers, just as Merleece was about to head out the kitchen door.

Merleece turned on her heels and said, "Did I forget one a' my jobs? I know it cain't be those tiaras you got on display in the big secretary. I dusted erryone a' them."

"Yes, I know you did. I saw you doing it. No, this has nothing to do with your work. No one in Rosalie cleans as well as you do." Crystal gestured toward the small kitchen table near the window. "Have a seat and talk to me for a few minutes, won't you?"

Merleece did not welcome the invitation—not by a mile. Whenever Crystal Forrest wanted to "talk things over," it invariably involved some social *faux pas* she had recently committed, and it meant that she, Merleece, would function as a sounding board until the issue was resolved in her employer's cluttered, flighty head. At such times, Merleece felt she was earning every penny of her very generous salary.

"What'd you do this time, Miz Crystal?" Merleece said, taking a seat while secretly enjoying the power she wielded in these situations. It was beyond amusing to her how Crystal almost viewed her as an oracle of some kind. Well, she was a Rosalie native, after all, and Crystal wasn't. As a result, Merleece was a touchstone who knew plenty about people— good, bad, and indifferent.

Across the table, Crystal settled in, arranging the décolletage of her expensive, royal-blue blouse and then touching the tips of her fingers to the top of her poofy hairdo for a quick primp. "It's Miz Helen Hope Williamson again. I always seem to be getting on her bad side. Honestly, I don't think she has a good side. I think it left a long time ago with her figure. Now, she's left with a good, *big*, back side."

Both women snickered. Then Merleece sighed, resigning herself to the long story that was sure to follow. "What about her and her big back side? I know you and her sit on erry committee in town together. What was the fight about this time? Flowers? Tiaras? What?"

"Merleece, you are something else. Your first guess was the right one. It's the Flowers-Under-the-Hill Committee that I just couldn't resist joining. It's brand-new, and I wanted to help beautify things for the tourists from the boats. After all, the first thing they see when they disembark is the riverbank. I wanted my *gahdnuh* to work the zinnia and poppy patches along Silver Street, using seeds from my *gahduns*, but Helen Hope won't hear of it. She thinks her *gahdnuh* is better, so they all took a vote, and Helen's man won out, even though he's a thousand years old. My Arden Wilson's in his prime, as you well know. I'm just beside myself, of course. She always wins in these situations, and you should have seen the smug look on her face after the tally. She acts like she rules the world, and I'm just a peasant in her eyes. Can you imagine? Me—a peasant?"

"You gotta face it, though," Merleece told her, pulling no punches. "Miz Helen Hope'll always have the advantage here in Rosalie. She was born here. Her mother was born here. Her grandmother and great-grandmother, they all born here. And back and back further than that to slavery times they go. She got the old genes, you don't. That's just a fact that you gotta face, and they's no way you can change it."

"*Genes!*" Crystal spat out. "No matter how much money you have, you can't buy genes. I do realize that, no matter how much I try to do for this town. Restoring Old Concord Manor to its impeccable state, contributing to the food pantry to feed the poor, sending some children to college with the scholarship money I donate to civic clubs, whatever it is. I try to do good. Genuinely, I do. But some still hold the fact that I came from *Al-benny* against me. What's an outsider to do? I think Miz Helen Hope just delights in putting me in my place. She's made a hobby of it."

Merleece leaned in, catching Crystal's gaze. "Lissen up, now, and lissen good. I know what I'm talkin' 'bout. I really don't see why you got to get so upset. Arden Wilson is doin' a damn fine job with those gardens a' yours. Now, you know I got my issues with him 'cause he really is a smartass and gets on my last nerve like he did when we both worked for Miz Liddie Langston Rose, but we both stay outta each other's way. So, be happy with what you got. Don't even worry 'bout who's growin' what up Under-the-Hill. You got the best-looking gardens in Rosalie, and well you know it."

"That's true, of course," Crystal said, brightening considerably. "My tours are the highlight of the Pilgrimage every spring. All the tourists who come through say so. They fill out my little comment cards, and not a one has had anything snippy to say yet. It always makes my day. I've decided to frame some of the best ones. Eventually, I'll have an entire wall of them to look at whenever I please."

"There you go. That's all you need. Frame 'em up."

"So, I shouldn't look upon this as a slight of some kind?"

"Hell to the no, you shouldn't. I tell my boy, Hiram, the same thing. Try to be who you are and do good at the same time. He's finally actin' like a grownup man over there at the Rosalie Fire Department. I thank the Lord for that, because I never thought I'd see it. Hard as it may be, you just gotta ignore Miz Helen Hope. Wear earplugs around her if you got to."

Crystal rose from her chair and motioned to Merleece. "Come, give us a hug."

Merleece complied, drew back, and said, "Here's my advice. Let Miz Helen Hope have her snooty genes. That's all she got."

Finally, Merleece was able to escape and head home for rest and relaxation. But once she began driving through town, something akin to an *aha!* moment surfaced. She had told Wendy not that long ago that she would try to think of certain specifics in the conversation between them that Wendy believed might have some bearing on King's murder. The session with Crystal Forrest had triggered it.

Genes.

But it wasn't that simple. The gist of the conversation fell into place. It wasn't just a matter of genes; it was *bad genes* that were the issue here. Merleece had told Wendy that if any family lasted long enough, that if there were enough generations to play genetic roulette with, that every once in a while, some truly bad genes creating toxic people would find their way into the DNA of individuals. Of course, Merleece realized that she hadn't been quite that scientific about it. She was no doctor doing important research that got written up all over the world. She'd just seen plenty of examples of monstrous behavior, even among the best of families she knew from her church. Then she thought again about her theory of "a woman scorned," and that rage she'd witnessed once between two women who seemed to have suddenly lost their minds over a man.

Merleece knew that she must give Wendy a call as soon as she got home and refresh her friend's memory about that particular conversation. "I gotta get home without runnin' red lights," she said out loud, sensing the importance of her recollection. But she was still alert enough to slow down and stop at the yellow light looming straight ahead of her. Traffic tickets were the worst.

Wendy and Ross had much to discuss over dinner that evening, so much so that her homemade andouille and sausage gumbo took a back seat for once. True, they downed delightful spoonful after spoonful, but the usual comments on its spiciness and great texture were missing, replaced by the developments that had taken place during the remainder of the day.

"So, I guess the crime lab doesn't make mistakes," Wendy was saying after taking a sip of her Chardonnay. "As in never, ever?"

"Nope." Ross paused his spoonful of gumbo halfway to his mouth. "Well, every once in a great while, maybe. But it's so rare, it's statistically inconsequential. And those little glitches get worked out quickly. No harm is done. I can vouch for that. Our criminologists take great pride in their work."

"Then Patrice's swiping of the glass was for naught."

"It appears so. We don't really have anything to bring the

guy in on for questioning. Unless Patrice wanted to press charges against him for assault, and she says she doesn't. She just wants to forget all about it and move on with her life. But if he shows up again, she is serious about getting a restraining order. That's where we do have jurisdiction. If Jimmers Tyson knows what's good for him, he'll stay away from Rosalie for good."

Wendy persisted, nonetheless. "But just because the guy's prints didn't match anything in the house doesn't mean he couldn't have confronted King, lost it, and pounded him to death anyway. The prints could have been removed."

"That was Patrice's train of thought," Ross added. "She made sure that we were aware of it. Offhand, I'd say that the three women who had some sort of relationship to or with King have all made sure that we were aware of certain things. Wyvonne has called all sorts of things to our attention from the very beginning; then, Bella was quite helpful in bringing forth that single hair of King's to absolve herself, or so she thinks. And let's not forget Patrice's contributions from the abortion story to this latest tale of seduction and assault. It's not provable so far, but the ringleader and group effort theory is still very much in play."

"Do you think Patrice could be playing you, playing all of us?"

"Possibly. We haven't ruled out the possibility."

"What about Ethel Kohl?"

Ross broke a baguette in half and said, "What about her?"

"She had a relationship with King. Kinda primal—mother and son."

"And?"

"She kept stubbornly insisting that she had killed her own son, and then there was the suicide attempt. I guess we are to attribute all that to her medical condition and nothing else? It just seems so drastic if she, in fact, did nothing."

Ross dipped the baguette into his bowl, made a throaty sound of approval as he took a bite, and then said, "I've given that a lot of thought, and so has your daddy. We both think that if by some remote chance, she actually did kill King, she would not have been in her right mind. She would be declared by her lawyer as of *diminished capacity*. A trial would end in sending her to an institution, and that's where she is now anyway. Well, not exactly an institution; it's a memory-care facility. But it amounts to the same thing. Jackson has seen to that. I don't think for a moment that he thinks his wife really did it. He just wants to protect her, as any good husband would, and I can't say I blame him."

Wendy caught his gaze intensely. "But that still leaves the possibility that if she didn't do it, then someone else may get away with murder. I know you and Daddy despise cold cases, and no one is comfortable with a murderer on the loose."

"Yes, we do hate our cold cases, but we do not consider this case closed by a long shot, regardless of Ethel Kohl's situation."

"Good. Neither do I. I'm glad to hear you say that, because I just know we're all missing something important."

"So, you told me you had some info to share with me? Something from Merleece, I believe you said?" He had a smug expression on his face, and Wendy called him out.

"You know better than to look like that. You always think Merleece and I are just a couple of gossips when it comes to all this. It's the closest you ever come to acting like a sexist, which you most definitely are not."

He immediately raised both hands in surrender. "Sorry. No offense intended. Proceed."

"Well, a conversation she and I had a little while ago came back to her, and I believe it may have some significance." Wendy then explained to him the entire concept of bad genes erupting here and there in generational terms and that it was impossible to predict the consequences of such an occurrence. And the snake in the high grass might not be easy to identify.

"Okay, that's a very interesting thought," he said in a serious tone. "It would seem to apply to the older families of Rosalie if you're gonna put it in those terms. The ones that have been around a while, like the Kohls and the Comptons, and people like Miz Helen Hope Williamson, but certainly not people like Patrice Leyton or Marcus Silvertree. I don't think Patrice's folks go back a ways—she's a recent comer, and I know Marcus is a transplant from the Delta. He's already made a big fuss about wanting to go back there as soon as he can. Pike even caught him trying to leave for Chicago and then Canada, if you can believe his story. The key word here is *trying*. He didn't even get to start up the car engine. Everything against Marcus Silvertree is still circumstantial, and then there's your testimony about his rushing out the front door. That oughta tell you how much the department respects you and your opinions."

Wendy looked extremely pleased and said, "I doubt the established family concept would apply to this Jimmers Tyson guy. I'd never heard of him before all this happened. Of course, there are lots of people in Rosalie that I don't know. But I am aware of all the families that have been here forever."

"I know you are."

After yet another sip of wine, Wendy said, "Suppose it was King who had the bad genes. That *time running out* revelation from Wyvonne Sidley implies something dark and mysterious going on in his life. We know it wasn't of a medical nature. So, what was it he was referring to? And I still can't get over the idea that he actually knew that someone was gunning for him, so to speak. There's something about the whole thing that's just not right. You know, even film noir-ish."

Ross looked bewildered. "I was hoping we'd gotten our hands on that ripple effect that would help us solve the case when we got that glass from Patrice, but no such luck. As much as I hate to say it, this case could go cold on us unless we get that real breakthrough."

Wendy couldn't resist giving him a wink. "Don't forget, you have me on your team. I may come through with one of my brilliant insights, and then we're all home free."

"I no longer put anything past you, sweetheart. Even though you stubbornly continue to resist your daddy's overtures to give up your journalism career and join the force, you might as well be on it with all you've done with some recent, thorny crimes."

She pursed her lips and wagged a finger playfully. "You know as well as I do that it's the gun thing. I just don't want to have to handle them. I will continue to solve crimes with my mind and the written word, not bullets flying through the air."

"You're good as gold with me," he said. "Besides, all three of us in law enforcement would be way too stressful."

CHAPTER 13

Greta Compton was beside herself at her daughter's unsettling news. What had come over her? The two of them were sitting in the parlor of Bella's cottage, having cocktails in the midst of what Greta thought was going to be a normal, polite mother-daughter visit. There was no reason to think otherwise, since Bella had sounded perfectly composed over the phone issuing the invitation. But once they got settled in, the dam burst.

"Your father, may he rest in peace, and I bought this house for you as a permanent home. We never dreamed you would ever think of selling it and moving away in some sort of conniption fit like you seem to be having right now. You need to give this second and third thoughts—or as many as it takes until you regain your senses. If you're wise, you'll listen to me."

Bella spoke up in her belligerent tone. "You never dreamed it because you thought I was going to marry and settle down here in Rosalie just like you did. And more specifically, you thought that I was going to marry King and that we'd have two houses between us as befits any grand family of Rosalie. Why, nothing less would do in the scheme of things in your world."

Greta had never seen or heard her daughter act this way. "What do you mean—*my* world? I can't believe what I'm hearing. Are you mocking being an old Rosaliean? Surely you can't be giving up your birthright. How many cocktails did you have before I arrived?"

"None, I am perfectly sober, and I am not mocking Rosalie by any means. That is not what this is about." There was prolonged silence after that.

"Are you going to tell me what it *is* about, then?"

"I more or less have. I don't want to stay here in this town any longer. I know you understand English."

"I heard that part. But I didn't hear anything else to justify it. Besides, I don't think you can move away until this horrible murder case is solved," Greta pointed out. "The police would view that with a great deal of suspicion. What on earth can you be thinking? Do you want to come off like some sort of fugitive from justice? I know you don't want that to happen."

Bella took a great gulp of her gin and tonic and said, "No, I don't. But I'm thinking that I can most certainly sell the house if I want. I have clear title. It wasn't a loan I had to pay back to you and Dad. It's mine outright."

"And where would you stay in the meantime if the case takes forever to solve, you sell the house, and have to move out?"

"With you, temporarily . . . unless you don't want me."

"That seems like a convenient paradox. I don't understand," Greta continued, more upset than ever. "You're acting like you want to wash your hands of Rosalie and all the privileges that come with it but want me to be your just-in-case backup plan. All of this seems so unnecessary and contrived."

"Frankly, I would like to start a brand-new life for myself. This old one just hasn't worked out so well. Is that so unusual?"

Greta steeled herself, struggling not to strike out verbally.

"In what way hasn't it worked out for you—that is, besides King leaving us all the horrible way he did? I admit that was a blow to everyone in Rosalie, but it doesn't necessarily have to be the end of the world for you or any of the rest of us. Life really does go on. It did for me after your father died."

"I'm aware of that. We both miss Dad. But if you admit that King's murder was a blow, then you should also admit that staying here in Rosalie only brings back memories of what once was and what might have been. Can't you understand that?"

Greta rattled her ice cubes in a distracted manner and said, "You've never really forgiven King for not actually proposing, have you? I'm not sure I have, either, for that matter. Ethel and I talked often about what was really going on in his head."

"Let's just say that it didn't exactly endear me to him when he wouldn't pop the question. Especially when he got involved with other people after that, and I know you can read between the lines. I was furious with him, to say the least."

"That much makes sense, but what about this business of exchanging single hairs in lockets," Greta continued. "Why didn't you ever tell me about that? It seems like the sort of thing you would divulge to your mother. I thought you and I were closer than that."

"King and I wanted to keep it private, something between us that no one else knew about. It was supposed to be a testimonial to our undying love. Then I had to trot it out to the police for obvious reasons—to clear my name, of course. It was humiliating to me."

"If you think it did clear your name, why are you now so intent on getting away? Are you hiding something further from me?"

Bella said nothing.

"Are you going to answer me or what?"

Bella shook her head.

"Now you've got me worried with all this stonewalling. Is it even remotely possible that you killed King in some moment of fury? How on earth could you get out of doing something like that? I don't think any amount of clever lawyering could save you, if that's what you're thinking."

Bella put her drink down firmly on the nearby end table featuring a lace doily in the center of it. "I won't dignify that question, but if this thing isn't solved, don't you think I'll always be under suspicion? Do you think I want to go through the rest of my life known as the Secret Murderess or something like that? I want to move to a new town and see new faces, meet new people that don't know anything about my life here. Maybe then I can get some peace of mind and get rid of this awful depression I have."

"And give up your social position here? You're overreacting, Bella. Get a grip. The depression, such as it is, will pass soon enough. If you have nothing to hide, then stay here and live your life among those who love and respect you. Does that mean nothing to you?"

Bella's glare was withering. "All I can tell you is that I want to get away from here—all the trappings, all the pretensions, all the expectations."

"Has your life been that awful? I think it's been rather privileged, and you know it. Pilgrimage Queen, Mardi Gras Queen, Wine Tasting Festival Queen—you've had everything you've ever wanted or needed and more."

The anger in Bella's voice rose to another level. "Your trappings, your pretensions, your expectations. Your wants and needs achieved precariously through me."

"What? I've never lived through you. I had my own achievements in my day. I know what it's like to be Queen of the Ball. Why am I even defending myself?"

"Oh, don't pretend that you and Ethel Kohl didn't have my life with King all planned out down to the number of grandchildren you wanted to spoil. You think I didn't know that? You think he wasn't aware of it, too? We both talked about the pressure you put on us all the time. Once the two of us started dating, you both ran with it and left nothing to the imagination. All you lacked was the wedding date and the design of my wedding dress. Oh, and how many tiers the cake was going to have, not to mention the flavor it was going to be. Almond, vanilla, or something totally different. Don't deny it."

Greta looked taken back, even sheepish. "We thought that's what you both wanted. We were only trying to be supportive. What kind of mothers would we be otherwise? It seems to me that we were both only following Rosalie protocol."

"I suppose that much is true, bless your hearts. But neither of us had any room to breathe. We couldn't make any mistakes in our relationship without you both coming at us with a reprimand. 'What's going on between you two?' you would say to me if I didn't give you a daily report. King said Ethel was the same way, always so solicitous. Do you know how wearing that is? You were both the mother hens of all time, clucking on endlessly and looking for your eggs."

Now there was hurt in Greta's eyes. "Goodness, what an awful description. I had no idea you were such an angry person with all these pent-up emotions."

"Well, you know what they say about pent-up emotions, don't you? They can explode into terrible rage at any time."

"What are you trying to tell me?" Greta said, sounding profoundly frightened. It took all the strength she could muster to keep from leaping to an unwanted conclusion.

But again, Bella went silent.

"You're going to say nothing further?"

"I don't think so. I've been as open with you as I can. You already know that I intend to sell the house and get out of Rosalie as fast as I can. You know everything that's pertinent."

"And is there nothing I can do to dissuade you from this crazy idea of yours?"

"Not at the moment," she said, picking up her cocktail to finish it off with a dramatic flourish. "I don't like the feeling of being cornered."

"And I don't like the sound of that, Bella."

"Sorry. There's nothing I can do about that."

Wendy had a sinking feeling when Lyndell summoned her into the editorial office the next morning. Call it her unparalleled instincts again, but she knew exactly what her boss was going to say to her.

"It's just too sad an ending to dwell upon right now," Lyndell was telling her from behind the desk, tapping her pen on the surface in distracted fashion. "The entire community has paid its respects properly, and I know for a fact they still aren't over what happened to King. How could anyone be? I just think we should leave well enough alone and not drag poor Ethel going into a memory-care unit out in the open in print. Those who are connected in any way to the Kohl family already know what's going on. You know how word gets around Rosalie. I know what our intentions were when I assigned you the piece, but circumstances have changed now. I think we need to back off."

"So we're canceling the piece, then."

"For now, yes."

"And that's final?"

"Consider this. I was also thinking that when this case gets solved, that won't be a pretty story to tell, either. I expect there will be shock waves all over Rosalie. So, let's cut the Kohls a break. We aren't a supermarket tabloid, you know."

Wendy had a hint of a grin on her face. "I understand. But you said *when.*"

"Wait . . . what?"

"You said *when* the case is solved, not *if.*"

Lyndell leaned forward smartly, as she often did. "I have every confidence in our husbands to bring it on home, don't you?"

"Yes, I do. But don't forget that I may have a say-so in this."

"If your success in the past is any indication, you certainly will. So just go ahead and save your draft. We may resurrect it at a later date, when things have calmed down a bit. Meanwhile, I got a call from a Miz Elsie McMichael about twenty minutes ago, and she thinks she may know something about Billy Caspian's death in the basement of Lacework House on Broad Street."

Her eyes wide with surprise, Wendy said, "That old story? But we've already put that to bed. I thought identifying the man's bones would be enough. I don't see how anyone could know the details of his death all this time later. I don't know how old this McMichael woman is, but she may be the only one left alive who was around at that time. Unless she's dug up a diary or something like that."

"I know. Go figure." Lyndell handed over a piece of paper. "But this woman was adamant that we hear her out. Here's her number. Give her a call. If she's a crank, just humor her. You know how to handle these things. She probably just has a crackpot theory, nothing substantial, I'm willing to bet."

Wendy rose and headed out, turning at the last second. "I wish I had a substantial theory about what really happened to King."

"Don't press, girl. Things have a way of coming to you when you're ready to receive them."

Ethel was sitting at her desk in her room, biding time before her afternoon bridge game. For the first time since King's death, she felt safe and protected in her cocoon. That was the most important thing, even if there were other matters to deal with, real or imagined. She hadn't been there long, but as a matter of record, she did not like the food at Seabreeze Place one iota. It was predictably bland, always under-seasoned, and no amount of complaining seemed to make a bit of difference. Not that she hadn't tried.

"Couldn't we have a bit more flavor in the chicken casserole? Haven't you ever heard of Tony Chachere's or Zatarain's down here? New Orleans isn't that far away, you know. Just get on the highway and head east until the trees are hung with Mardi Gras beads. This just tastes like cream of nothing with noodles," she had told the server at her table, a small Hispanic woman named Inez who never looked her in the eye, appearing to be afraid of her. "And could you pass that along to the chef?"

But nothing ever came of that, or any of the other complaints she passed along. The chef was always too busy to talk to her, she was told, but Inez did say with some authority, "Most of our residents don't like the spicy foods. It would upset their stomachs, and that's not good. I'm sure you can understand, Miz Ethel. We have to take that into consideration."

It was likely the truth, but Ethel's palate remained unsatisfied. On the other hand, there was bridge, which Ethel enjoyed very much with three women who were decent players. Well, most of the time. She had read a note on the community bulletin board about a fourth for bridge being needed and that anyone interested was to check in with the activities director. So Ethel did just that, and she had already observed that Barbara never counted trumps that were out properly and was always getting surprised by rogue trump tricks; Hulda was too aggressive with her bidding and got set more often than not; Laronda talked across the table too much and had developed a system of winks and finger taps during the bidding. But they were all a passable diversion, for the most part, and Ethel was pleased that her knowledge of the game largely remained intact. Odd, how that worked. It did not come and go like some of her faculties.

The sad part, which almost made her rethink playing the game with the ladies in the first place, was that bridge also made her remember King and his parties; in a thousand years, she would never get over his death. That had torn at the very fabric of her soul. How could it not? It also made her want to die. So, she had drunk that bleach to end it all, because the truth was just too much to bear. She didn't even care that the church regarded her attempted suicide as a sin. She would face the consequences head-on rather than going on living this way.

Nonetheless, the change of venue made her feel safe at last. If she was to live much longer, at least she would be safe during the time allotted to her. That much had been accomplished.

There was a knock at her door, followed by a melodic, singsong voice. "Are you decent, Ethel? Girl, it's time for our game out in the common room."

"Come on in," Ethel said.

The door opened to reveal Laronda Givens, the bridge blabbermouth of all time and the only woman of color in the group, dressed in one of her long, flowing outfits, poofed and sprayed brown wig, and rings on every finger of both hands. Those same bejeweled hands made great clunking sounds when she collected tricks. "We don't want to be late, you know."

Ethel glanced at the atomic clock above her desk, which Jackson had given her as a present for her big move to Seabreeze Place. "You won't ever have to wind it," he had told her. "It operates on a signal sent from somewhere in Colorado. I forget exactly where."

She hadn't understood the concept at all, and even wondered at times if the clock might explode, vaporizing her. Atomic? Didn't that have fearsome nuclear connotations? But of course, she decided she was being silly, so she accepted the gift in good faith, even though she cringed every now and then when she observed it and walked past it very quietly.

"We'd be ten minutes early if we left now," Ethel said to Laronda.

"I know, girl, but you know by now that I like to be sure and claim my seat facing north."

Ethel wanted to shake her head but smiled instead. Everyone humored Laronda's belief that if she didn't sit facing north, she wouldn't win anything—not a bid, not a leg, not a game, not a rubber. So no matter who ended up as partners with whom, Laronda was always accommodated, even though everyone also knew about her secret signals and such. They just didn't let on that they did, probably due to the fact that Laronda's cheating didn't help her much. A natural at bridge, she was not. Like the others, she was just in it for the socialization.

On the way to the common room, Ethel found herself exhaling both mentally and physically. It had nothing to do with Laronda or the others or the relaxation of the game itself. It amounted solely to her safety. She was tucked away, hidden. and out of danger—including safe from herself—and that was all that counted. Now, on to the pleasantries of a genial game of bridge.

Wendy and Merleece were meeting for lunch at the Simply Soul Café on the north side of town, where people of color cooked and served the food to Rosalieans of every sort, including tourists from the boats who sometimes arrived by the busload. Greens, beans and cornbread, along with egg pie for dessert, usually prevailed as menu favorites, and the two women had quickly placed their orders while the stock-in-trade B.B. King music played in the background as usual.

"I'm glad Miz Crystal let you come," Wendy was saying. "As I told you over the phone, I had something on my mind to run past you, and I very much count on your perspective."

"Lissen, Strawberry," Merleece said, leaning in with an air of authority, "I didn't need that woman's permission. You best believe that. I just told her I wanted to have lunch with you, and that was the end of it. Story over. I got it like that at Old Concord Manor. I work hard, but I get left alone, too. I tell you, best job I ever had—best pay, best perks, best erry-thing."

Wendy's laugh was more like a hiccup. "Miz Crystal's a mess, I know that, but she means well. She just doesn't know how to pull off whatever it is she's trying for. She'll never convince everybody in Rosalie that she's been here for three hundred years and counting. If she'd just calm down and relax and let everybody appreciate her good qualities, but she's too insecure and high-strung for that."

"I heard that. Anyways, what'd you wanna run past me? Bet it's about that poor Mr. Kohl's murder, am I right?"

Wendy took a sip of her tea and said, "Yes, it is. Daddy and Ross seem to be at a dead end with the case. Everything is circumstantial at best, but I think my brain ought to have come up with something definitive by now. But it hasn't quite happened. The thing is, every time you and I get together in situations like this, you come through for me with some clue pulled out of the air, and then I run with it."

Merleece frowned, putting her elbows on the table. "Now what kinda pressure is that to put on me, Strawberry?"

"No worse than the pressure I'm putting on myself. Once I got into this sleuthing business, I just couldn't stop anytime one of these peculiar crimes happened. So, here I am again."

"I hear what you sayin', but suppose I happen to be fresh outta clues pulled outta the thin air? Then what next?"

Wendy flashed a smile. "Then I'm no worse off than I am now, spinning my wheels and downright disappointed in myself that I can't see through the veil of mystery surrounding this case. There are things I can't share with you, of course, but I know I'm missing something critical."

"So, nothin's come of that big 'gene' discussion we had? Or the one about the 'woman scorned'? You seemed to be pretty excited about all that. No good, then?"

"I wouldn't say that nothing's come of them exactly," Wendy added, unfolding her cloth napkin and putting it in her lap. "I have the feeling that they both do apply. But in unexpected ways, and in ways I haven't yet been able to adjust to make sense of them. The pieces of the puzzle just don't fit yet, and I'm frustrated no end to be so stuck."

"My advice is to just be patient. You tryin' too hard. My granny used to say to me all the time, 'Back away when you cain't think right. Get off it for a while, and go do somethin' different. Have a drink. Bake uh applesauce pie. Take a walk 'round the block. Sew on a button. Outta sight, outta mind. Then, it'll come to ya.'"

"Your granny sounds like a very wise woman."

"She was that. Mahmoo's only fault was she was so stubborn 'bout errything that she wouldn'a run out the house if it was on fire. She'd've let 'em spray the hose on her while she was in her favorite chair watchin' her favorite show on TV. I mean, she had her schedule to keep day and night, and she wouldn't budge from it no matter what."

Both women laughed just as their waiter arrived—a lean, young black man with long, multi-colored braids and a million-dollar smile.

"Ah, I'm happy to see you ladies are in very good spirits,"

he said as he placed their plates of greens with salt pork, pinto beans, and pepper cornbread in front of them. "Laughing is great for the appetite, and I trust our food will only make you happier."

"It always does," Wendy said. "I've been hooked for a while now."

"Since I brought you here that first time," Merleece added, as the waiter made a seamless exit. "Been a while now, but I wanted to show you what real soul food was like."

Wendy took her first bite of the highly seasoned greens. "I never get tired of these. I'm totally addicted forever."

Later, over their slices of egg pie, Merleece said, "Have I come up with anything brilliant yet over our lunch, Strawberry? I haven't kept track, you know. Too busy with the good food."

"You probably have. What usually happens is that I find myself reviewing our conversations and then whatever it is pops up, waving its hands and saying, 'Here I am. Pay attention.'"

"So it's like that, huh?"

"I exaggerate a little. But I swear it seems to work that way. Something you say in an offhanded way triggers something in my brain."

"I got that part down," Merleece said with a big grin on her face. "And even if nothin' does pop out at you, we had this delicious lunch together and our girlfriend time."

Wendy raised her tea glass and said, "Let's toast to that." Then they clinked rims as Wendy finished her thought. "To girlfriends together forever!"

CHAPTER 14

Wendy's next inspiration in her determined effort to assist her father and husband in their investigation of King's murder occurred in the middle of the night; specifically, with the light of the full moon slanting in through the bedroom window. She sat bolt upright but was hardly content to keep her idea to herself. That was never her style. So she vigorously shook Ross out of his sleep and was greeted with a growling bear as a result.

"Whah . . . whah, what?"

"I want to explore one of my hunches until it's clear I'm right or wrong, one way or another," she told him.

He continued to be grouchy, still facing away from her, cradling one of his pillows. "Couldn't it at least have waited until morning? Don't you know what time it is?"

The blue-green numbers on their digital clock read: 2:12 a.m.

"Yes, of course it could have waited. But I'm way too excited to wait until the sun comes up. And anyway, don't you want me to share all of my hunches with you in a timely fashion? You've never complained in the past. Besides, I don't want to argue with you, I just want you to listen."

With a sigh of resignation, he turned to face her. "Okay, I

admit you've been spot-on with your insights in the past. I've just not usually been asleep when you shared them. So, go ahead, whatcha got, sweetpot?"

"I've been marinating a while and—"

Ross tried to mute his laugh but couldn't. "Please don't use that word unless you're planning to cook something."

"Smart aleck," she said, giving him a playful kick under the covers. "Okay, then, I've been *thinking* a while. Is that better?"

"Much. Proceed."

"But before I get to my new thought, I was reviewing recent conversations I've had with both Lyndell and Merleece, and both of them brought up a very valid point. They said that if you mentally press too hard, you won't get the result you want. Sometimes, you just have to let things go. I was going to say *marinate* again, but I want you in a good mood. Anyway, Merleece summed it up perfectly. *Out of sight. Out of mind.* So, I've been mentally relaxing, so to speak. Even meditating."

Ross managed to sound both tentative and polite. "Ohh . . . kaaay."

"Don't overwhelm me with your enthusiasm."

"No, now that I'm fully awake, I'm interested to hear what comes next after all that buildup."

"The deal is that I'm going to get an appointment with Dr. Pevey as soon as I can."

That caused Ross to sit up against his pillow and gently clear his throat. "You woke me up for that? Wait . . . do you think you're sick? Please tell me you're not."

"Of course not," she said, veering into scolding. "I want to understand more about Alzheimer's."

"Sweetie, he's a busy man. You can go online and read up on it yourself."

This time, Wendy pounced. "I'm told the worst thing you

can do when it comes to medical conditions is to go online. There's a wealth of misinformation out there, and people drive themselves crazy thinking they've come down with everything they find, no matter how extreme. There is no substitute for going to a real doctor."

Ross sounded amused. "I'll give you that one. I did that myself once when I was in college. The online thing, I mean. I was convinced I had mono, but it was just a bad cold."

"Mono, huh? Kissing too many of those Ole Miss women, I'd guess."

"You'd be guessing wrong. I had one girlfriend then, but let's not go there."

"Agreed." She took a deep breath and continued. "So, what I thought I'd do is to tell Dr. Pevey I need more medical input for a feature I'm doing for the paper, and if he could make time for you and Daddy, he can make time for me."

Ross's lighthearted tone continued. "I married the most determined woman in the world. No doubt about that."

"Thank you. It's true, of course." Wendy took the time to fluff up her pillows, having no intention of shutting down the conversation. "By the way, I forgot to tell you that Lyndell's also shelved our piece on the Kohl family for now, but I'm betting she'll reinstate it once we get this case solved. Rosalie will demand comfortable closure, in any case."

Ross folded his arms and gave out a little snort. "I'm sure they will. Now can we go back to sleep? Or do you wanna roam around the house conjuring up all the questions you're gonna ask Dr. Pevey?"

"Don't be so snippy. I think this is very important, even if it's counterintuitive."

"Why counterintuitive?" Ross tried to avoid a frown but couldn't. "You lost me there."

"I mean that sometimes we disregard the obvious and

think it offers nothing. For instance, alibis. Who has them? Most everybody doesn't—just Jackson and Ethel vouching for each other. I'm taking a stand right here in the middle of the night in bed to say that at least part of our case will be solved when I finish with Dr. Pevey. I'll explain later, if all goes as expected. Meanwhile, if you and Daddy haven't asked Jackson if the name Jimmers Tyson sounds familiar to him, I think you should. There is an indirect connection there that should be explored, even if it's a dead end."

"Okay, if it makes you happy, we will. I'll mention it to Bax at the station this morning." Then he went silent for a while before raising a slight point of contention. "I can tell you already what Jackson is gonna say if we bring up Jimmers Tyson. I mean, there's always a chance he knows something about the man, but I think he'll insist once again that Marcus Silvertree is the one we should be locking up. On that, he hasn't wavered; and as you know, Tyson's prints didn't match any the crime lab found at Kohl Place. Still, Tyson hadn't entered the equation every time we previously interrogated Jackson, so your point is well taken. We should ask him and observe his reaction closely."

"This case is frozen. We need to thaw it out."

"As I've said before many times, I could swear you were on your daddy's payroll the way you dive into this headfirst." He leaned over and kissed her briefly on the lips. "And despite my grouchiness right now, I can assure you, your help is fully appreciated."

"A woman always likes to hear that about every aspect of her life."

He returned to his "facing-away" sleeping position and said, "Great. Now can we go back to sleep?"

"Back to sleep, we go," she told him in a breathless, seductive tone. "After all, my brain needs its beauty rest."

* * *

Wendy was more than grateful that her reputation—not to mention those of her father and her husband—preceded her. The prominent Dr. Pevey had been most accommodating, quickly returning her voice message.

"Tell you what," he had told her over the phone. "You just drop by tomorrow around 7:30, a half hour before we officially open, and I'll be happy to answer all your questions about Alzheimer's before I get into my regular clinic hours."

Once ensconced in his tidy little office, and with an eye to their time constraints after a few preliminaries, Wendy got to the point with her pen and notepad at the ready. "I'm particularly interested in the difference between hallucinations and delusions in these patients. They're not the same thing, are they? I mean, they sound like they might be, but I'd like for you to clarify that for me, if you'd be so kind."

Dr. Pevey's long, narrow face with the high cheekbones brightened as he pointed an index finger toward the ceiling in imitation of a lecturing professor. "You are absolutely correct. They're quite different. When an Alzheimer's patient has any kind of hallucination, it may be either visual or auditory in nature; but in either case, they see or hear something that is simply not there. They may see bright colors, animals, or strange figures they can't identify. Or they may hear fantastic, disturbing noises or voices. Whenever that happens, my advice to loved ones is always to be gentle with them, never abrupt or argumentative. Ease them back into reality as best you can."

"And with a delusion?" Wendy said next, writing as fast as she could.

"It's a form of paranoia. That a sense of danger lurking may be very real to them, even though they don't see or hear anything under such circumstances. The power of suggestion can be wielded quite effectively either way, before, during, and after. The wrong word or phrase can heighten the delusion, while the right word can lift them out of it."

"That makes sense," Wendy added. "Although I think it might be frightening to wield that kind of power over anyone."

"It's often quite unintentional at the start of the episode," Dr. Pevey continued. "The art of walking on eggshells comes into play in dealing with these patients. Even the most well-meaning of their loved ones can stumble and make things worse. The upshot here is that it's extremely upsetting for a spouse or other family member to see someone disappear bit by bit, knowing they are helpless to stop it. It's very frustrating to endure."

"I can imagine how stressful that's been for Jackson Kohl. I'm surprised he's been holding it together as well as he has."

Dr. Pevey made a soft, clucking noise, and there was great sadness in his voice. "I've been physician to Jackson and Ethel since right after they were married, and in my wildest dreams, I would never have expected their lives together to end the way they have. Murder and a terminal disease, and now, Jackson left alone with such tragedies. He doesn't deserve such a fate, considering all he's done for this town. And King was a chip off the old block. Both fine men, dedicated to the community. I was more than eager to cooperate with your father and husband regarding medical records. I believe I'm speaking for a lot of Rosalieans when I say that this town will never be the same until this horrible crime is put to bed. Practically every patient I see has some comment to make, and it's not like I bring up the subject in the first place. I have medical work to do."

"Don't worry. The solution will come," Wendy said, dropping her pen and notepad in her purse. "And you've done your fair share of helping the cause, I assure you."

"Thank you, Wendy," he said. "As for Jackson Kohl, perhaps he'll let his faith sustain him during this difficult period of his life. I go to the basilica, too, and the Kohls almost never missed Mass on Sunday."

* * *

Ross was getting ready to refuse Jackson's offer of a drink after he'd entered the slave quarters for the informal interrogation he'd arranged. He'd figured they would both be more relaxed outside of the impersonality of the station.

"It's not that I wouldn't like a little libation," Ross said. "It's just that I never drink on the job. But please, you go ahead and mix one for yourself."

Jackson lost no time in fixing himself a bourbon on the rocks, and soon the two of them were seated next to each other on the living room sofa. "So what was it you wanted to talk to me about? Is there some breakthrough?"

"Not just yet. But we've had a few developments, and I'm here to let you know about one."

Jackson took a sip of his drink and sat up straighter. "Go ahead, please."

"Does the name Jimmers Tyson mean anything to you?"

Jackson jerked back slightly. "Why, yes, I believe it does. King mentioned him to me once in passing, and the look on my son's face wasn't pretty, I can tell you that. It had somethin' to do with King's relationship with that Patrice Leyton, but he wouldn't go into detail with me on it. Just that this Tyson fellow was trouble. His mother and I never could figure out what he was up to with that Patrice—well, I guess we did in a way, you know, but it was better left unsaid."

"Say no more, sir. But is there anything else you can tell me about Jimmers Tyson? I might as well tell you that he was in town when your son was killed. He admitted as much to the very same Patrice Leyton."

Jackson took even an even bigger swig of his drink. "Is that so? Have you brought him in and questioned him? He coudda had it in for my son every bit as much as that Marcus Silvertree, to my way of thinking. Had to be a man on the rampage, the way I see it."

"He's left town, but we do have samples of his DNA, and it doesn't appear he was in Kohl Place while he was here. We do have a few unidentified prints, but most of them are compromised, and we have no way to track them down at this stage."

"We all know evidence can be erased easily enough," Jackson added. "My money's still on Silvertree, but I'd track this Tyson fellow down if I were you. I know you wanna see justice done, and I don't have to tell you how I feel."

"The whole town is with you, sir, if it helps to know that."

Finishing off his drink, Jackson suppressed a belch and said, "No, it doesn't help much. I wish it did. Nothin' helps much. It's all a mess, a nightmare, and I didn't see it comin.' I swear I didn't. One second, you're on top of the world, and the next, life as you know it is over. Gettin' hit by lightning couldn't be any worse."

Ross wondered if Jackson had had a couple of other cocktails before his arrival when the man slammed his glass down on the coffee table, hung his head, and sucked up air as if it were his last breath.

"I don't know how we got here," he continued. "Ethel down there, and King wherever he is, and me left with my business and my reputation. It seems damn little to be left with now. Damn little. Maybe it's all I deserve in this life."

The interview was deteriorating fast, so Ross decided to pull up stakes. "Once again, I'm so sorry for these losses you've sustained. Have you thought about getting some help with your grief? Maybe a counselor, maybe your church. They might make a difference."

The amount of anger in Jackson's voice was sudden and virulent. "My church, my church. Damn my church and everything it stands for. Damn them for the guilt they make me feel, that they made King and Ethel feel, namely that none of us are good enough and have to change our basic nature, that we can't make our way in life without them. Damn all that, and damn the damage it's done!"

Ross was speechless but saw a hint of embarrassment in Jackson's face.

After a bit of silence, Jackson said, "I . . . really didn't mean for all that to come out the way it did, but it's done. I'm all knotted up inside. I've had trouble sleeping. The only thing I can do that helps is to drink."

Cautiously, Ross said, "You don't have to explain." He rose quickly from the sofa. "I'm gonna leave you now. All I can do is wish you peace of mind. Meanwhile, if you should think of anything else, just anything at all about Jimmers Tyson and your son, or anyone else for that matter, please don't hesitate to get in touch with us down at the station."

Jackson rose to show him to the door. "I don't know that there is anything more I can tell you, but I promise to let you know if I do."

As Ross walked once again along the garden path that Ethel had landscaped so many years ago and had come to splendid fruition, he could not ignore the insight pressing in on him from the conversation with Jackson. It was a well-known fact that the Kohls were devout Catholics, particularly Ethel and King. Why then this sudden and vociferous attack on the church by Jackson? Was it generated by his profound grief over what had happened to his family, or was something else involved? Of one thing Ross was certain: He would run the development past his Wendy, the better to stimulate her savant, puzzle-solving gifts. There was no mistaking that Jackson Kohl had sounded and looked like he wanted to burn down the basilica with a thousand torches but without a scintilla of regret.

* * *

Over glasses of Rosalie muscadine wine at the kitchen table that evening, Wendy and Ross were comparing notes—with Wendy holding forth first.

"You and Daddy should put this much behind you regarding the case: Ethel Kohl believed she killed her son because she was suffering from a delusion that she did the deed. Unfortunately, it was part of her disease and her ongoing deterioration. Jackson did the right thing in entrusting her care to Seabreeze Place. It had to be done. So, let's once and for all dismiss the idea that Ethel Kohl killed King. It never happened, except in Ethel's troubled brain, the poor woman. I wanted to get that out of the way before we went any further."

"I'll go along with that," Ross said, raising his glass before taking a big sip. "I take it you came to this conclusion because of your visit with Dr. Pevey. He's a pretty persuasive and authoritative man, and I'd be inclined to abide by his advice and counsel."

"Yes, I view him the same way."

"Anything else?"

Wendy seemed hesitant at first but finally dove into a monologue. "Well . . . it's just that . . . I've been trying to figure out how Jackson is getting through all this tragedy; but then, Dr. Pevey mentioned how devoted the Kohls were to their church and that Jackson's faith was probably serving him well now. It was a nice thought to send me on my way, don't you think? I've never considered myself all that religious, but I know that some people are to an extent I never could be. I'm just too curious about the universe to settle for dogma. Daddy's always encouraged me to question and then listen cautiously."

Ross put down his glass as his face clouded over. "Okay, I understand that part, but I think we may have a problem."

"What do you mean? A problem with what I just said?"

"No, I mean that far from singing the praises of his faith, Jackson went off on a tirade against his church. He seemed to be blaming them for what had happened to his family, not whoever it was who killed King. I coudda sworn that he was ready to ram his fist through one a' their stained glass windows. How can you possibly blame a church for all that's happened? It doesn't make sense. That is, if he really meant it, and in my opinion, he wasn't faking his diatribe."

Wendy looked startled. "That *is* peculiar. Even if it's a form of grief, it's peculiar."

"That's what I thought. The more I think about it, the more I come to the conclusion that Jackson just wants someone or something to blame, and since we haven't arrested Marcus Silvertree—or Jimmers Tyson, who he did remember a little bit, by the way—he's lashing out indiscriminately." Ross then further explained the exchange he had had with Jackson about Jimmers Tyson.

"It was secondhand, maybe even third-hand, information at best," he concluded. "That kinda stuff is not all that helpful, especially when it comes from someone under the influence. I'm just thankful Jackson wasn't driving around in that sort of foul mood."

"You've given me a lot to think about," Wendy told him, as they both finished off their wine and together began fixing their dinner.

But that night in bed, Wendy decided upon her next step, this time without the excess of waking Ross. Tomorrow, she would once again seek the counsel of Father LeBlanc at the basilica.

CHAPTER 15

It was clear to Wendy that Father LeBlanc regarded her presence in the rectory with a certain amount of skepticism, maybe even a hint of disdain. She was certain she could read his mind: *I wonder what she wants now. Did I not make church doctrine clear enough last time?*

No matter. She intended to maintain her focus. She could also spot a forced smile and demeanor a mile away, but she was driven by the conviction—perhaps even some sort of premonition—that something urgent was afoot, and she intended to see it all through to what she hoped would be a salvageable result. As she had on her previous visit, she followed him into his office, took her seat, and began her story.

"As you know, Father, I'm not Catholic, but I have my concerns for a man who is very much so, Jackson Kohl." She let her opening statement sit there for a short time, noting that the lines in Father's face softened somewhat before she continued.

"I think he is having a definite crisis of faith and needs your help. My husband tells me that on a recent visit to the slave quarters behind Kohl Place where Jackson is living, he attacked his church verbally—your church as well—in no uncertain terms. Ross said he'd never witnessed such a bitter outburst in his life, and he's seen his share during his career in law enforcement, believe me. It appears Jackson's almost blaming his son's death and his wife's medical confinement to a memory-care unit on you, in a manner of speaking. I guess I mean the generic you—as in you and the church taken together. I thought you ought to know all of this, just in case you didn't already."

Father sank back in his chair and made a temple of his fingers—almost, but not quite, a prayerful gesture. "No, I was not aware of that at all, Miz Rierson. The last time I saw Jackson was at his son's services, where he was very much in crisis, as you know. He has not been to confession or church since, though I encouraged him at the services to call on me if he needed me. Offhand, I'd say that these tragedies in his life have gotten to him, as they would anyone with a heart and soul. But those are the times when he should seek consolation from the church the most, not lash out with a vengeance. It's very concerning for me to hear this, and I'm glad you brought it to my attention."

Wendy's smile was on the tentative side. "I imagined you would say something like that, but I wanted you to have all the information so you could decide what, if anything, you should do next."

Father averted his eyes briefly and then said, "The reality is that I can't force Jackson or anyone else to seek me out. They must come to me and the church of their own accord without being coerced. Our communicants must want to participate and not be dragged screaming into what we offer. Heavy-handedness doesn't get the job done."

"That's an interesting way of putting it," Wendy added, surprised at how committed she was to pleading on behalf of a man she really did not know all that well, his wife and son being the ones who had had the more meaningful impact on her. "But if you knew one of your parishioners was physically ill and needed your comfort, you would go ahead and visit them then, wouldn't you? Why would this be any different? Maybe it's not my place to say so, and I hope I'm not over-stepping my bounds here, but being proactive might be a good idea."

Father actually broke into a genuine smile, a far cry from the forced one he had generated upon greeting her. "Miz Rierson, have you ever considered becoming a practicing Catholic? Your generosity of spirit moves me greatly. I know a few of my communicants who could follow your example."

"Thank you for that compliment, Father, but for now, I think I'll stick with being a somewhat lapsed Presbyterian. But you'll be the first to know if I change my mind."

Father had obviously entered his comfort zone, because he started laughing out loud. "Understand that mine is an ecumenical laugh, and I appreciate your honesty." He sat with that for a moment and then leaned forward. "And in this particular case, I agree with you. I don't think it would hurt at all for me to pay him a visit and see what pastoral care I can offer him. It might be an advantage for me if I could, but I simply don't read minds long-distance. You've acted as a spiritual helper here, and I'm grateful."

Wendy managed a soft sigh of relief. "Good. Glad I could help. I feel a little better now."

"So Detective Rierson really feels Jackson is at a very low point, does he? Sometimes, people get so confused or turned around that they forget to ask for help anymore. Or they think they don't deserve it when they fall on bad times. They think they're being punished for something real or imagined. I can only hope that he'll be willing to see me, whether I go there or he comes here."

"Well, don't worry," Wendy added. "I know there are

certain things you can't divulge to me. You've made that clear. But would you at least let me know that you've seen him and tried to help him through this crisis he's having?"

They rose together, and Father shook her hand. "I will do that, Miz Rierson. You know, I've long admired your father as our chief of police. There's no better a public servant in Rosalie. Well, maybe your husband's also right up there, from what I've heard and seen. In any case, I believe I see where you get that admirable character of yours."

Wendy found herself blushing, something that most people found utterly endearing in a redhead with a few freckles here and there. "What a sweet thing to say to me, and I can only hope I've ordered up just the tonic Jackson needs."

"I'll keep you posted to the extent I can."

"Thank you. I'll look forward to that." It was then that she noticed a small picture of Father on his desk that she had failed to spot before. He was dressed in martial arts garb, striking an aggressive pose. "By the way, that's a very impressive shot of you. Is karate a hobby of yours?"

"Not so much anymore," he told her. "When the spirit moves me, so to speak. You see, I had a previous life before I decided to go to the seminary. Not everyone is born knowing where they belong and where they can do the most good. I actually had a little martial arts studio—Emile's Disciplines and More, I called it—and I was going gangbusters with my classes. More people than I could handle, really. Then, I came to the decision that I needed something more fulfilling in my life, so here I am. Don't ask me why it happened, but I had a shift in priorities and switched from disciplines to disciples. The upshot is that I can defend myself quite well in most circumstances, although it hasn't come up since I changed professions."

Wendy offered up a brief but genuine laugh. "I don't

doubt that for a second. I've found in my line of work that the best way to understand anyone is to learn their backstory. That's always the 'meat and potatoes' of who they really are."

"Believe me," Father added. "I'm in the business of hearing backstories, right and left."

Wendy was sitting in her cubicle back at the paper later that afternoon when the call came through.

"I wanted you to know that Jackson agreed to see me at Kohl Place, and I was delighted," Father LeBlanc told her. "As you can see, I've wasted no time based on what you told me. I'm going over there in just a few minutes to see what I can do for him and perhaps put him at ease. I promised I'd let you know about any breakthrough to the extent I could, and I believe it's come sooner rather than later. Again, I want to thank you for telling me about his crisis. You're a good person, and there need to be more people like you in this world."

Wendy blushed again, as she had earlier in the day in his presence, and thanked him. She sat with her endorphins for a while after the call officially ended. Unfortunately, she knew from personal experience that that kind of feeling usually didn't last forever. Some other mundane business often butted in.

Shortly thereafter, she came out of her glow and happened to notice that she hadn't called up Elsie McMichael about the Billy Caspian piece she'd done a little while ago. The note that Lyndell had handed over to her was still pinned to her handy "to-do items" corkboard over her computer that featured restaurant takeout menus, as well; but with everything else going on, and her mind on King's murder more than anything else, she had managed to ignore the note. Truth to tell, she didn't want to contact this woman and listen to what surely amounted to journalistic pabulum. Reluctantly, however, she braced herself and made the call.

"It was somethin' my grandmother, Tootie Lee, told me

when I was just a little girl," the thin, high-pitched voice at the other end was saying after manners were made.

Stoically, Wendy said, "Yes?"

"Well, that Lacework House on Broad Street belonged to Mayor Lindsey Hoskins back then. He's no longer with us, of course. He's gone to his reward. If there was one waitin' for him, that is. That's the thing, you know. Tootie Lee told me that she heard that Billy Caspian was havin' an affair with the mayor's wife, and when the mayor found out, he just exploded with rage and killed Billy and then buried him in the basement. She swore by the story, and I believe it, too."

Slightly more interested, Wendy said, "Did your grandmother go to the police with it?"

"No, she said she didn't wanna get involved."

"That's all your grandmother knew? Through hearsay?"

There was a pronounced sigh of disgust at the other end. "I wondered if you'd react thataway, but Tootie Lee said the person who told her this was a church-goin' woman who never lied about anything. She was practically a saint, everybody said. The other thing Tootie Lee said to me was that what happened to Billy Caspian was like Daniel bein' led into the lion's den—only nothin' of a higher nature saved him. And furthermore to that, he didn't know what hit him when Mayor Hoskins lured him down into that basement and then whacked him with a shovel. It made sense, 'cause they did find a shovel down there buried with him, though it seems kinda stupid to me not to just throw the murder weapon away somewhere completely so it couldn't be found."

"That sounds like a blow-by-blow description—almost like it was recorded on camera. Is there some sort of film or picture available?"

The remark clearly went over Elsie's head. "What? Film? You mean like Kodak or Polaroid? Do they even make 'em anymore? I don't think they do."

"Never mind. That's all very interesting and colorful," Wendy said, trying to be as diplomatic as possible. "But what I'm getting at is that I don't suppose there is any proof of any kind? This happened so long ago that the authorities will need evidence to look into this any further."

"None that I know of. Just word a' mouth. But I believe it."

"Why are you coming forth with this now?"

There was an awkward pause. Then, a frantic flood of words. "Well, part of it was that article you wrote about the bones they discovered. Like to have made me faint away to the floor just picturin' 'em. Skeletons, they creep me out no end. Never did like Halloween like the other kids. 'Course, I wudd'n that crazy about candy anyhows. I tended to put on weight back then, and then the dentist told me I had too many cavities and all. And then there was that awful murder of that handsome King Kohl. That made me shudder the same way. I just thought . . . well, what's wrong with doin' your civic duty? If nothin' comes a' what I just told you, so be it. But I leave it in your hands at this point."

Wendy desperately wanted to end the call, so she lied. "I see I have another line lighting up, Miz McMichael, so I thank you for the information. We'll get back to you if we need anything further. We have your number. Have a nice day. Goodbye." And she hung up.

Wendy took a deep breath and then shook her head slowly. It was just as she had figured: hearsay and gossip that went back almost eight decades. No room for that in journalism.

On the heels of her disdain, however, something of a *savant* nature clicked inside that unique brain of hers. Merleece, Lyndell, Wyvonne, Bella, Patrice, and now this gossipy woman looking for her fifteen minutes of fame, had all led the way and massaged her gift. Words and phrases appeared on her front burner like enormous screen credits:

Rage
Daniel
Lion's den
Bad genes
Explosions
Power of suggestion
To hell with the church
Bleach
Time running out
Single hairs

And just as suddenly, *she knew*. She knew in a way that conventional law enforcement could not know. Not quite everything yet, but the urgent part. Inadvertently, while thinking she was doing the right thing, she had set in motion a resolution that might have fatal consequences. At the moment, she did not know which was racing faster—her heart, or her thumbs as they texted Ross:

Send patrol car to Kohl Place asap; case going down fast; Father LeBlanc & Jackson Kohl in slave quarters

Ross's response was nearly immediate: *where are u? r u okay?*

fine; at paper; savant at work; could be possible life & death situation there

Pike & I headed over now

Hurry

That much was done. There wasn't time to go into conjecture and hunches and all the rest of it with Ross. Wendy headed briskly to Lyndell's office to tell her where she was going, but her trusty editor wasn't there; tracking her down in the lunchroom or bathroom didn't seem like a great priority at the moment. So she quickly scribbled a note and left it on Lyndell's desk:

> *Breakthrough in Kohl case—headed over there now—Ross notified—get in touch with Daddy for more info.*
> *Wendy*

With that out of the way, Wendy headed to the parking lot, but she couldn't seem to walk fast enough. She didn't care that Ross would probably have told her to stay where she was until they had everything under control. Her brain was operating at warp speed, while her legs seemed to be in slow-motion mode. Was she stuck in some sort of alternate reality quicksand? She glanced down at the asphalt just to make sure it hadn't liquefied on her. It was all because she knew she wasn't wrong now. What lay ahead was possible disaster that would tear the town apart further. Perhaps Ross and company would be in time.

CHAPTER 16

Father LeBlanc was sitting on one end of the expensively upholstered living room sofa in the slave quarters, while Jackson had settled into his trusty recliner nearby, sipping on something clear, neat, and tall. But despite the liquor intake, Father didn't think his parishioner looked relaxed or comfortable at all. Both his face and voice came off as strained, even tortured.

"I'm telling you the truth when I say that I'm near the end of my rope," Jackson was saying. "It's really all over for me. I'm alone, on my own. There's nothing you can do about it, either. King went first, now Ethel's as good as gone. What I did was for her own good, though. She'd suffered enough. Maybe that'll count for something—that I did the right thing where she was concerned."

Keeping his composure as befit his station in life, Father said, "What you did seems above reproach. Now, if you'll allow me, I can give you my advice and counsel. And if you'd like, we can have confession right here and now. Unburden yourself, if you need to."

"Just as simple as that, is it? The old standby cures all that ails?"

Father drew back, somewhat surprised. "Life isn't simple.

It's full of twists and turns that we frequently don't see coming. We both know that. But there are sacred ways we have of dealing with our mistakes, and you've always taken advantage of them in the past. It seems to me you've at least tried to become a better person. I don't think I'm wrong about that."

Jackson took a healthy swig of his drink and stared Father down. "You think so, do ya? Then tell me, whaddaya do when the past bites you in the ass big time? When everything you thought was the right thing to do backfires on you."

"I don't know what you mean, Jackson. Could you elaborate a bit for me, because I don't see where you're going with this."

"I'm not sure you really want to know. But since you called me up and more or less insisted on this little tea party of ours, I'll go ahead and explain it all. Because, you see, I have nothing left to lose." He finished off his drink, smacked his lips loudly, and continued. "Oh, sure, there'd be those who say I still have the real estate business to run—the best in town. Always has been, always will be. And let me say once again that Marcus Silvertree never even came close to achieving what King and I had built up through our hard work. Silvertree's a wimp, out of his league. You'd think I'd feel sorry for him, but I don't."

"Is that what this is going to be about—the rivalry with Mr. Silvertree?" Father said, frowning. "Offhand, I'd say you won that contest."

"You'd be right. We did. But as for the accusations I've made against him, he was the obvious fall guy. I thought the man was a waste of molecules, even a bit of a sissy, so why not accuse him? And, yes, I did set him up. Only, the Rosalie Police Department is hard to fool, lemme tell you. They never would arrest him. I kept pressing and pressing, but they wouldn't take that last step."

Father did not like where the conversation was going, but

he felt that he had an obligation to at least listen to one of the most generous communicants in his parish. "I certainly agree with your opinion of our police department being tough on crime. Captain Winchester runs a tight and professional ship, and his daughter is quite the professional reporter—and with a good heart, I might add. I wish all my parishioners cared about others the way she does."

"I guess so," Jackson said. "But what this is really about is that the church up and bit me in the ass, and I can never forgive you, or the church, or anyone connected with it. You took my son away from me. Someone's gotta pay."

The rising anger in Jackson's tone truly alarmed Father, so he immediately sought to calm him down. "I'd like for you to take a deep breath to try and steady yourself. I'm here to listen to you, not to judge. Try to keep that in mind."

The ploy didn't work, and Jackson said, "That's what you think. The part about judging me, I mean. You haven't heard anything yet."

"Then tell me what I need to hear." At that point, it suddenly dawned on Father that he had left his cell in his car. From an emergency communications standpoint, he was defenseless.

"For starters, you won't think I was such a saint when I tell you that I suggested to Ethel that she was the one who had killed our son. Over and over, I did it. 'Have you forgotten what you did in a fit of anger?' I'd say to her. 'Have you forgotten how you came to me with the sad truth that morning?' She was susceptible to the wildest ideas once she had left the threshold of reality behind with her condition. She couldn't distinguish the truth from a lie easily anymore, and it was easy to convince her of anything. The bad days had started to outweigh the good ones by a lot. I guess I was laying the groundwork to get her out of the way. But I did promise her that she would be safe when all was said and done. Maybe some part of her had already realized the truth about King's murder. It had already happened when I woke her up that morning, and we had breakfast together before the commotion started. But who would believe anything she said in her mental state? She was the perfect scapegoat, but I was pretty sure she wouldn't be punished. She's where she needs to be. I give myself a pat on the back."

With a look of horror on his face, Father said, "Why would you do something like that to her, Jackson? What could you possibly have been thinking? Did you really think you could live with yourself?"

"I was doing everything I possibly could to deflect and to direct suspicion away from myself, yes. I don't consider this a church confession, because I've had it with the church. This is just one man talking to another man. But the fact is that I killed King. I killed my own son, and I can never take back that moment of rage when I rushed over and ripped that plaque off the wall. King had no idea what I was about to do, and by the time he realized it, he was dead. I moved fast during those moments of rage. I hit him as hard as I could three times. Three for the number of grandchildren I wanted and expected him to give me. Is that so wrong?"

"You can't be telling me the truth," Father said with some authority. "I know you aren't capable of something as heinous as that. Your grief has gotten way out of hand. This is a mental health issue that you have to resolve, every bit as much as the one Ethel had. You must seek help."

"You may be right. Maybe I'm mental. But I still did it, Father. I did it as sure as you are sitting here on my sofa. And I did more than that after I'd savaged him with his own awards plaque, which he got because of all the hard work I'd done before him. He didn't live in a vacuum, though he apparently thought he did. He just inherited all the good feelings from the community when he started assuming more responsibilities. But he didn't want to keep doing that. Hell, no, he didn't. Because I'd already done all the hard legwork for him, and he just wanted to throw it away for blessing people."

"He wanted to do more than that," Father said, continuing to remain as calm as he possibly could. "I don't know if I can make you understand what it's like when you choose religious life."

"No, I don't suppose you can. You say you gave up a successful business. But I assume you were not married and did not have a family."

"That's correct. I was single."

"Well, I built my business for my family and wanted to see it continue. So that's why I did what I did, and I surprised myself with how clearly I was thinking to cover up what I'd done." Jackson thrust out his chest and sucked in air. "Yes, I was panicked and still seething with rage, but I still had my wits about me, emptying his trash can, full of all his lists and such that he told me he was composing about what order to choose for his big revelation. I guess you could say that King was on the anal side. Maybe took after me in that respect."

"I think he wanted to do the right thing by everyone in the end," Father said. "That was who he really was."

"I'd expect you to say that. He was confused—that's who he really was, thanks to you. So, after I killed him, I went into the kitchen, shredded those wads of paper in the disposal, and continued on my tear. I put on some of Wyvonne's latex gloves, wiped down as much as I could everywhere with her bleach, and wonder of wonders, even remembered that Wyvonne had told me about the sentimental hairs that King and Bella had exchanged. King had told her about them in one of his many boozy sessions with her, and I knew where he kept his silly little locket hidden. *Why not implicate Bella, too?* I thought. *She hadn't convinced King to marry her. She hadn't advanced my cause, or Ethel's, too.* As for Wyvonne, Father, I think

King did more confessing to her than he ever did to you. He had loose lips when it came to that strange little girl with the 'every shade of crayon' hair. And then, I texted Marcus and Wendy Rierson to set them both up—one as the killer, the other as a witness. I mean, I was sharp as a tack, incriminating as many people as possible. Give me some credit. I was damned good, don't you think? Now, are you ready to judge me?"

"I don't know what to say to you anymore. I don't feel like I know you at all, and I thought I knew you so well from all those years as being your pastor. Haven't you had any feelings of compunction over what you did?"

Jackson rose from his recliner and walked quickly toward a hallway that led to the downstairs bedroom that he and Ethel had shared. "Yes, here and there. Perhaps I haven't handled what I did as well as I thought I'd be able to after the fact. But this has all come to a head now. Don't move. Wait right there. I have something to show you that'll convince you that I'm telling you the truth and nothing but. I can see that a part of you still needs to be convinced. Let's put an end to that, shall we?"

Father's anxiety soared exponentially. He rarely felt in over his head in dealing with his parishioners, but suddenly, he did. And it wasn't just a matter of anxiety. There was a sense of imminent danger crowding in upon him, so much so that he seriously considered leaving the premises without even saying goodbye. Should he bolt for the door while he had the chance? It was only a few feet away. He sensed that he had only a few seconds at his disposal. Furthermore, what Jackson had just told him had not taken place during an official act of confession; there was an outrageous element of pride and not contrition involved. So he was not bound to keep it confidential. The police, he reasoned, should know about it pronto and take it from there. What a time to forget having his phone in his coat pocket! Was his oversight a form of being tested? Furthermore, would he survive this test?

All thoughts of running away vanished, however, when Jackson reappeared in the hallway doorframe moments later, pointing a gun his way. Father gasped, sprang up from the sofa, and said, "What's that for? What are you doing? Jackson, you need to think very carefully now. You don't want to make things worse than they are already."

"It's very simple, Father. I've decided I'm gonna shoot you with it. Then I'm gonna shoot myself. A very quick proposition that will bring all this to an appropriate end. Though maybe a little messy, and maybe Hell will be waiting for me, but it'll be better than the Hell I'm living. No matter how many prayers you throw at me, you'll never be able to get inside my head and make things right."

Father tried to sound as low-key as possible, even though the adrenaline in his blood was running wild. "Killing me and killing yourself is no answer to anything. It will just make matters much worse. Somewhere deep inside, you know that. I simply won't believe you have no semblance of a moral code left."

Jackson waved the barrel of his gun around carelessly and started rambling. "What I know is that the church is the one that's really responsible for my son's death, not me. If you think hard enough, you'll realize what I'm saying to you is true, because you've known all along about his new ambition, according to what King told me the morning I killed him. You were the very first to know what he was up to. He'd texted me around eight that morning not to wake Ethel and to come to his office right away, because he had something life-changing to tell me. He said he would tell Ethel later, so why would I not come with that kinda approach? I thought he might have some brilliant new idea for our business. He had his entrepreneurial moments. Why wouldn't I want to be in on that as soon as possible?"

Jackson took a quick breath and continued. "And then, King told me what he really wanted to do. He seemed to be proud of himself. 'I think I can accomplish far more doing this,' he told me. And I said to him, 'What am I supposed to do with the business without you?' King just shrugged and said, 'Whatever you want to. I'm out of it for good.' And that's when I had to kill him. He had his mind made up. He wouldn't budge. I pleaded with him again before I moved behind him toward the wall. He wouldn't hear of doing anything else with his life, and he sealed his fate. So I didn't want him in my life anymore under those conditions. He was telling me he wouldn't be passing along my genes. He had a duty to do that. He would be forsaking the family line. There would never, ever be any grandkids for me to spoil. He was leaving real life, as far as I was concerned. I was outraged. He was rejecting my life's work and the work I expected him to continue doing. What was it all for if I couldn't have generation after generation continuing my work? Genes are everything, you know. Ethel's family had the tall genes I'd always coveted. Look at me; look how short I am. But my King was tall, and he was supposed to carry on the tall, proud line. How could I ever forgive him for turning his back on his own blood for the church? You can't understand. You have no children. You're out of the mainstream with all your rituals and sacred certainties. You don't know how a family is supposed to work. Easy for you to shrug off leaving everything important behind the way King was gonna do."

Father knew that he dare not inflame the situation further, and he softened his voice to just above a whisper. There was a real chance he might receive a bullet in the chest for uttering the wrong words. "I really want to understand your position in all of this. You probably think that the entire world is against you, but you must believe me when I say that I am your friend, not your enemy. Please, put your trust in me now. It's vitally important that you take that leap of faith."

"You just *think* you're my friend. But you're really not. You did your job too well. You knew the truth and what was coming and did nothing to discourage King. You made him proud to turn his back on his family and follow you."

Feeling slightly weak in the knees, Father said, "It's true that I did approve of what King told me he was going to do. I hadn't known all that long when he obviously told you that morning. But you have to understand that King told me his plans during a particular confession in which he listed a whole host of mistakes and bad decisions he'd made. Some I already knew about; others were brand-new to me and nothing to dismiss. His past was checkered, but then that's true of just about everyone walking this planet. I cannot break the seal of the confessional under any circumstances, but I hardly thought his life was in the balance. Why would I go there?"

"No? Then what did you think when you heard he had been murdered? Did you think you should come forward then?"

It did not take Father long to dredge up the feelings of devastation that had permeated every cell of his body when he had first heard the news. He had worked hard to convince himself that it had nothing to do with King's decision. How could that possibly be? It was, after all, joyous news for the church. For some church and its communicants somewhere—after he left the seminary and inherited a parish to shepherd. Surely, there was some other justification for King's murder; one that the Rosalie Police Department would soon discover, bringing that person to justice.

"I thought a dreadful crime had been committed, and I fell into immediate despair. It seemed insane to me. At first, King had planned a party to announce his decision, but then, I advised him to tell everyone that needed to know on a one-on-

one basis. So, he ended up canceling the party at the last minute, and it appears you were the first he told the reason for it. He would have gotten around to everyone in good time."

There was a hideous-looking smirk on Jackson's face, a contortion that made him nearly unrecognizable. "Yes, King and his lists. I was the first, but no, you don't get off that easy. I can picture you influencing him, confession by confession, absolution by absolution, luring him into the promise of eternal salvation and wiping the slate clean, until . . . you broke him, the part of him that lived in the real world of reproduction and continuity, until he wanted to become just like you. Someone with no faults and above reproach."

"I am *not* that someone. I have never pretended to be. And I said nothing to him along those lines. He thought for himself. He came to his decision of his own free will."

"You coudda fooled me. I'm sure you gave him your blessing. I can just picture you right now, with that unctuous act of yours."

"I may have in a pastoral way, but I performed no such sleight of hand with your son about his ultimate choice," Father said, this time with growing indignation. "Now that you know the truth about him, I must emphasize once again that he definitely made the decision to start his life over and become a priest of his own volition. That's hardly an easy decision for anyone to make. It's not to be entered into and taken lightly by anyone. More than once, he told me in our ordinary talks outside of confession that he thought time was running out for him based on the wrongs he'd done in his life to date, and the way he'd treated women, the times he had taken them for granted and not considered their feelings, the things he'd done for them that he shouldn't have done, in particular. He was truly contrite. I can tell the difference between someone who's genuine and who's faking it. He also told me that he knew it would be tough to turn his back on the business and you, of course, but he was bound and determined to try for a different kind of existence. He was worried about his ultimate destination. Can't you put yourself in his shoes?"

Sounding as tortured as he looked, Jackson said, "The ultimate destination, huh? You know, Father, after all these years, I think I've come to the conclusion that there really is no destination in store for any of us, so why not do what we want in life? What does it matter in the end? Why not do everything you can to sell every house on the block and never look back? After all, you can't take the house with you. You can't take the money with you. You can't take anything with you. So why not enjoy it all while you can? I'm sure you don't agree with that, but why couldn't you have just left him alone? More to the point, why couldn't you have left me alone today? And don't you dare say that 'God' sent you here. I hate that kind of arrogance. You don't run the world, you know. You just think you do."

"No, I don't think I run the world by any stretch of the imagination, and I won't say anything like that to you," Father added, suddenly infused with a certain strength of purpose. "An actual human being sent me here to help you, and she was right in her thinking to do so. We need all the help we can get in this life."

Jackson had a pronounced sneer on his face. "Well, I started to turn you down when you called me up. It was the last thing I expected. But then I thought to myself, 'Why not? Jackson Morris Kohl, you're gonna off yourself soon, so why not take Father LeBlanc with you?' Hell, I figure that two murders and a suicide aren't any worse than one murder. They're all wrong in the first place, according to the way you live, Father, so what do numbers matter?"

"It's not a matter of numbers. It's a matter of having a moral code."

"You're big on that phrase, aren'tcha? You're running it

into the ground, as far as I'm concerned. Not only that, but
you've buried it six feet under."

"No, it's my life's work."

Jackson's body stiffened, as if obeying some unheard military command, and he cocked his pistol. "Here's a bulletin for
you. Your life's work will soon be over."

As Wendy rushed through the city toward Kohl Place, the
weird symmetry of it all began to settle in, although she continued to chastise herself for being so slow-witted about it,
too. She had been there, nearly at the beginning of the case, as
an unwitting pawn, and now she intended to be there for
what she was certain would be the finish line, with critical information at her disposal. It simply could not be otherwise,
even though she knew Ross would not like her putting herself
within range of any sort of danger. She knew better than that
but could not help herself. He would just have to keep scolding her about it, and maybe one day, it would finally sink in.

The concept of *rage* had been the overweening factor in
her epiphany, not a woman or women scorned. Merleece had
been well-intentioned as usual, but she had missed the mark
on this one, and as a result, Wendy had spent far too much
time analyzing which of the females in King's life had had the
unmitigated and wicked gumption to do away with him for
hurts and sleights, or worse, real or imagined. Her unparalleled instincts eventually told her that Wyvonne, Bella, and
Patrice lacked such abilities at their cores, though they all had
their moments of vulnerability and pettiness that did not serve
them well. That initial "woman scorned" line of thinking had
also led to the absurdly rocky conclusion that Ethel Kohl
might have killed her son. Poor Ethel. Wendy could only
hope she would find peace of mind at Seabreeze Place until
the end of her days. That much, at least, was a blessing.

Of the male suspects, Marcus Silvertree's status had reeked

of a setup from the get-go, including Wendy's realization—
and Ross's, as well—that she, herself, appeared to have been
set up as a witness by a cleverly timed text. Jimmers Tyson, on
the other hand, had had the misfortune to show up for his so-
called reunion with Patrice Leyton the wrong week of the
year; Wendy had reckoned that he had been guilty of nothing
more than bad timing—and perhaps some manhandling that
Patrice had rightly rejected in no uncertain terms. Good for
her, and good riddance to him.

Lost in the wide net of red herrings cast was the one person, female or male, that everyone had mostly overlooked because of the genuine anguish he seemed to have projected to
everyone from the very beginning and through the visitation
and services—King's father. His tirade against the church had
found its way finally into her savant neurons because it ran
completely against the grain of his known, pious, community-
spirited personality. Something had to give, and it was the
previous illusion that fell as surely as King had fallen to his father's wickedness.

And then, thanks to her sessions with Father LeBlanc and
discussions of doctrinal practices, it suddenly occurred to her
that King and the church together had likely done something
to displease Jackson. No, not displease—more like light his
fuse and cause him to explode. To her horror, she also realized
what she had done in sending Father to the front line to fight
a fierce enemy—the well-camouflaged but thoroughly toxic
male that she now believed Jackson Kohl was.

"What have I done?" she said out loud in frustration,
waiting for a light to turn green. "Come on, signal, come on."
Halfway believing that it could hear her, she could have
sworn that it was stuck, and she was getting ready to send the
car into the intersection in careless fashion before it finally
changed.

She knew that all her puzzle-solving prowess had no control over how fast Ross and whoever else on the force reached Ground Zero to avoid some sort of unwelcome detonation. Texting would likely only distract them. Then she switched the imagery in her head to something even worse: A cornered toxic male could amount to a millennium-era dragon breathing fire, and Wendy could only hope that Father wouldn't get burned beyond recognition.

There was a look of panic on Jackson's face when he first heard the sirens, causing him to ask a stupid question. "What the hell's that?"

But Father wasn't about to do or say anything to annoy the man with the cocked gun still pointed his way. He was in the midst of a terrifying freeze-frame. "Police—maybe an am-bulance—would be my guess."

"Coming here? Did you call the police before you came here? Are you working along with them? How dare you!"

"No, I didn't call them."

"You're lying."

"I make it a practice to try very hard not to do that."

"Always full of the high road, aren't you? And you made it so irresistible to my son. You took the continuation of my family away from me. Those weren't your genes to throw away like they were nothing. Who gave you the right? You had no claim to them. And then you made a big mistake in coming here with all your self-righteousness. Now, you've forced my hand."

Father steadied himself and continued to plead calmly. "I came here to help in good faith. That is always my intention with my parishioners—no less so with you."

"That pious talk won't save you. Nothing will." As the sirens grew louder, Jackson motioned to Father. "Come over here and stand in front of me now. Do as I say, or I'll shoot you where you stand. If they come through that door, you'll be my hostage, and that'll be the end of it."

In a matter of seconds, Father found himself with one of Jackson's arms around his neck and the other holding the gun to his temple. He could feel and even see his pulse pounding in his eyeballs, and he began praying silently. If these were to be his last moments on earth, he would not betray his training and see it through to the end.

Jackson continued his rant. "I'll say it again. Just know that if the police are coming for me, you're dead as soon as they rush through that door. They'll find two dead bodies on the floor—yours and mine. You go first, then me. Are you ready for your big moment? All this time and all these years, you've been talking the talk with your homilies and posing from the pulpit while smiling away. Are you ready to keep your mouth shut at last and walk the walk?"

Father said nothing, continuing to mouth his prayers.

Then, the wailing of the sirens stopped, and time itself seemed to stop for Father when Jackson moved the end of the barrel closer to his temple.

There was already a small crowd gathered on the sidewalk across from Kohl Place, buzzing with great agitation among themselves while Wendy pulled up and parked her car halfway down the block. With its blue lights still flashing, Ross's police car was stationed smack in the middle of the street, effectively blocking it, but he was nowhere to be seen. It was clear to Wendy that he and his partner were already closing in on the slave quarters in the back. She got out but chose not to get any closer to the crowd. Instead, she stood frozen once she reached the sidewalk, listening to the nosy comments from those closest to her who had arrived earlier.

"What on earth do ya think's happening?" she could hear

one older, heavyset woman saying with a certain undisciplined excitement in her tone.

"You suppose it's one a' those drug busts?" another younger-looking woman near her answered, similarly excited. "They say drugs are takin' over the world now."

"A drug bust at Kohl Place?"

"I dunno. It's not as crazy as it sounds. First, a murder. Now, this—whatever it is. You think you know people. And in this neighborhood, too. It's such a shame. I'm afraid to go out at night now."

Wendy was sorely tempted to walk over and chastise them for indulging in such a gossipy session while lives might very well be at stake in the slave quarters, but a probable ensuing exchange ran across the projector in her head like a ticker tape:

"Who the hell are you? You don't live in this neighborhood," the heavy woman would say to her if Wendy dared engage her.

"Yeah, what's it to you? You're just here for the thrill," the other woman would say.

"No," Wendy could picture herself responding. "That would be you."

And then an ugly, protracted argument would follow. Onlookers would join the fray, and who knew how it would all end? That was more than enough of a disincentive to keep Wendy firmly in place, though still resenting all the rubbernecking. What a useless but predictable practice that was, particularly around car wrecks. This was even worse, in a way, because it was very personal to her.

Then a shot rang out, and the crowd variously gasped, screamed, and jumped, nearly in unison. Wendy's head jerked back—but in silence—because although her beloved Ross may have been out of sight, he was hardly out of mind. Had he or his partner fired that shot? Or had they been fired upon?

There were times when she truly despised having a husband in law enforcement and worrying about him every minute of every day as a result, although she had had plenty of practice as her daddy's daughter. Her mother, Valerie, had once told her when she was twelve that the spouses of police officers had to be nearly as strong as they were—it was essential that they avoid living their lives in fear. They must never go there and spend a lot of time fretting, even if they felt hollow inside much of the time.

That startling gunshot continued to echo in her brain, so Wendy moved back slightly and leaned against the car hood for support as the worst-case scenario gripped her brain. Was she going to faint? Then she made it to the passenger's side door and got it open just in time to collapse on the front seat, hitting her head on the steering wheel as she lunged forward. Somehow, she remained stuck in that position and passed out—with the horn protesting loudly to everyone nearby.

When Wendy came to in emergency room triage at the hospital, things half-remembered—or were they imaginary?—swirled inside her head. A gunshot ringing out. The thought that Ross was in danger. Father LeBlanc in danger, too. Flashing lights and a gathering crowd. Gossipy buzzing among people with nothing better to do than gawk on the sidewalk. Until the most important item emerged again.

"Ross," she finally said. "Where's Ross? Where's my husband?"

A nurse—very young with a blond ponytail, reassuring smile, and wearing aqua scrubs—appeared at the left side of her bed and said, "Miz Rierson, your husband is waiting outside the curtains. Would you like to see him? He's a very happy man right now, I can tell you that."

Wendy felt a wave of relief inundating every nerve ending of her body. "Please, please. Let me see him right now."

The nurse went over, pulled back the curtains, mumbled something, and Ross entered with the biggest smile she'd ever witnessed on the face of the love of her life.

"Hi, sweetie. You're gonna be just fine. That bump on your head will go down in a few days, the doctor says. Your numbers look great right now. BP, oxygenation, everything. You've just got a headband of a bandage up there. While you were still out, they drew your blood and checked out a few things. All you have to do now is just relax. Things couldn't be better."

Everything crystallized even further for her, causing her to gasp. "Never mind me. What about you and that gunshot, you and Jackson Kohl and Father LeBlanc and—"

He gently took her hand, careful not to disturb her hookups to telemetry, and made a series of shushing noises. "Now don't you worry about anything. No one is dead. No one is even hurt. I'm right here with you holding your hand, aren't I?"

"I . . . I just lost it when I heard that shot ring out, and then I felt dizzy, and I don't remember much else after stumbling to the car."

"A couple of the ladies in the crowd heard the horn blaring, ran over, and dialed 9-1-1. Of course, you shouldn't have even been there, you know. You've got to learn how to keep yourself out of harm's way a little better, because you conked your head on the steering wheel when you fainted. But this is not a time for scolding. Just the opposite—it's a time for giving thanks."

That only increased Wendy's frustration. "Yes, but I want you to explain everything that happened. Starting with who was with you in the patrol car. Was it Pike?"

"Yes, it was Ronald," Ross said, nodding. "He's just fine, too. He's down at the station now. He sends you his best. Not a scratch on either one of us."

"And nobody's hurt? Not Father LeBlanc? Not even Jackson?"

He shook his head. "Nobody, noway, nohow."

"So tell me everything that went down. It's not about me now, it's about you."

Ross let go of her hand and pointed toward the curtains. "First, there's someone else that wants to speak to you, but just briefly." Then Ross called out, "Father? You can come in now."

On cue, the curtains pulled back to reveal Father LeBlanc, smiling almost as broadly as Ross was. "Hello again, there, Miz Wendy Winchester Rierson. The doctor and nurses tell me that you're in great shape. There's nothing to worry about. Right now I'd say God's in His Heaven."

Ross stepped back a bit to allow Father to approach Wendy's bed, and she said, "You're also safe, I see. I was so worried when I realized I'd sent you on a very dangerous mission. But I did recover my senses in time and sent Ross out to the rescue, thank goodness. It seems like the angels were on your side."

"Yes, my prayers were answered when it counted," Father said. "Although I know I did have a little something to do with it. Anyway, it all turned out well in the end. Perhaps in a way you would never have imagined."

Somewhat puzzled, particularly by the exaggerated smiles of the two men in the triage room with her, Wendy said, "Will one of you tell me how it all went down before I explode?"

Now it was Father who stepped aside, pointing to Ross. "I'm sure you want to do the honors, Detective Rierson."

"I do, indeed," he said, once again lifting Wendy's hand gently, and this time he kissed it. "Sweetheart, you're between five and six weeks pregnant. Didn't you realize you were late?"

Suddenly, all thoughts of what had happened in the Kohl Place slave quarters disappeared. Was she really hearing those words after all this time? Was their long journey of frustration at an end? Then, a very dark idea crossed her mind.

"Am I dead, or am I just dreaming?" she said. "Is this triage room real? Are both of you real or just apparitions? And, yes, I knew I was late, but that's happened before, and nothing's ever come of it. Let's just say that I was preoccupied. Subconsciously, I'm sure a part of me didn't want to get my hopes up, either. There've been too many disappointments for both of us."

"That may be, but I assure you, we are flesh-and-blood real, and you being pregnant is real," Ross said, turning his head briefly toward Father. "It turned out to be one of those days where everything happened fast and all at once. Some of it not so good, but some of it wonderful beyond belief. Sweetheart, we are gonna have our baby at last. I haven't told your daddy yet, but can you imagine how over the moon he's gonna be? I thought we could tell him together in person—he and Lyndell, of course."

"Yes, I can imagine it easily. Seems like he's been waiting on this longer than we have, and Lyndell hasn't exactly been patient, either. Although lately, she's backed off a little."

"Glad to hear it. Meanwhile, the doctor ordered up and an x-ray or two for that nasty bump of yours, but if everything checks out, I'll be taking you home soon," Ross told her, "and we can get on with our lives like this never happened."

Then he leaned in and kissed her gently on the cheek, and she was at a loss for words. All she wanted to do now was to experience that verb, that word that Ross wasn't so fond of— *marinate*—for a while. Just to marinate in the exuberance of the moment. There was nothing wrong with the concept. She wanted it to go on forever. Those other matters, those details, all the rest could wait.

CHAPTER 17

"Wait until I get you home and I get you settled," Ross kept telling Wendy as they drove away from the hospital after the x-rays had shown that there was nothing particularly troublesome about her injury. It was angry looking, to be sure, but nothing that time would not heal. "Then I'll tell you the rest of the story. Don't you want to have something to look forward to? Besides, you have nearly eight months of patience ahead of you. We both do."

She actually pushed out her lower lip and pretended to be upset with him. "Which is going to be longer for me than for you. That's the way these things work, you know. You're a cheerleader on the sidelines at best."

He took his eyes off the road just long enough to flash her the most affectionate smile he could manage. "Rah, rah, rah! But you have to know that I certainly didn't mean to be flippant with my remark about patience. I don't consider that my part is over by any stretch. Just let me pamper you like the doctor said and start waiting on you hand and foot. That should be every loving husband's privilege, you know."

She beamed right back at him, because during such moments, she secretly thought he was adorable. "Okay, but the second after you've set me up like a crown princess, I want the full story on what happened at Kohl Place. You've been acting like this is classified information, and I need security clearance or something. This isn't good for my pregnant disposition."

So once at home, he moved quickly to get her settled, propping her up in bed with a tray containing water, her meds, and a single orange daylily from the front yard flower bed in a tall vase, all of it resting on the nearby chest of drawers. Now it was time for her payoff at last.

Wendy played at scolding him. "Don't leave out any detail, either. No matter how incidental you think it might be. I need closure, and I need it now."

"Actually, Pike and I didn't have all that much to do when it came time for action," Ross began, sitting on the edge of the bed and getting into library story time mode. "I wish all our assignments were that easy to handle, if you can call confronting people with firearms easy. As it turned out, Jackson had already revealed to Father that he had actually killed King, his very own son—and I'm still trying to fathom that one. I can't imagine stepping off that cliff with a good outcome. Jackson was also threatening to kill himself and Father, too, as his grand finale—another murder, plus a suicide in the making, he said. We'd just gotten to the front door of the slave quarters, and I'd shouted, 'Rosalie Police Department!' when we heard the gunshot. We thought the worst had happened at first and that we were too late, but then Father LeBlanc cried out, 'It's okay, it's safe to come in. Everything's under control.' And it really was, because—"

Wendy interrupted, sounding just like a little girl figuring out a fairy tale. "Wait . . . I think I know what happened. Karate saved the day?"

"Good guess. How could you possibly know that?"

She then patiently explained to him the backstory of Father's martial arts studio before he'd opted for the seminary and a completely different direction for his life. "Human beings are so much more complex than we could ever believe," she concluded, looking extremely pleased with herself. "Every single one of us."

"Makes sense, but I thought you were psychic for a minute there. Anyway, Father told us that he elbowed Jackson hard in the stomach," Ross continued, "and then immediately gave him one of those karate chops that brought him to his knees. The gun went flying out of Jackson's hand, but it went off because it was cocked. Somewhere even now in those slave quarters, there's a bullet lodged in a wall or in a painting or maybe even up in the ceiling. But in any case, no harm was done, thanks to Father's quick thinking and physical prowess. I remain very impressed with the man. As you say, we are all very complex."

Wendy executed a nearly silent, mini-applause gesture with the tips of her fingers. "Yessss! There's more than one way to deal with the bad guys." Her mood quickly grew more somber, however. "So my brainstorm about Jackson being involved up to his eyeballs was spot-on. I certainly hate being right about it at this point, because it's beyond gruesome when you think about what actually happened, but I also feel guilty about putting you and Pike and Father LeBlanc in danger. That's why I just had to jump in the car and go to the scene. You keep telling me over and over again that I'm too reckless for my own good when I get involved in these investigations, and I suppose you're right. I know I'm too impulsive at times."

"We'll worry about that at some later date. One person can only get into so much trouble, but your instincts weren't misguided at all. It's hard for me to believe it even now, but Father repeated to me and Pike what Jackson had already told him at gunpoint. It was King's intention to abandon their real estate business and enter the priesthood, leaving his past behind and wiping the slate clean. It's not hard to see how difficult a decision that was for him, leaving behind everything he had ever known. Apparently, Jackson couldn't forgive the fact that his son wasn't willing to carry on the family line. At that point, he lost it and went on a rampage with the awards plaque, then tried to implicate as many people as he could, including poor Ethel. Except maybe he did the right thing by her and moved her to safety in the end. Maybe there was a tiny shred of decency left in the man."

Wendy's tone was permeated with sadness. "I don't know. It hardly seems enough, and I certainly don't trust his motives even in that. But there's no doubt that Ethel is safe now, and perhaps it's best that she never knows the truth about Jackson and King in her remaining years. What she doesn't know surely won't hurt her. Merleece's idea of *bad genes* popping up now and then in families wasn't far off the mark. I just wish I'd figured out the context sooner. If I had done that, would you and Daddy have acted on it and then followed through?"

"Sweetheart, don't go there. You more than did your part, as usual. All of us were fooled to some extent. Of course, I'd like to think that if Father hadn't known karate, Pike and I would have made a difference somehow. It's not like we haven't had showdowns before with armed suspects and won the day. That's how we earn our keep."

"I'm sure you would have done a bang-up job." She paused, repressing a grin. "Oops, I didn't mean to use that phrase like that."

Then she managed a little shudder. "I don't want to even think about what could have happened to either of you, though. It just blows my mind. Here I am, pregnant with our first child, and the idea of a parent killing a child seems like the very worst, cruelest act I could ever imagine. So beyond the pale to take out one of your own. I mean, there Jackson was with that shiny, civic-oriented reputation and plaques galore all over his walls, fooling everyone including Father, and behind it all was an inconceivable monster concerned only with his own damaged view of himself. I'm going to have to stop thinking about it so much and move on."

Ross took her hand as if warming it between the two of his and said, "Yes, let's don't dwell on it any longer. It's over and done with. Unfortunately, the Kohl family is over and done with, as well. But we have new life to bring into the world."

"I'm happy about that, of course," she told him. "We're part of the cycle of life, the eternal balancing act. But one last thing to satisfy my curiosity and then we can drop it: what do you think will happen to Jackson when this comes to trial?"

Ross took a moment and then said, "I doubt *diminished capacity* will work in his case, though his lawyer might try it and throw Jackson on the mercy of the court. It certainly would have worked for Ethel had she actually been the one who did it. But it's difficult for me to envision a jury being the least bit sympathetic to what Jackson did and the reasons he gave for it. No matter how you position it, it was pretty nasty and cold-blooded. No, I think prison without parole is much more likely."

"What about the death penalty?"

"Up to the judge, I'd say. Anyhow, as we've both admitted, we need to say goodbye to all that and focus on what's ahead for us. For instance, how and when do you think we should tell your daddy and Lyndell about the baby? I haven't told Bax, and I don't see how you could have had the time to tell her with everything's that happened recently."

"You are absolutely correct. As it happens, I was totally preoccupied with being out cold." Wendy offered up a devilish grin and pointed to her forehead. "Why don't we have them over here for dinner tomorrow so I can show off my new, bandaged hairdo?"

"Couldn't you take it off, pretty up a bit, and try to camouflage? You know, create some bangs or something like that, the way you women do so well."

She shot him a look of disbelief. "Men! You make me sound like some sort of spy and a master of disguise to boot. You should know by now that I'm not that vain by a country mile. And, by the way, I don't want you treating me like I'm made out of crepe paper from here on out. I'm as strong as I ever was, so for starters, we can both contribute to this meal of our grand revelation, just like we both contributed to the baby."

"Ain't biology great?" he said, matching her sly smile.

"Takes two, last time I checked," she answered, pointing toward her belly.

Of course, Wendy knew the subject would come up after she and Ross had shared the good news with Bax and Lyndell at the dinner table the next evening. Over the white wine and caprese salad course that Ross had concocted and poured, to be exact. Except that Wendy had promptly deferred to lemon water for obvious, prenatal reasons.

"I'll definitely miss the grape," she told everyone, cocking her head with a smile and raising her water glass immediately after the news had been dispensed. "But we must consider the greater good. These vintages and I will get a temporary separation, of course. But at some point, there will be a grand reconciliation—within reason, of course."

Effusive congratulations, hugs, and kisses followed, with much rising up out of chairs and leaning over and shuffling about for a short while; but it did not take long for a puffed-up Bax to tackle the inevitable.

"Thought about any names yet, daughter a' mine?"

Wendy and Ross briefly exchanged glances, but she took the floor, full of good cheer. "We have, indeed. We were thinking of honoring you, Daddy, and Ross, too, if it's a boy. How does Ross Baxter Rierson sound to you? That was our first take."

"Wow!" Bax said. "What an honor, kids!"

"Wait . . . before you get too excited, there's a smidge more to consider," Wendy added, spearing a piece of mozzarella to go along with the slice of tomato that was already on her fork. "Ross is thinking of calling him R.B.—a child that comes with initials. What do you think of that? Too impersonal? Too macho?"

Bax's smile shrank just a bit, but he kept the enthusiasm in his voice. "R.B.—sounds like a private detective to me. I kinda like it, now that I think about it." Then he raised a hand in the air. "Hold on, though. That's not very far removed from R&B, as in the music you hear at Simply Soul. B.B. King, for instance."

Lyndell chimed in, sounding highly amused. "What's wrong with that? When you come down to it, who doesn't love B.B. King? But I highly doubt that anyone will stick an ampersand in there like that. Unless it's a nickname from his school pals on the playground. Nicknames happen to just about everyone at some point. So what if his little friends do come up with something like that? On the other hand, if he wants a career in journalism, R.B. Rierson sounds like a great byline to me. Or the perfect pen name for a great American novelist." She paused and turned toward Wendy. "And if it's a girl?"

Wendy smiled at her but then focused on her beloved daddy. "I'd like to honor Mother, if you don't mind. Valerie as a first name, and a middle name to be announced when the spirit moves us. But I'm leaning toward calling her Valerie. I still miss Mother so much, and I know you do, too."

"I think that'd be beautiful," Bax said, choking up slightly. "Just beautiful."

"But you understand that nothing's set in stone," Wendy added. "We have the right to change our minds, trimester by trimester. We just thought we'd let you know how things stand at this early stage. And who knows? If we have twins, we could end up using both names."

"They'd have to be the fraternal type to pull that off," Bax said, wagging his thick brows. "There's no history of any kinda twins on my side of the family. What about you, son-in-law?"

Ross frowned while clearly trying to review things in his head. "Nope. None that I know of, but I can't go back very far where my family is concerned—either side of it. Both proudly blue-collar, I guess you could say. I have to admit I've never been all that high on genealogy, and neither were my parents, which I guess is considered a sin in Rosalie."

Wendy waved him off vigorously. "That's not the exaggeration you think it is. Rosalie is guilty of overkill in that area. It's great to be proud of who you are and where you come from, but it's not okay to hit other people over the head with it and make them feel that they're somehow inferior. We're all on different journeys. And it's even worse when it's done subtly or behind someone's back with a snotty remark. I overhear way too much of that at cocktail parties and even over a game of bridge out at the country club. At times, I feel like rapping knuckles with a ruler."

"You're right about that," Lyndell said. "Since I came here several years ago, I've had to learn the hard way. I've apparently stepped on lots of invisible toes by just including certain people in the same sentence. My goodness, the fuss that was made by equating this one with that one, and I didn't know why at first. I only knew that I'd stepped in it, and I won't go into details. I'm proud to say I've remained calm and objective through it all, however. That seemed to win people over, and I do consider myself a part of Rosalie now. I have definitely paid my dues."

"You definitely have, and the fact is that you're a great editor with some pertinent insights," Wendy said. "Just the new blood this town needed, and everyone's the better for it. You set the bar very high, and that's always a good thing."

"I thank you for that. By the way, when do you see your ob-gyn? I'm sure you can't wait," Lyndell added, winking at the compliment she had just been handed.

"A week from Friday was the first date they could work me in," came the reply. "Which is actually very soon, of course. It's no secret that women are always having babies right and left. I'm so excited. I can hardly wait to follow every single instruction down to the letter. This is going to be the healthiest baby ever, I can promise you that, even though I had the occasional glass of wine when I didn't realize the situation. It bothers me a little to think about it."

"I wouldn't worry. I've never seen you overindulge. And you can work at the paper as long as you want," Lyndell said. "Or as long as the doctor says you can. I'm a huge proponent of maternity leave for those who work for me. I think employers should be much more flexible in that regard, and we're well into the millennium. By the way, your job will be waiting for you after the baby comes. It'll all definitely be up to you."

Wendy perked up even further. "Just knowing I still have options means a lot to me. I'm going to play it by ear, if you don't mind."

"I don't mind at all. Whatever you want and need."

"Music to my ears," Wendy said, nodding graciously.

* * *

Wendy was well into the second trimester when she got the unexpected, sobering news. Lyndell called her into the editorial office, asked her to take a seat, and began. "There's no easy way to say this, but I just received an e-mail from my contact down at Seabreeze Place. I asked them to stay in touch with us about Ethel in case we wanted to revisit a story on her down the road. You never know. Unfortunately, dear Ethel died in her sleep last night. It was a somewhat of a surprise, because she hadn't been having any acute problems to speak of, other than the condition she's been fighting all along, bless her heart. I knew you'd want to know as soon as possible. I'm still trying to take it in, myself."

Wendy felt a combination of shock and sadness plunging to the soles of her feet. "Thank you for letting me know. At least Ethel was in the right place there at the end. Her struggles are over. I have the feeling that life was harder for her than we'll ever know."

"I suspect you're right. Of course we'll run her obit, but we'll have to rely upon her closest friends to help with that since Jackson's in prison, and we've had more than enough of him to last us a lifetime," Lyndell continued. "He's had more than his miserable fifteen minutes of fame, and I think I'm going easy on him with that remark. I'm just glad he didn't do any more damage than he did."

"It could easily have happened. Anyway, since I interviewed her, Greta Compton would be the one to consult there," Wendy said. "She and her husband were great friends with the Kohls on almost every level. Perhaps she can fill in the blanks a bit for us."

"I'll let you handle that since you had the initial contact," Lyndell added. "We can get the rest from public records and the church. I'm sure Father LeBlanc can help us out and do her justice."

Wendy was looking down at her baby bump as she spoke.

"So the Kohls really are gone for good. They'll just be Rosalie memories from here on. Unfortunately, some of those memories will be cringeworthy, and that's a shame. I'll always feel that Ethel and King deserved better than that, but none of us really knew what a monster Jackson was."

"It's definitely not the legacy anyone would have envisioned just a short time ago. By the way, the rumor is that Marcus Silvertree may not head back to the Delta after all. Supposedly, he'll give the real estate business a try again now that he won't have any competition. I'm not sure people will cotton to him right off the bat because of the circumstances, but Rosalie will certainly need someone who can buy, sell, and flip houses. Someone has to step into the vacuum, but he'll have to be very diplomatic about it and proceed cautiously. What Jackson did was enough of a shock for everyone. Marcus should let his better angels guide him."

Suddenly, there was a sharp intake of air from Wendy.

Lyndell leaned forward solicitously. "What is it? What's wrong?"

"It's the baby," she said. "Just kicked for the first time. Right now, this very second as I'm speaking. Kicking up a storm."

Lyndell clasped her hands together joyously. "And I got to witness it. What an honor. Talk about being at the right place at the right time."

"Nothing like some good news to balance the bad."

"I haven't asked lately, but does your ob-gyn say everything is still copacetic? I think I already know the answer to that, though."

The question immediately chased the sadness from Wendy's face. "Absolutely you do. Nothing but perfect test results and great sonograms, copies of which Ross has framed and taped in his locker down at the station. Would you believe it? He says that every time he opens it, he gets a glimpse of his future over the long haul. A brand-new person to bring up in this crazy world of ours, and he tells me over and over again that he can't wait to get started. He definitely understands the big picture and feels more than equal to the task. Isn't that the sweetest thing ever? Sonograms as locker room pinups. He says he doesn't even mind take a ribbing from the guys. Some of them are fathers, themselves, so they've been there and done that, and they're always giving him tips on what to expect."

"That's just the sweetest. Ross will make a wonderful father. I just know it as sure as the two of us are sitting here shooting the breeze."

Wendy pointed to her hair as if she'd just had a crown placed on her head. "You certainly don't have to convince me. He makes me feel like a queen with the way he coddles and cuddles me every day, even though I keep telling him not to treat me like I'm made out of spun glass or hanging from the ceiling like a chandelier. 'I'm not going to break,' I keep reminding him. But I secretly crave all the attention he lavishes on me. He really doesn't overdo it that much. I'm exaggerating just a little tiny bit out of the love I have for both him and the baby."

Lyndell wrinkled her nose briefly. "Go ahead and let him spoil you. This is a special time of life, and you'll want to savor every second. You've been looking forward to it for a while now."

Wendy jerked back her head once more, clearly mesmerized. "Oops! There she goes again. This series is even stronger than the last one. She definitely wants attention, and she's got it. She's on the radar now—a permanent blip until she comes in for the landing."

"Bax says you're still planning on calling her Valerie," Lyndell said, chuckling. "But no nicknames, he insists. No Val or anything like that—just plain Valerie."

"I agree with that. Daddy's pretty traditional, as you know, and Ross and I want to please him. He wants another Valerie in his life after all this time. Not that he doesn't treasure you, of course. Don't misunderstand. I'm thrilled he has you in his life, and I'm just as happy the two of us make such a great team here at the paper, too."

Lyndell made a circling gesture near her temple with her index finger. "Believe me when I tell you that I've had some real prima donnas who couldn't be told squat at some of my other editorial jobs. They thought every time they sat down at the computer, they deserved to win an award, but it doesn't work that way. What they wrote while they were on the staff at the school paper wasn't even close to reality. Some stories just don't make the grade—just too blah—and I'll never forget something my own father told me once about success. He said that the important thing to do was to concentrate on the effort, and that over time, the results you wanted would show up."

"Plus, a good reporter never stops learning."

"You're so right. Same for a good editor. But back to your dear daddy. You should see how he walks around the house humming some little tune all the time. Or when he shaves. The little ditty is not anything I can identify, you understand. Just a collection of happy notes that his brain has strung together for the hell of it. I know exactly what's going on, too. He's dreaming about that granddaughter of his on the way, of course. I bet he's got everything planned for her all the way through college."

"Probably, but Ross and I will have our say. That's the thing about Daddy," Wendy said. "He's tough and strong and always stands up for his beliefs, but underneath it all is a big teddy bear of a man with a sentimental streak a mile wide. He's always been a man that has no trouble showing his emotions."

"You don't have to tell me," Lyndell added with an expression of delight, rapping her knuckles on her desk. "I get the privilege of sleeping with him every night."

Wendy focused on her baby bump again, gently touching her belly with the palm of her hand in protective fashion. "Lucky you, but I keep wondering if this one here will inherit my puzzle-solving abilities. Or maybe her grandmother's artistic talents. More acrylic masterpieces for my wall. Who knows? Maybe a combination will come through. You just never know what you'll get with genes, do you?"

Lyndell drew back smartly. "True enough. But suppose she wants to be a detective on the police force, guns and all, just like Bax really wants you to be, but you never quite co-operate with him. For the record, I'm glad you don't and continue with your excellent journalistic skills on my behalf. But what would you say to your daughter if that turns out to be her choice? Bax can be a very persuasive man, as you well know. I keep waiting for him to stop bugging you, but that doesn't seem to be in the cards."

Wendy's generous smile spoke volumes by itself. "I'll proudly tell her that she can and will be anything she wants to be, and I have the feeling she'll choose wisely."

"Just like her ambitious mother did."

"Yep," Wendy said. "I'm right where I should be in life— totally ready for the next exciting chapter."

ACKNOWLEDGMENTS

My heartfelt thanks for this, the fourth novel in my A Bridge to Death Mystery series. I always start with the Kensington team in New York: John Scognamiglio, editor; Carly Sommerstein, production editor; and in the Art Department, particularly Kristine Mills. I can always count on them to turn out a superior product for my readers, and I am never disappointed.

At my agency: Jane Rotrosen; Christina Hogrebe is my guiding light; and Meg Ruley, my original lighthouse keeper. My research for this project was greatly aided by Theresa Thevenote, director of the Avoyelles Parish Library System in Marksville, Louisiana. She verified a number of doctrinal issues for me so that I was on solid ground when creating the character of Father Emile LeBlanc.

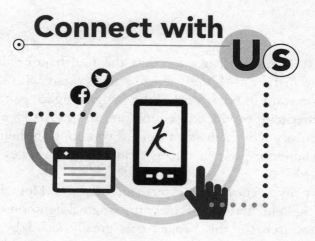